Both Barrels Vol. 2

Both Barrels Vol. 2

EDITED BY

**Ron Earl Phillips
Jen Conley
Christopher L. Irvin**

Reloaded: Both Barrels Vol. 2
Copyright © 2013 One Eye Press LLC

This book is a work of fiction. Names, characters, places, and incidents
either are products of the author's imagination or are used fictitiously. Any
resemblance to actual persons, living or dead, events, or locales is entirely
coincidental.

Cover art, "The Child" © 2013 Joseph DellaGatta
boston-joe.deviantart.com

ISBN-13: 978-0615875514

www.OneEyePress.com
www.ShotgunHoney.net

Table of Contents

Table of Contents

"It is the most satisfying thing I can think of, to write a scene and have it come out the way I want. Or be surprised and have it come out even better than I thought."

ELMORE LEONARD

Foreword

Daniel B. O'Shea

As if I didn't already feel old enough, I guess I'm now the professor emeritus of Shotgun Honey. The old codger in the miss-matched clothes who's been relegated to foreword-writing duty.

But it ain't like age is slowing everybody down. Hell, this collection starts off with another ass-kicking tale from Patti Abbott, who's been kicking asses since half you punks were still pre-cum in your Daddy's dirty boxers.

In a way, though, Shotgun Honey's all about the young Turks – and about keeping up with them. It's a place where a lot of new voices cut their teeth, voices that pretty soon are tearing a big, bloody chunks out of the crime fiction herd. It's a place where we old farts can feel young again, try something new, shed our old dog hides and trot out some new tricks, make sure we don't rust, maybe sometimes show these punk kids we've got some fight left in us yet.

Kent Gowran kicked this thing off a few years back with a bright idea—take the usual 1,000 word flash fiction finish line and move it back a third. Shotgun Honey forces writers to boil every story down to its essence, to take the already strong coffee that the vile bastards you'll find in this collection were cranking out and distill it down to a lean, nasty espresso of carnage. If you like your fiction black, you're in the right place. If you're looking for a goddamn soy mocha latte, then go catch the trolley to cozy town. You're in the wrong neighborhood.

When you take the type of talent that accepted that challenge and delivered stories with that lean and hungry look and then you let them off their leashes, let them run down some bigger prey, this collection is what you get.

So gird up your loins, crime fans. You'll laugh, you'll cry, you might puke a time or two.

But you won't be bored. And you might never feel safe again.

Daniel B. O'Shea, 2013
Author of PENANCE

A White Funeral

Patti Abbott

"Do you know what your grandmother said to me on the last day of her life," Adele asked Kay, adjusting the tablecloth so that each side had a twelve-inch drop. "I'm sure I've told you this before." Her tone was faintly accusatory, as if Kay had solicited the story.

"What?" Kay lay on the sofa waiting for the phone to ring, watching idly as her mother walked from one end of the table to the other.

"Well, she was in the hospital and I came in, bringing a few drugstore items: a packet of bobby pins, Woodbury soap, spearmint gum, and the latest issue of *Photoplay*. I even remember Dorothy Gish was on the cover. Some people thought Dorothy was the more beautiful sister, but Lillian was the better actress."

"I think I've heard that."

"She was sleeping," Adele continued, "but she woke up when I opened the drawer to put her things away. And that's when she said it." Adele stopped abruptly to place a pair of blue and white candlesticks in the center of the table. "Don't they look nice on the white? I know these candlesticks are from Woolworth's, but they look genuine on my grandmother's linen tablecloth."

"Look, Mother, you got it wrong. Tonight's nothing special." Kay sat up suddenly, glancing at the phone as if he—Roy Tyson— might be listening. "I don't know where—"

"Well, suddenly your grandmother sat right up," Adele interrupted, "looked me straight in the eyes and said 'Del, you look like hell." Adele moistened her fingers and straightened the wick on one of the candles. "Make sure you have a book of matches handy tonight. I don't think the table lighter has a drop of fluid in it."

"Maybe she was making a humorous poem."

"What? No, she wasn't making a poem, Kay. And now I do remember telling you this before, because you said the exact same thing. She may not have said Del. It might have just been, 'You look like hell.'"

"You always put the Del in."

"I was taken by surprise, of course," Adele continued, "and said, 'Look, Mother, as it happens, I'm on my way to the beauty parlor this minute. I was just dropping these things off first—these things for you!' Adele pulled out a chair, checked the seat for crumbs and continued. "Anyway, she just closed her eyes then and died."

"Did you know right away she was dead?" Kay obediently fed her mother the next line in the script that surely sat in some drawer.

"No, I thought she'd just drifted off. I wonder if she'd any notion those were to be her last words." Adele sighed. "She always said things like that to me. Now my brother, Carleton, well, he could do no wrong. We had to track him down at a bar to give him the news of her death. I remember taking the #23 trolley car up and down Germantown Avenue, hopping off at all his favorite watering holes. That reminds me, Kay. I heard they're going to start phasing the trolleys out. It won't be Philadelphia without the sound of those trolleys."

"Good. The tracks ruin the streets. Have you ever tried to drive over them?"

Adele was standing over her now—as thin and upright as a flagpole. From her prone position, Kay could feel her mother's strength pulsing through her body, heaving in her chest, making Adele's hands tremble with energy. It threatened to well up and run right out of her like a bolt of electricity.

Unaware of her power, Adele picked up her dust cloth. "Let's see it was 1922. I've already lived ten years longer that she did."

"Rheumatic fever, huh?"

"Came down with it as a child and after that she was never very strong." Adele droned on, recounting the story of her mother's illness.

When the hell was that call coming anyway? What had Roy said? Two, three? Kay felt ill with anticipation. "I'm going to take a bath before Billie gets home."

"In the middle of the afternoon?"

Down the hall, Kay took off her clothes, crammed them into the pink hamper that separated the two single beds, and walked naked down the hallway. In the bathroom, she poured a generous amount of bath salts into the tub and turned on the tap. Over the sound of the water, she could hear Adele running the vacuum, diligently crashing into a wall every few seconds, pushing the old Hoover with such fervor it made the floorboards groan. Anyone but her mother would have put a radio on and listened to music while she cleaned, but Adele preferred the sounds of her own efforts to those of Eddie Fisher or Peggy Lee.

And then the phone rang. "It's him," her mother said a second later from behind the door. "What's his name?"

"Tell him I'm in the bath." His call was nearly an hour late. Let him wait now.

"That doesn't seem like a very genteel thing for a mother to say to a strange man," Adele fretted.

"For God's sake, Mother. He takes baths too." Kay turned off the water hard enough to make the pipes squeal. "Never mind, I'll take it." She stood and dried her wet hand on the towel.

Adele sighed with relief and stepped away from the door as Kay came barreling past her naked. "I'll just get out of your way then."

"Did he cancel?" Adele asked after Kay hung up. Sounding fearful yet somewhat titillated by the possibility, she stepped out of the kitchen and handed her daughter a towel.

"No, he didn't *cancel*," Kay said, wrapping the towel around her middle like a man would.

"Where did you meet this fellow anyway?" Adele asked. "There's something about his voice...Unsavory, I think you'd call it. Like Fred McMurray in *Double Indemnity* or maybe it's Raymond Burr in *Rear Window*. Look, I have a thousand names of nice men stashed in my phonebook. Fellows who are perfectly willing—eager even—to go out with you. Only the other day, Mrs. Brewer told me her nephew—"

"For Pete's sake, Mother. I don't need you to find dates for me. I told him dinner was in the oven."

Adele laughed. "That'll be the day."

"I can cook."

"When was the last time you cooked?"

Kay paused. "Look let's not get into this right now."

Kay knew Adele would put out the best spread she could and let Kay take credit. That was the kind of strange thing Adele did on her quest for a father for Billie.

Arrangements had been made for Roy to come at eight-thirty, when Billie would be fast asleep. Adele was scheduled to visit her friend, Dottie, just down the block. A pan of lasagna sat in the oven; a salad awaited dressing.

"What if he asks how I made it?" Kay asked, hovering over her mother's final touches. "I can never keep all those cheeses straight." She felt the worry lines creep across her face and smoothed her forehead with her hand. "Romano?"

"Ricotta. And he won't ask," Adele told her, buttoning up a sweater despite the heat. "No man gives a thought to where food comes from." She was gone then, only the familiar smell of her Jean Nate cologne wafting behind. Kay stood in the kitchen for a minute panicking, wondering how she'd get the lasagna out of the pan. Then she remembered the pie-shaped utensil her mother used.

"Hello baby," Roy said a few minutes later, framed by the doorway. He wore a light blue colored pinstriped suit with an open-collared, starched white shirt. He smelled of Bay Rum cologne and was definitely the type of man who attracted her: tall, well-dressed —at ease in his body and not afraid to show it. The men her mother usually came up with looked like elementary school principals. She gave a quick glance toward the bedroom door and let him kiss her in the extravagant way he had. Like he was trying to pour himself into her mouth, and as usual she felt dizzy afterwards, as if he'd sucked all the oxygen out of her. There was no doubt he took kissing seriously. It wasn't just a prelude to sex since they hadn't gotten that far yet. He seemed content to take it slow, which suited her too after the disastrous six weeks she had with a boyfriend last fall. No one had told her that some men make unusual requests. Things that on the face of it have nothing to do with sex as far as she could see.

In the eight years since her husband Bill's departure, Kay had probably dated forty men. She had slept with six of the forty, but mostly with Don D'Amato, a sweet guy her mother had actually found in the Reading Terminal. Don was a cheese monger who always smelled faintly of Limburger. He wore a ridiculous Bavarian outfit to work in his miniscule booth at the marketplace, a buxom blonde woman named Dora or Norah dispensing hunks of cheese beside him, and annoying German music playing in the background. Once she had seen Don in that venue, things deteriorated at a fast clip much to Adele's regret.

Roy finally came up for air, took a seat on the sofa and looked around. "Sheesh, you keep a clean house."

"Make yourself at home," she told him, looking for a magazine to hand to him. She could feel a line of sweat dripping between her breasts, she was so nervous. "I need to check on your dinner."

Damn, she sounded just like the waitress at Littleton's Diner. She rushed into the kitchen and opened the oven. It seemed surprisingly cool for an appliance cooking their dinner. Did the thing turn off by itself when the meal was done? Except it wasn't done, she discovered, when she poked a finger inside the lasagna. Would Roy know what was wrong and be able to fix it or would the whole thing only serve to betray her ignorance of housewifely tasks? She could call her mother, but the phone was in the living room and he'd hear the call, perhaps even hear Adele chiding her. Maybe she should just dash down the street and ask Adele?

"I need to borrow some salt from next door," she said, popping into the living room. "I'll just be a minute." Roy, who'd discovered the TV and was already watching a variety show, nodded. "Take your time, honey" he said generously. "I never eat till late."

She hurried down the street, and after battering uselessly on Dottie's front door, realized the women were probably in the backyard. With Philadelphia row houses, getting to the rear meant circling the entire block, and she took the longer route, not wanting to cross Roy's field of vision. The two women were heading into the house when she finally arrived, folded chairs under their arms.

"For God's sake, you have to relight it!" Adele gave a dramatic sigh, looking meaningfully at her friend so Kay couldn't help but know the subject of her ineptitude had been discussed at length. "Okay look, I'll show you how to do it on Dottie's stove."

"Ooh, mine's electric, Del," Dottie said apologetically. "You just turn it on and you're off."

Adele looked at Dottie as if she was being difficult on purpose. "Well, I can tell you how to do it—or draw a picture, I guess. Or maybe I should just come home with you."

"My neighbor has a gas oven," Dottie remembered suddenly. "Mrs. Murphy— just next door."

"Well, let's be quick about it," Adele said. "No telling how long he'll wait."

The three women hurried over to the Murphy's house and knocked on the backdoor. "You know, I don't even like to think about having a strange man alone in my house. I left my best gold earrings on the tray on my bureau." She threw an annoyed glance at Kay when Dottie's back was turned. "What do you really know about this fellow anyway?" She looked over at Dottie. "She met him at the hairdresser's, Dottie. What kind of man has his hair cut in a beauty parlor? And I tell you, I didn't care for his voice on the telephone. Not at all. What was the word I used to describe it earlier? Whatever it was, it caught it perfectly. I hate it when I can't remember something clever I said."

The Murphy family was eating dinner. "We usually eat at six," Celie Murphy said, waving them into the tiny kitchen. Her girth took up much of the available space and they huddled by the stove. The family of five was jammed around the kitchen table, eating peach shortcake. "I can't think why we're so late tonight...oh, look," Celie said a second later, "I forgot to turn the oven off when I took the meatloaf out. It'll never relight right away."

Mr. Murphy, a burly gray-haired man, rose from the table suddenly, nearly lifting it off the floor, his napkin waving from his collar. "Do you want me to come light it for you, Kay? Or I can show you how to do it on paper?" He hiked his pants up and threw his napkin down on the table as if it were a gauntlet.

"He's an engineer at the phone company, Kay," Celie said proudly.

Kay listened patiently as the four adults offered tips on how to light a gas stove. Feeling somewhat confident finally, she sailed out the door, wondering whether Roy had given up and gone home. She'd bet anything he hadn't touched her mother's dimestore jewelry.

When she got back to the house, Roy was sitting in the living room with Billie, in a crisp pair of lavender shorties, perched on his lap. One bony leg draped each side of his thigh. She looked up at her mother half-asleep. "I heard Uncle Miltie," she told her excitedly, "and it's not even his night. He's visiting Jack Benny."

Her head, sweaty from sleep, nestled in Roy's neck. It looked wrong there. Everything looked wrong though Kay couldn't say why. Roy did look a bit like Raymond Burr, for one thing.

"She came rushing out of her room," Roy said, placing Billie carefully on the floor and rising. "Berle's voice, I guess."

"Billie doesn't usually take to strangers," Kay said, still vaguely uncomfortable. "Billie, you go back to bed. I'll be in to check on you in a minute."

"But Uncle Miltie's coming back on—" Billie had begun when Kay gave her a look that sent her running.

"I'm sorry I was gone so long. I meant to be right back but...."

"I didn't know you had a daughter that old," Roy interrupted. "I had pictured her as a baby."

"She's only nine. I don't know what she said, but I'm sor—"

"They're so cute at that age," Roy continued. "I could fit her foot in the palm of my hand." Had he tried that, Kay wondered. A chill went down her spine. Though Billie could be flirtatious with strange men, Kay remembered. Roy was still talking. "So she flounced into the room like a junior Scarlett O'Hara. I had to laugh. We hit if off all right."

Why was he still talking about Billie? Now a lone drop of perspiration ran down the middle of Kay's back. She looked at his face closely. It was red; his lips seemed plumped up somehow.

A guarded look now crept over Roy. "She's just a kid, of course and I'm not around kids much—I probably don't know how to compliment them. What's okay to say to their mothers."

Kay could think of a lot of things that were okay, but none of the ones she'd just heard. Roy stood in front of her, slumping and damp. He'd never looked so unattractive before. Weasely even. Maybe she should check the tray on Adele's bureau, but she had the feeling it wasn't jewelry that interested Roy. A sharp needle pierced Kay's brain with little stabbing pricks, and she took a deep breath.

"Roy, I was just about to tell you the oven's broken so I won't be able to make dinner after all." The words came out of her mouth surprisingly easily. "I was hoping it could be fixed but...."

"We can go out somewhere, Kay" he offered. "I know a great spot—"

"I don't have a babysitter. You know—I thought we were staying in tonight and wouldn't need one." She eyed the bedroom and his eyes followed hers with that slightly unfocused look men got after several drinks. Had he been drinking before coming here? He only smelled of cologne. Could cologne cover the smell of alcohol?

He leaned in for a kiss at the door, his usual move, but she nudged him away. His face finally registered the brush-off, and he turned to go.

"I think I hear Billie," she said easing the door closed. "Coming, honey." She pressed her back against the door until she heard his car start up.

Billie was sitting up in bed, reading the *Five Little Peppers and How They Grew.*

"I like your new boyfriend, Mommy," she said as soon as the door opened. "He laughed at the show. He's got a funny—"

"Billie, you know better than to sit on a strange man's lap," Kay interrupted. "Whose idea was that?"

"Mine, I guess."

"Are you sure?"

A pause. "Sort of. He was sitting on the sofa where I usually sit. I think he might have patted his knee," she added suddenly.

Kay swallowed. "What did he do while you were sitting on his lap?"

"He watched the show." Billie frowned, working hard to give her mother the right answer—the one that would end the questioning.

"Nothing else?"

"Well, he bumped me up and down a couple times, like his leg was a bucking bronco," Billie told her. "I'm too old for that but I didn't say it." She paused. "It kind of hurt me." She looked down at the affected area and frowned.

"Do you want me to read you some of that book?" Kay asked, either not willing or not able to ask the next question. *Did you tell him that it hurt? What did he do then? Did he do it more? Did he offer to rub the sore place?* These things would occur to her in the years ahead. Instead that night she thought this: *Roy may just not have known that nine-year olds don't play horsy. It was possible.*

Billie looked surprised. "I'm too old for that too, Mom. Gran stopped reading to me in second grade."

"Can't I read to you this once?"

"I like hearing it in my head. I'm used to that."

"Well, don't read too long. You're up way past your bedtime already."

"Mom," Kay said softly into the receiver a minute later.

"Still didn't light?" Adele sounded tired. Apparently her energy was not as infinite as it appeared.

"What? No, it's not that. I sent him home."

Adele sighed. "He did do something awful, didn't he?" Her voice was growing shrill. "It wasn't my jewelry, I hope. If you'd just let me...."

Kay could feel her mother shake her head then; she could picture the downward turn of her mouth, the droop of her shoulders.

"Could you just come home?" Kay asked, breaking off a piece of the bread on the counter and sticking it in her mouth. "I don't want to be here alone."

"Is Billie okay?"

"Fine. It's just me. I got the heebie jeebies somehow."

"For God's sake, Kay! You're supposed to be an adult." Adele sighed. "Heebie jeebies! I'll be along home when we're done with this game of rummy. I don't like to disappoint Dottie. I thought you could get along without me for one evening."

"Just come when you can." Kay hung up and sat there quietly for a minute. The light under their bedroom door had gone out and the house was completely silent except for the sound of Jack Benny saying something to Rochester. She rose and pushed the heaviest chair in the room in front of the door and sat down on it. After a few minutes, she pulled the chair away from the door, opened it, and started down the steps. It was almost but not quite dark. When she got to the sidewalk, she stopped, not even sure where she was going, what she would do. Finally, she sat down on the stoop and began to cry. That felt about right. Remembering suddenly the nearness of her daughter, she muffled the sobs with her arm.

The Howl at the Park

Hector Acosta

"Get the dog, Bait."

"I got the last one, you do it. And stop calling me that."

Bobby turned around and glared at me from under his green trucker's hat. He kept the van idling, a hand caked with dirt and grime on the steering wheel. "You da' one that wanted to come along, so you do as I say."

I flipped him off, and quicker than a knife wound, he had my finger in his hand. Wasted no time in twisting it.

"You got that?" he asked.

"I got it, I got it," I said as I wiggled around in the torn, vinyl backseat.

"And what's your name?"

"Screw you!"

"Try again." He bent my finger back and a squeal that shamed me ran out of my lips.

"Bait!" I shouted, red faced and all. Bastard.

I saw a flash of yellow when he broke into a grin and released my finger. "Atta girl. Now go squirrel up that dog."

Sliding the van's door open, I stepped out into the cool, Arkansas night. The slight chill in the air sent goosebumps scurrying up my naked arms and legs, making me almost turn back to get my jacket. One look at Bobby though and I knew better.

I rubbed my arms up and down while I looked around. Dix Hills was on the north side of Little Rock, a small, hoity toity neighborhood full of two and three story houses. The fresh coat of paint that was applied at the start of every summer caused the houses to shine real pretty in the moonlight.

"Christ almighty, will you move your skinny ass?" Bobby said, poking his head out of the driver side's window.

Can't believe I ever had a crush on his front tooth missing ass. I flipped him off, and this time was fast enough to pull my hand back before he snatched it.

"Girl, I swear I'll leave you."

He would too. Just last week, Bobby and Ray had gone for a pick up, only for Bobby to come back alone a few hours later, muttering about how that was the last time he took his meth head of a brother out on a run with him. It took Ray most till sun up to walk his pockmarked dumbass back to the trailer he shared with my second cousin Leigh-Anne.

That's when Bobby came and asked me if I thought I'd be better than a meth-head at the job. I said yes, figuring it beat hanging around the kitchen and listening to the old ladies talk about the sons they had up north in Pulaski County Jail, or down south dead and buried in the cemetery.

The lawn had a slight give to it that reminded me of the bouncing house the church had put outside of their parking lot two summers ago. The grass felt strange, with none of the sharp pebbles and bits of glass that my shoeless feet were so used to stepping on. I kept my eyes down and ignored the flicker of lights that washed over me as I ran.

The lock on the gate was nothing fancy, just a chrome thing like the one that I had on my locker at school. Bet I could have jimmied it open in no time, but Bobby was in no mood to wait, so I took a deep breath and scaled up the wooden fence. Not much different than climbing up a tree.

The dog was waiting for me on the other side.

"Hey there, boy. How you doing?" I whispered, digging into my pocket and coming out with a handful of cut up hotdog pieces.

The tiny brown and white thing sat in his haunches and tilted his head, staring at me with a set of cigarette butts he had for eyes. Dumb dog must have caught the scent of the hotdog, because as soon as I stepped closer to him, he started to wag his tail.

Weren't nothing at all for me to reach down and pick him up. Couldn't have weighed more than five, maybe six pounds, which was good considering I was gonna have to climb the gate again to get out.

"Come on now, stop wiggling," I hissed, extending my hand out and grabbing the top of the gate, while keeping the dog tucked between my other arm. Stupid thing kept trying to get loose, his head tilted down and nose buried in my pocket. "I ain't got no more food," I hissed.

Took longer than I would have liked, but I finally managed to clear the fence and make my way back to the van. The dog continued to be worry free, tail wagging in excitement while he licked my fingers.

"We good?" Bobby asked.

I plopped into the back seat and presented him the dog, who just swiveled his head and looked back at me, his constant panting making it seem like he found this whole thing hilarious. "Yep. What type of dog you said he was again?

Starting up the van, Bobby shrugged. "Some stupid name." he said, slowly driving the van away. "Shit something or other."

"Yeah. Shit Sue. I think that's it. What a weird name huh?"

"Ain't like it makes a difference."

The dog licked my face before sighing and lying down on my lap. I didn't correct Bobby.

§

Dog didn't last no more than two minutes against Bobby's pit.

When we first dropped him in the circle, the stupid dog headed right back for me, standing on his hind legs and pressing his paws against the chicken wire.

"Dog likes you," Bobby said. "I hazard he can tell how much you two have in common."

I didn't say nothing, just kept my eyes on the circle. First time I'd been allowed out here, and my whole body tingled with anticipation. It felt like when I'd gone up to the state fair and rode the rickety wooden roller coaster, the excitement building at the pit of my stomach just as the cart neared the highest point, and then washing over me and making me close my legs when it plunged down.

The dog stopped pawing at the fence when Bobby's pit entered the circle. The pitbull was a mean old animal that Bobby had never bothered to name. Big too, its coat an ocean of black with occasional islands of scarred pale flesh that no one had bothered to do much about.

Anything with some sort of sense would have known this was

an animal none to be messed with, so of course the shit dog just wagged its tail and headed right for it.

Quick as its master had been with me, the pit lunged for the dog, thick bits of drool glistening from its gums as its jaws opened. With the deadliness of a bear trap, it clamped down on the dog's furry neck.

The small dog yipped and kicked its legs, which was nothing to the pit, who shook him harder. Blood splashed on the ground, where it would settle and become just another stain to be ignored.

"Look at that killer instinct. Mikey ain't gonna have nothing on me this weekend. Kill 'em dog! Kill em!"

My stomach clenched as the pit shook the small dog one last time and threw him to the side of the cage, where it just laid there, fur matted with blood and dirt. To my surprise, I heard him give a small whine, and saw his chest slowly, so slowly, rise and then fall.

"Got a good one this time. We might get another session out of it," Bobby said, spitting a wad of tobacco into the circle. "Maybe it wasn't a bad idea taking you, Bait."

He walked around the circle and picked up the muzzle hanging from a tree branch. Snapping his fingers, his dog's demeanor completely changed. It turned to face Bobby and crouched down, its growl mixed with a whine that to my ears I reckoned sounded a lot like the dog it almost killed.

"Oh shut the fuck up already," Bobby told it and unlocked the gate, stepping into the circle and approaching the dog. With a practiced motion, he had the dog muzzled in a matter of seconds.

"Git the other one and take him to the cages," he said. "I'm gonna find Mikey and tell that peckerwood we should double what we got on this fight."

I waited till Bobby was gone before I threw up the frozen waffles I had for breakfast this morning. Wiping my mouth with the back of my sleeve, I looked over to the dog, who was not quite dead, but a whole distance away from alive. Truth be told, I considered just leaving him here out in the open. Come nightfall, a fox or some other animal would finish the job that the pit had started.

But I only got halfway out of the backyard before I turned around, stepped into the circle, and picked the dog up as carefully as I could.

Looking down at him and having him look back up at me with wounded eyes that weren't as dark and vibrant as before almost made me throw up all over again. Swallowing the bile building in my throat, I carried the dog to the cages.

Dogfighting was the newest thing in the trailer park. Before that there'd been the card games that always ended in fist fights, the drag races that had to stop due to no one having a good enough car to actually give a damn about, and even a sad, blow uppy attempt at a meth lab or two.

I'd lived here in this place my whole life, passed around from family to family when my ma and pa died. Or ran away. Or went to jail. I'd been too young to remember, and the story told to me changed as often as the sofa I slept in.

The shed was at the very end of the park, right next to the skeletons of a burnt out trailer. The aluminum walls caught the sunlight in a way that reminded me a bit of the way the fresh paint of the Dix Hill houses had grabbed the moonlight. The door was closed, but I didn't see no lock on it. Inside, the stench of shit and urine slammed into my nostrils. The stench would have sent me reeling were it not for the dog. Because of him, I held my breath and continued.

It was a whole other type of black inside. I'd slept outside plenty of times to know darkness, but this here was different. Felt almost like a real thing, something that could grab me and stuff me into one of the cramped, rusted cages that lined the walls. Already I was sweating from the heat. Most of the dogs inside hardly paid any mind to me, but there were a couple, as scarred as Bobby's, that growled when I passed them by. Settling on a cage by the back, I lined it with some newspapers I found on the ground and gently set the dog down. He barely stirred when I did so, just gave another small whine.

I watched him for the next few minutes before leaving and coming back with a small bowl full of water and some leftover Wal-Mart rotisserie chicken I found in the kitchen of someone's house.

"Here, eat." I said, setting both things right by the dog's nose.

The dog instead just raised its head and gave my outstretch hand a lick, before lowering it once again and sighing.

The sigh is what did it. I dunno, something about that sound just made me all sorts of angry. It was like the dog was blaming me for everything that had happened. Wasn't my fault his owner didn't think enough of 'im to put him somewhere safe when they left town. Wasn't my fault that this is the life he was born into.

"Stupid animal," I said, rattling his cage and stomping away, trying to ignore the tears streaming down my face.

§

That night I didn't got almost no sleep. Don't think no one at the park did.

It was the stupid dog's fault. Even four trailers away I could hear it howling, a low, pitiful wail that arced into the night and made the windows of the living room I was in vibrate. Who knew that such a tiny little thing could make such a ruckus. Soon enough, the other dogs joined in too, the sound spilling all over the trailer park.

Somehow, after who knows how long of tossing and turning on the sofa, I finally fell into a weird sort of sleep, the howling pressing into my ears and burrowing deep inside me, into a place I didn't even now I had. If you guessed I dreamed, you'd be wrong. There was nothing inside that head of mine when it hit the armrest of the sofa except relief.

When I woke, I did it with jolt. Light streamed into the room and cut through my haze. Blinking, I checked the cracked clock on the wall and realized it was almost noon. Took me only a second after that to realize I heard no more howling.

I ran for the shed.

Getting the doors wide open to let as much light in as I could, I headed for the back. The other dog's stares pressed down on my shoulders while the center of my chest twisted up into a knot as I scanned the cages.

His was empty.

"There you are, girl. Been looking for you all day."

"What you want Bobby?" I asked, still looking at the cage. His bowl and the chicken I left were still there, and I moved them out of the way—in a stupid hope that maybe the dog had been hiding behind them.

"Just wanted to tell you that I won. Made a sweet fifty bucks out of it."

"Great."

"Dog's fucked up, but he'll be okay. Probably anyways. Wanted to see if you wanted to go out like in a couple of days for some more dogs. Yeah?"

I closed my eyes and wished there was a way to close my ears too.

"Bait, you heard me?"

"Yeah, Bobby I heard ya."

"So? You wanna come?"

"Sure."

"Cool. Don't think we should hit Dix Hills though. But there's other places."

The next part, I didn't want to do, but I knew I had to. "Hey Bobby? What happened to the dog?"

He pointed to a pen holding his dog. "I told you, he's fucked up, but should be alright."

"I'm talking about the other one. The one we..." I almost said stole, but the word lodged in the back of my throat and refused to come out. "The shit sue."

"Oh, that one. Animal was dead by the time I got here. Guess he wasn't as good as we thought. Serves him right for all the noise he made last night."

I think I nodded, and he kept talking for a while, before slapping my ass and leaving me alone in the shed.

I don't know how long it was before I moved again. I do know that once I started moving, it only took a couple of minutes to open up most of the cages. Some of the dogs scattered at once, while others just pressed themselves against the back of their cages, as if freedom was a scary thing to them.

Having done that, I walked over to Aunt Clara's nearby trailer and went inside. Two things I knew about aunt Clara: one, she could usually be relied on to sleep through most everything thanks to the pink and blue pills and whiskey she downed them with, and two, she kept a rifle in her living room closet.

I thought the thing would have been heavier, but it weighed less than the dog I held last night. Clara kept it nice and oiled up which was a surprise. She also kept it loaded, which wasn't so much of a surprise.

Returning to the shed, I walked over to the only cage I hadn't unlocked.

Bobby's dog hadn't even been cleaned after the fight, specks of blood all over his fur. The dog laid at the back of the cage, and when it sensed me approaching, raised its head and watched me get closer.

Now, I probably was doing the dog a favor, doing what I aimed to do, but I don't want you thinking I did it for that. When I rested the rifle on my shoulder and pushed the barrel into the cage, all I was thinking of was how it'd killed the little dog. How it killed the bait.

The kickback of the gun almost put me on my ass. If setting the dogs loose hadn't stirred everyone already, this would. Nothing rouses people up from sleep like the sound of a gun going off.

Didn't bother to look at what was left inside the cage now. Resting the gun on the ground, I left the shed.

I left them all. Left the cages and the trailers, the dogs and the people.

A mile out and I could still hear howling in the distance.

All Alone

Erik Arneson

October 29, 1951

Lust blazed across Oscar Cain's eyes as he watched the newest burlesque dancer at The Troc. Slouched in a red velvet padded seat, he forgot to blink as he took in every detail of her legs and breasts and the numinous way those legs and breasts swayed on stage. She was less than half his age, but many of the dancers were equally young and that didn't stop him from patronizing The Troc at least once a week. It surely didn't stop him from thinking the lewd thoughts inspired by this alluring girl, the platinum blonde Cherry Wilde.

As Cherry Wilde left the stage, Cain stole another sip of bourbon from the flask tucked in his suit jacket. He stood up, made like he was brushing lint off his trousers to conceal his arousal, and walked to the lobby.

The ticket seller, Mabel, sat alone in a cramped rectangular booth. The only interaction she had with customers was through the narrow slot where they slipped her cash and she gave them tickets. Mabel was rapidly approaching 60, a fat woman with small, angry eyes hidden beneath unkempt eyebrows. Her gray hair was so consistently unruly that Cain wondered where someone went to get a haircut that bad, or did she cut it herself.

"Big Will in today?" Cain asked.

Mabel answered with a grunt and a nod toward the manager's office. Cain crossed the worn red carpet in the lobby and turned the knob of a wooden door with a peeling coat of white paint. It was locked. He pounded on it with his open palm. Flakes of paint fluttered to the ground.

"Beat it!" Big Will yelled from the other side.

Cain yelled back, "Get off your ass and open this door!"

Big Will opened the door a few moments later, wearing drab brown pants and matching suspenders over a faded blue button-down shirt, half-buttoned, with prominent sweat stains at the armpits. Cain, in his tailored three-piece suit and snap-brim fedora, didn't understand how any self-respecting man could present himself like that. Even at The Troc.

Big Will greeted his visitor with a clammy handshake and a forced smile. He seemed to get bigger and balder every time Cain saw him. The man must be carrying more than 350 pounds on his five-foot-six frame. Waddling back to the oversized wooden chair behind his desk, Big Will asked, "So what do you think, Cain?"

"That little Cherry's as sweet as you promised."

Big Will sighed. "Yeah. When do you want to meet her?"

"Tonight. What's her real name?"

Big Will pulled out a yellowish handkerchief that was probably clean and white, once. "You make me nervous, Cain, you know that?"

The left side of Cain's mouth turned up in a smile. He enjoyed seeing his power cow people. "You can handle some nerves if it means staying in business, can't you?"

Sweat and grime accumulated on Big Will's handkerchief as he wiped his face. He told Cain the dancer's real name, Susan Hayes. "Her shift ends at seven o'clock."

"Perfect," Cain said. "I have some business to take care of. I'll be back to pick her up for dinner."

§

Cain embraced his occupation, a bagman working for a boodler in a city run by thieves. An imposing man who took pride in his physique, he spent his days visiting businesses across Philadelphia and glad-handing the owners – threatening them when necessary – to make sure they understood that although Barney Samuel was down to his last weeks in office, he was still Mayor and deserved their respect. Preferably in the form of cash donations.

Samuel, a Republican, wasn't running for re-election. This complicated Cain's work, as did the campaign being run by the self-styled reformer and current city controller Joseph Clark. Clark was trying to become the first Democratic mayor of Philadelphia since 1884 by convincing the citizens that their city government was corrupt to the core. Walter Annenberg's rag, the *Philadelphia Inquirer*, was in bed with Clark. It might all be true, and in fact Philadelphia's reputation was such that many who traveled in political circles referred to it as the City of Brotherly Loot, but Cain had a sweet deal going and no interest in seeing it end.

Cain entered Dabrowski's Hardware in the Port Richmond neighborhood. Jack Dabrowski was helping a customer, so Cain browsed the high-shelved aisles until he found the hammers. He tested a few before selecting the one that felt best in his hand. The wooden grip was just the right diameter and the tool was well-balanced, the nicest hammer he'd ever held. Cain walked back to the front of the store and stood near the cash register.

The customer was a man who looked to be in his 70s and said he needed a wire fence to keep rabbits out of the garden in his back yard. Dabrowski carried the fencing to the register, chatting with the customer the entire way. When he saw Cain, he stopped mid-sentence.

Cain smiled. "Nice to see you, Jack."

"I...uh..."

"Go ahead, finish helping the nice gentleman."

Dabrowski, a short man who had been a wrestler in high school three decades earlier, nodded and moved to the other side of the register. He accepted the man's money and asked the part-time clerk to carry the fence to his house, five blocks away.

When he and Dabrowski were alone, Cain said, "I thought we had a good relationship, Jack. But I'm wondering, was I wrong about that?"

"Were you wrong?" The shake in Dabrowski's voice and hands betrayed his fear, pleasing Cain. "Your idea of a relationship is I pay the fire marshal, the plumbing inspector, and anyone else you send, over and over. What do I get in return?"

Cain shrugged as though the question mystified him. "You get to operate your business unimpeded." Cain thumped the head of the hammer into his left hand while he spoke. The steady rhythm matched the relaxed cadence of his voice. "Jack, do you know why I'm here today?"

Dabrowski's right eye twitched.

Cain swung the hammer with a flourish, bringing it down onto a pile of pamphlets next to the register. Dabrowski flinched.

"What are these?" Cain asked.

Dabrowski didn't respond.

"Do you not understand the question? I know you're a Polack. Are you retarded as well?"

Dabrowski's nostrils flared and he threw a wild punch. Cain caught Dabrowski's fist in his left hand and shook his head.

"I didn't want it to come to this, Jack," he said, squeezing hard enough that Dabrowski took a sharp breath and gulped. Cain shoved Dabrowski's hand down onto the counter next to the "Joseph Clark for Mayor" pamphlets and pushed it flat.

"Flat is best," Cain said. "Trust me when I say it'll be much worse if you move your hand."

Cain held onto Dabrowski's wrist and raised the hammer. Dabrowski inhaled sharply and turned his head on the downswing but didn't move his hand. The hammer pulverized the bone in his pinky. Dabrowski held back a scream and tried to yank his hand away, but Cain's grip was stronger. The hammer raised again and this time landed squarely on Dabrowski's wedding band, deforming the ring and the finger inside it.

Cain loosened his grip and Dabrowski jerked his hand away, using his other arm to cradle it like a newborn baby. Tears dripped from both eyes. He tried, slowly and carefully, to remove the ring from his smashed finger. It was too bent to come off.

"I know it's painful, Jack, but I'm not unreasonable," Cain said. "I only went for two fingers because I respect the fact that you have a family to feed. And I believe we can rebuild this relationship. For starters, you won't be spreading this crap for Clark anymore. Right?"

Dabrowski stared at Cain, but only for a beat. "Right."

Cain nodded. "Good. Sorry about the ring. I should've had you take it off first. I recommend using some bolt cutters on it. And see a doctor about those fingers, Jack. I'd hate for you to lose them." He turned the hammer in his hand. "Thanks for this. A fine tool, indeed."

§

Cain tossed the hammer into the backseat of his 1950 Cadillac Coupe de Ville, a black hardtop. He drove to his favorite lunch spot, the Mayfair Diner, and sat in his favorite booth.

Joan, his favorite waitress because she was young and her uniform was always a little too short and a little too tight, poured him a cup of coffee. Cain looked her over, top to bottom and then back to the top, and smiled. She was petite but well-rounded in the right places.

"The usual for you today, Mr. Cain?"

"Unless I can get you instead."

Joan giggled and walked toward the kitchen. Cain's eyes lingered as he imagined her dancing at The Troc. Before she left his sight, Detective David Morris of the Philadelphia Police Department appeared at Cain's table.

"We have a problem," Morris said.

"No 'Hello'? No 'How are you today'? What's this world coming to when we can't make time to be civilized?"

"Hello. How are you? Now listen good, Oscar. We're about to get thoroughly fucked."

Joan gasped at the curse. Neither of the men had noticed her return. "David," Cain said, "I think you startled our lovely Joan with your coarse language."

"Oh, that's alright," Joan said with a nervous smile. "Your usual, Detective Morris?"

"Sure, doll. Thanks."

Both men watched Joan wiggle back to the kitchen.

"Tell me about this problem," Cain said.

Morris leaned forward, his voice an insistent whisper. "The grand jury's getting real close."

"Is that all? Relax. Folks in this neighborhood, hell, folks all across the city – they want to gamble. We're providing a service."

"You know the grand jury's looking at more than gambling, and not everyone's strong enough to hold out when they feel the thumbscrews. And heaven help us if Clark takes over City Hall next month."

"Sometimes I think my friends have all gone crazy. Republicans have run this city for damn near 70 years. That won't change."

"That so? You see today's *Inquirer*? They endorse Clark right on the front page, and the next two pages spell out everything: the tax office embezzlement, the parking lot operators stealing cash, even Ellis's suicide, for God's sake."

Cain waved it off. "Proof that Annenberg's lost his mind. Doesn't mean the voters are losing theirs."

"I hope you're right, but I wouldn't stake so much as a dollar bill on it. Anyway, here's our immediate problem: Raymond's been summoned to the grand jury and he's been acting all sorts of strange. Spent a lot of time visiting a lawyer. I think he's turning state's evidence."

Cain took a deep breath. "When's he testify?"

"Sounds like the day after tomorrow."

Cain folded his hands under his chin and closed his eyes. Without opening his eyes, he said, "We'll visit Raymond after lunch."

"To do what?"

Cain opened his eyes. "What do you think?"

Morris shook his head. "Jesus. You really are a callous prick."

Cain reached across the table, grabbed Morris's necktie and pulled him forward until they were nose to nose. "You think I like this?" he asked through gritted teeth. "The three of us have been pals since grade school. But we have to protect the Mayor, and I'm not going to jail, either. Besides, I know you wouldn't have told me what you did unless you're certain that Raymond has turned. And if Raymond's not on the team anymore..." Cain let the words hang there as he released Morris's necktie.

Morris coughed weakly and buried his head in his hands. "Jesus," he muttered.

Joan appeared with a bright smile, carrying two dishes. "Here you go, gentlemen. Liver and onions for Mr. Cain and the meatloaf for Detective Morris."

§

Cain knocked on the door at Raymond Lawson's home near the Bridge Street Terminal in Philadelphia's Frankford neighborhood. When Lawson answered, Cain noticed his eyes widen as he recognized his visitors.

"Oscar, David. What brings you here?"

"Simply saying hello to a good friend," Cain said.

"Yeah," Morris said. "How are you, Raymond?"

Lawson's eyes narrowed. "Good. A little busy."

"Too busy to invite us in?" Cain asked.

Lawson hesitated. Cain used his shoulder to nudge Lawson out of the way and stepped inside. Morris followed on his heels. Lawson glanced outside and closed the door.

Cain looked down the hallway toward the kitchen as he hung his fedora on the coat rack. "Where's Julia?"

"Still at the high school. She has detention duty this week."

Cain nodded slowly. "Must be tough on you," he said.

Lawson shrugged. "What must be tough?"

"Getting yanked into a grand jury isn't fun for anyone. How you holding up?"

Lawson stared at Cain. "I'm handling it."

"Good," Cain said. "How about we head to the basement for some of that nice whiskey of yours?"

Lawson hesitated, then his shoulders drooped. He led the way to the basement.

Cain and Morris sat on adjacent stools at the bar Lawson had built himself. Cain folded his hands on the polished red oak countertop and sat motionless. Morris couldn't keep still. He ran his hands through his hair, cracked his knuckles and crossed his arms.

From under the bar, Lawson pulled out a bottle of whiskey, then two glasses. "Straight or on the rocks?"

Cain stared at Lawson. "Perhaps you should have the first drink, Raymond."

Lawson nodded. He poured the whiskey into a tumbler and drank it in a single gulp. "You've heard," he said.

"Did you expect otherwise?"

"I hoped otherwise."

"Damn it, Raymond," Morris said. "What the hell are you thinking? It doesn't have to go down like this. Right? Cain, tell him it doesn't have to go down like this."

Cain continued to stare at Lawson.

"Listen," Lawson said. "I'm the sorriest man here about it, but yes, it does have to go down like this. If I had a play, I'd make it. But I don't, and we all know it."

Lawson poured himself a second whiskey.

After he gulped it down, Cain said, "I give you credit for handling this like a gentleman, Raymond. I'll have one for old times' sake."

Lawson shrugged and grinned. "I won't have much use for it soon anyway, right?" He reached under the bar. With his left hand, he pulled up a clean tumbler and set it down. With his right, he pulled up a Smith & Wesson .38 revolver and fired a shot at Cain.

Cain fell to the floor, disoriented. He left ear hurt. He grabbed it and felt blood. As Cain scrambled to hide behind a sofa, he heard a second shot, then a third and a fourth, then silence.

He called out, "You don't have to do this, Raymond!"

No answer. He examined his left hand, which was smeared with blood. He felt his ear and wondered where his earlobe was.

"Raymond!" He heard only breathing, nothing else. "David, you okay?"

Morris gasped like he was in pain. "I think... I think I got him."

Cain called out again. "Raymond! I'm going to stand up. Don't do anything you'll regret."

From his knees, Cain peered over the back of the sofa. He didn't see Lawson anywhere. He stood and saw Morris on the floor, holding a hand to his stomach, blood spreading in a dark stain on his baby blue dress shirt. Morris nodded, indicating that Lawson was behind the bar. Cain listened closely but heard only Morris's wheezes. He looked over the edge of the counter. Lawson's lifeless black eyes stared back at him.

"You got him, all right," Cain said. "Deader than four o'clock."

"I need an ambulance," Morris said. "I'm shot bad."

Morris's face was pale, covered in a sheen of sweat. His eyes were desperate. He was barely in better shape than the corpse behind the bar.

Cain picked up the empty tumbler from the bar and held it to see his reflection. Most of his left earlobe was missing. He felt the part that remained and grimaced from the sting caused by his touch. Cain grabbed a dish towel from the counter and wiped his fingerprints off the tumbler, the bar, and the stool. He looked around and concluded that he hadn't touched anything else.

"Don't worry, David, I'll get an ambulance," Cain said.

He took the towel with him and climbed the stairs back to the first floor, where he retrieved his fedora from the coat rack. Outside, none of the neighbors were in their yards. He walked quickly to his car and drove home. He figured Morris would soon join Lawson in hell, or purgatory. Neither had earned a place in heaven.

§

It was quiet in Cain's row house mansion near the Art Museum. Standing under the spray of warm water in his shower, he considered what had happened. It had been, on balance, a good day. He would miss Lawson and especially Morris, but his first priority was to protect himself and his second priority was to protect Mayor Samuel. Getting Lawson out of the picture did both. His earlobe had bothered him at first, but the more he thought about it, if he had to lose some piece of flesh, an earlobe was just the thing.

After his shower, Cain bandaged his ear and shaved. He was confident his date with the dancer Susan Hayes would go well. Dates with the girls that Big Will hired always went well. As he stood at the mirror and slapped on his Old Spice aftershave, he debated whether he should call her Susan or Cherry. Susan, he decided, at least until things started to heat up.

§

In The Troc's lobby, Cain saw Mabel in the ticket booth reading *LIFE*. She didn't bother to put down the magazine, he didn't bother to say hello. He continued to Big Will's office and knocked on the door.

"Beat it!" Big Will yelled.

The door was unlocked this time, so Cain let himself in. Big Will was behind his desk with a nearly naked brunette on his lap. "Oh!" she screamed, startled, when Cain stepped in.

"Damn it, Cain, can't you hear?" Big Will pushed the girl off his lap. She scurried to pick her clothes up from the floor.

"Hell, Big Will, how was I supposed to know what you're up to?"

The dancer used her clothes to shield her breasts. Big Will sighed. "Viv, go tell Susan to come in here." The girl nodded and left through the office's back door, which Cain knew from experience led to a hallway that led to the dancers' dressing room.

"What happened to your ear?"

"Cut it shaving," Cain said.

"You cut your ear... shaving?"

Cain stared at Big Will. Before long, Big Will got the picture. He pulled out his handkerchief, wiped the sweat from his forehead, and said, "Yeah, I see how that could happen."

Susan Hayes entered, wearing a thin white sweater that clung to the bullet bra underneath like Saran Wrap. The top interested Cain so much that he didn't immediately notice her cherry red pants, also form-fitting.

"Susan, my girl! You look exquisite," Big Will said. "Allow me to introduce you to Oscar Cain. He works for Mayor Samuel and has been a great friend to me and The Troc through the years."

Susan extended her hand to Cain. "It's a distinct pleasure to meet you, Mr. Cain."

Cain removed his hat and kissed the back of her hand. "The pleasure is distinctly mine." And he meant it, particularly when he heard Susan giggle.

§

During the drive to Bookbinder's at 2nd and Walnut, Susan couldn't stop talking about what a great car the Coupe de Ville was. At dinner, she went on and on the same way about the restaurant, the maître d', the wine, and the lobster Cain ordered for her because he believed it was an aphrodisiac.

As they waited on the sidewalk for the valet to bring his car, Cain turned to Susan and smiled. "There's an incredible view of the city from my roof," he said. "Would you like a peek before I take you home?"

"Oh," she said, biting her bottom lip and swaying her hips ever so slightly. "I should get home. I have another long day tomorrow. It's not easy on the legs to dance for so long."

"If anyone has the legs for it, you do," Cain said. "This'll only take a few minutes. We can go to the roof, I'll show you the best view of downtown, then I'll take you right home. What do you say?"

Susan's eyes twinkled. "I'll do it!"

Less than 15 minutes later, he parked in front of his Green Street mansion. He helped Susan out of the car, and her wide eyes took in the three-story building's ornate wooden entry doors, the arched window above them, and the large stained glass windows on the second floor.

"You live here?" she asked.

"Home, sweet home." Cain opened the black wrought iron gate that led to his yard and they approached the front door. "Come in."

In the entrance hall, he gave Susan a brief tour, especially showing off the large parlor, decorated with deep burgundy Victorian wallpaper and fine leather furniture. He made sure she noticed the large, gold-framed photo of him and Governor Thomas Dewey of New York.

Cain showed off his bedroom on the second floor, pointing out the large four-poster bed. "The most comfortable bed in

Philadelphia," he said. "I bought the mattress and the silk sheets from a European importer in Manhattan. The finest quality."

As they reached the door that led to the roof, Cain asked, "Are you ready for the best view of downtown?"

Susan nodded enthusiastically and they walked into the cool night air. Susan gasped and ran to the waist-high brick wall at the edge of the roof, where she stared at the mosaic of lights glimmering against the night sky.

"Gorgeous," she said, her voice barely louder than a whisper. "I love it."

"I've seen those lights thousands of times," Cain said. "But..." He paused.

Susan faced him. "But?"

He grinned his most charming grin and said, "Their beauty pales in comparison to yours."

Susan blushed and Cain's heart raced.

"Come here, baby," he said as tenderly as he could manage. "Let me feel your face on my hand." He caressed her cheek.

Susan smiled an unhappy smile. She pulled away. "Mr. Cain?"

"What is it, doll?"

"I don't mean to be disrespectful, but I hope you didn't bring me up here thinking that, you know, that things were going to happen between us."

Cain wasn't concerned. He had faced this kind of reaction before. He slipped his hands around one of hers. "Susan, relax. We're going to have a great time. And I'll take care of you. You know that, right?"

She nodded weakly.

Cain leaned in for a kiss. Susan pulled her hand out of his and made a move for the door that led back inside. Cain grabbed her wrist and jerked her body to make her look him in the eyes.

"Susan, don't leave me here all alone," he said, trying to mask his anger. "Didn't the other girls talk to you?"

Her eyes drifted down. "They said if I showed you a good time, you'd take care of me. Maybe help me get a better apartment, things like that. They never said anything about what you're suggesting."

He could no longer hold back his ire. "You dumb broad, what exactly do you think 'a good time' means?" He pulled her close, his lips brushing against hers as he spoke through his teeth. "Listen to me. I can make you or break you, and I will enjoy it either way."

"You're hurting me," Susan said.

Cain loosened his grip enough to stop the pain but pulled her back to the edge of the roof overlooking downtown. "Just look at that romantic view. How about we start with a little kiss, doll?"

Susan blinked, smiled a little and said, "Okay."

Cain knew he had broken her. Other girls had been difficult, too, but eventually every one of them gave in. He released her and leaned forward. Just as he closed his eyes he felt her hand whip across his face. His eyes jumped open and he grabbed her wrist again.

"That was a mistake," Cain said.

With his free hand, he slapped Susan. Her head twisted violently and she screamed. He slapped her again. She fell to her knees and sobbed.

He let go of her wrist but stood over her and asked, "What the hell made you think that was a good idea?"

"I'm sorry, Mr. Cain. I'm so sorry."

He shouldn't give her another chance to get it right, she had used up all of her chances. But she was truly spectacular in that sweater, and he desperately wanted her in his bed despite the red blemish spreading across her cheek. He extended a hand to her and she took it.

"I'm so sorry," she said as she started back to her feet.

"It's alri...," he said before Susan cut him off with a powerful knee to the groin. Cain doubled over in pain, unable to catch his breath. She brought her knee up again, this time to his face. His nose cracked and a line of blood sprayed across the brick wall. He fell backwards, cursing the strength of those beautiful legs.

"No one," she said, wiping the tears from her eyes, "treats me that way. One other man thought he could, but not even my father got away with it. And as nasty and despicable as he was, you're not half the man."

Cain coughed and struggled to take a shallow breath. "Do you have any idea..."

"I've got a lot of ideas," Susan said. "First is that you've said enough."

She kicked him in the throat, the point of her three-inch heel connecting with his Adam's apple. Cain couldn't breathe at all now, and he worried that she'd crushed his windpipe. Susan grabbed him by the hair and pulled him to his feet. She bent him over the wall, giving him a bird's-eye view of the alley below. All Cain could think about was getting air to his lungs.

"This can only end one way, Mr. Cain. I know what you'll do to me otherwise. So if you have anything to get right with the Creator, now's the time."

He turned his head as much as her grip would allow and spit on her leg. The white bubbles of his weak spittle stuck to her cherry pants.

"So be it," she said, and lifted his legs to push him over the edge.

Cain's body was barreling through the air before he fully understood what was happening. Comprehension took hold between the second floor and the first, when he wondered if he'd be reunited with his buddies Morris and Lawson. And just that quickly, Oscar Cain's head landed on the pavement, his skull shattered, and Mayor Barney Samuel lost the best bagman who ever worked the streets of Philadelphia.

The Trouble with Sylvia
Cheri Ause

Since her body showed up, it seems like all anyone ever wants to talk about is Aunt Syl. A lot of folks still don't believe us, but we say see for yourself, it's in the paper. So we show them the article, and then they give us that *look*, you know the one that says "Are you people evil or just plain stupid?"

Of course, there are the ones who like to point fingers, although they never say word one to our faces. Like that old busybody Mrs. Willis, the one who used to play bridge with Sylvia every Thursday afternoon? She straight out told all the ladies at the Ji-Max Card Club that we did it just to spite Sylvia. Imagine that. In all my forty-seven years, I've never heard such a thing. Like anyone would ever do anything like that on purpose.

Sylvia was always one to go her own way and on every occasion was the first one to tell you to mind your own beeswax. That's the word she used, *beeswax*, although what bees had to do with anything I never knew. Whatever plans she might've had for monkeying around behind closed doors, she sure wouldn't tell us, and I'll swear to you now, we'd be the last to give her any what for. So when she turned up missing—now isn't that the dumbest idea you ever heard—*turned up missing*? Shouldn't it be "*went* missing" and "*turned up* found"? You can't "turn up" and be "missing" at the same time, I think you'll agree.

Anyway, Sylvia "turned up missing." In fact it was her brother Cecil, my uncle, who was the first person to bring it up—him always being the one to keep account of everybody and everything, don't matter if it's his business or not. We was all sitting around watching *Dancing with the Stars*, talking about how the show was probably rigged so that cute little Bristol Palin would get almost to the end and then have victory snatched away from her by some Hollywood type.

That's when Cecil up and says, "Where's that Sylvia got herself off to? It's been days since I've had to listen to her yap about isn't it her turn to pick what's on TV." He nodded toward Sylvia's empty wing-back chair. "A body could get real used to the quiet," he says. "That and not having to watch any more of them snooty public TV shows."

Then Phyllis, you know Phyllis, she married Cecil last year. She's fifty-five and a pretty good catch for someone as old as the hills. Of course, there is that fortune my dad said Cecil's supposed to have hidden in a mattress somewhere, but that's just a story. I know because I have looked everywhere for it, and if he's got more than two nickels to rub together at the end of the month, it'd be news to me. Anyway, Phyllis said she'd noticed that Sylvia's coffee cup had been left hanging untouched on the mug rack for what seemed like days. She just figured Sylvia was away on one of those solve-a-mystery weekends, but when she got to thinking about it, it was already Thursday and that'd be a pretty long weekend.

We looked around the house some at that point, and it did seem kind of strange that her winter coat was still hanging in the hall closet even though it was the middle of February and 25 degrees on a good day. We knocked on the door to her room, but there was no answer, so we just went on about our business figuring she was going on about hers.

At the same time, there *was* a peculiar smell coming from somewhere in the house. Phyllis accused me of putting things down the toilet that didn't belong. "You know how these old pipes in this house back up," she said. I said the only thing that got backed up as far as I could tell was Cecil and maybe she ought to check what she was putting down him.

Another few days passed and wouldn't you know, Christina Peterson, one of Sylvia's mystery weekend friends, called saying she hadn't heard back from Sylvia yet and needed to know that very day if Sylvia was planning to go with them on another one of their "getaways," this one on a train. Why those people want to hang around some mildewy old mansion or ride around on a dumpy train all weekend pretending to be Shylock Holmes or whoever, I just do not understand. I guess if the food's good enough it wouldn't be too bad; otherwise, why would you spend all that time trying to find a fake murderer when you could be with your family playing a nice game of Parcheesi or working a jumbo jigsaw puzzle together?

Of course, as soon as I told Christina that Sylvia wasn't home, right away she got her undies in a bunch and wanted to know where she was. I could just hear her blood pressure rising when I told her we didn't know. Then I added, that although it obviously didn't mean much to her, we thought better than to pry into Sylvia's private life. So Christina starts in on me, jawing about all the unanswered phone messages she'd left with us and asking what kind of family doesn't know where someone is for two weeks. To be honest, it wasn't till I heard the words "two weeks" that I counted back and realized the last time I saw Sylvia was the day after my hair appointment, which was, in fact, two weeks earlier. That's when I just laid the phone down on the bench and let Christina finish that conversation with herself.

Turns out when Christina finally figured out I was gone, she hung up and called the other old mystery spooks. The next thing you know they're all standing on the front porch demanding to know what happened to Sylvia and what we knew. That got them nowhere, especially with Cecil, who told them it'd be best if they'd just go on home and stop bothering us, that he was in charge of the family and had everything under control.

When they heard that, they got right back up on their high horse and went straight to the sheriff's office. I got this next part from Franny Morgan, his dispatcher. The sheriff told them he'd look into it but he probably couldn't do anything being that Sylvia was an adult and old enough to go wherever she wanted, whenever she wanted, and with—or without— whoever she wanted. "People up and walk away all the time," he told them. "In February?" they said. "Yep, in February too."

All that badgering must have finally got to Phyllis because she decided she was going to get to the bottom of things. She figured we should look for clues in Sylvia's room, whether Sylvia would approve or not. She said it would be kind of like our own little mystery weekend.

"You should invite the spooks," I told her. "At least they've had some practice at ciphering signs."

But Phyllis would have none of that. "I don't want that bunch scuffing up my freshly waxed linoleum."

I said I'd help search Sylvia's room, but Phyllis said I'd have to wait in the hall. She didn't want me "contaminating the scene."

As soon as Miss CSI opened the door, we figured out where the smell was coming from. "That darned Sylvia," Phyllis says. "She's been sneaking food into her room again and letting it go bad." She took a hankie from her pocket and bunched it up over her nose before going in. I followed right behind, figuring as a blood relative I had every right to be there too.

The bed was made up real nice with that frilly new comforter and the pillow shams Sylvia bought at the Target January white sale. Phyllis snooped under the bed and I must say looked disappointed when she didn't find any dirty dishes or spoiled food. Next she opened the closet. Everything there was neat as a pin too.

"What's that?" I said.

"Where?"

"Right there." I pointed to the space between the chifforobe and the wall. "What's Sylvia's shoe doing back there?"

Phyllis, who never thinks any room is tidy enough and is always on the lookout for anything you put down for one minute and don't pick up again right away, went to investigate.

She tugged at the dark-brown *Aerosol* and then stood up real quick. "This isn't Sylvia's shoe."

"Well, what is it? It sure looks like her shoe."

"It's Sylvia."

That's when we discovered for ourselves that Sylvia was stuck in between the chifforobe and the wall. She was all purple and green, and stuff was oozing out from different parts of her. I won't trouble you with more details. So we called the sheriff, and after he showed up, he called the fire department and the EMTs and his deputy and the coroner. It was quite a hullabaloo.

And now everyone keeps talking about the whole mess even though there's not much of anything more to tell. Contrary to what you might have heard, the D. A. is not filing charges at this time. His investigators said it was all just an accident most likely brought on by Sylvia herself. It turns out she probably dropped her black onyx spider ring, one of those trashy pieces of jewelry she always liked to wear on those mystery weekends. It must have rolled behind the chifforobe and she must have squeezed herself in after it, because that's where they found it—just inches past the tip of her outstretched and desiccated hand.

The Release of Degredation

Trey R. Barker

"Get it off, bitch." A wolf's howl. "**Now**."

"I take it off now—" She winks. "And you won't stay for the punch line."

"Don't want no fuckin' punch line...want some tits."

Instead, Bridgette bares a flash of tat. Snakes up her right arm toward her chest. Gives a demure smile to a bored audience. Piano player bangs out some bullshit that feels like a jagged crank trip. Lighting changes from lurid greens and blues to purples and reds.

She eyes Seanny. He's sitting with the new girl.

She's an assembly line girl...we all are.

Bridgette touches the empty holster hiding between her breasts.

"So I told him." Eye contact with a couple of men. They don't want the sophistication of burlesque. They want the strip and do it quick. "Marriage was a fine institution." Heavy breathing and sweaty foreheads. Eyeing her boobs while unzipping and hauling out their broken johnsons.

Another wink. "A fine institution." Her voice breathy. "But I'm not ready for an institution."

Piano player pounds away. A few obligatory laughs. She dances and spins fast to raise her skirt. Give 'em a flash of skin, let 'em see the tattoo slithering toward her crotch.

She says, "An old Mae West line. I stole it."

Strolls across the stage, a come-hither look on her face. The men all think it's sensual. She believes it's slutty and low-rent, exactly what Seanny wants. "A friend of mine once said, 'Good performers borrow...great performers steal.'"

"Goddamnit, get nekkid!"

Ignores the catcalls, the men pawing at her shoes as she passes.

"So I stole the line." Bridgette runs a hand over her left breast—the men go wild thinking she's going to expose herself—and pulls a key. "Then I stole his car."

They throw a wall of 'boos.'

"And fifty bucks."

Seanny is at the bar, new girl riding his arm like a heated dog rides a leg. Gonna end quick for me, Bridgette thinks. Got the new gash on display; eyes glaze over when he looks at me.

How long do I have left, Seanny? Three nights? Five? A week?

Doesn't matter. He'll be dead and Bridgette will be gone. Touches the holster. Gone and back to the burlesque Mama taught her. Song and dance, mystery and seduction, detailed costumes rather than naked, jazz rather than boozy country or hair-metal.

Stares at the crowd, at Seanny, at the new snatch. Wants to cry. Wants to be done.

But doesn't know where Mama's gift is.

"Damnit."

§

"Gotta show more skin. How many times I tell you that?" Seanny paces the dressing room, rubs his cock.

"You hired me for burlesque, Seanny," Bridgette says.

"Hired you for tits."

Swallows his insults, softens her face. "You're right, I'm just tired."

"Tired and bitchy," Seanny says.

"So who's the new girl?"

Seanny waves his hand. "Might dance. Wants to be part of the show. Ain't no thing."

Smiles his lop-sided grin. Thinks it's so fetching. Believes it seduced her, got her into his car and then into his club. Used it to grease her skids, promise her high-class burlesque shows all over the country. Used it to put her with another woman.

She's dead now. The other woman. Too much of Seanny's candy. Bridgette will be, too, if she isn't careful.

Two months ago Bridgette had been the new gash. Now Seanny has his newest chick and pretty quick, he'll suggest a duet, make lavish promises about high-dollar theaters and audiences, then give Bridgette too much candy and the new girl would be the solo star.

Seanny offers a few pills. "Need a little set me down? Cure that pissiness."

"I'm good."

"My lovely Bridgette, you know the score. We're making a killing here, ain't we?"

The killing's all yours and I'm on your leash.

His lizard tongue wets his thin lips. His hands travel to her breasts. "Love my Bridgette. Big words, big hair, big tits, big ass."

She lowers her head deferentially. "Thanks to you."

Gives her right breast a painful squeeze. "A little surgery, fix you right up. Christ the money will roll in."

"Big words, big hair, big tits, big ass."

"Damn straight."

He waits, she undresses. Her back to him so he can't see the holster. Gives him her sweaty panties and bra. He sniffs. "Lucky eBay." He winks. "Might have to sweat up a set for me."

Throws on some clothes, gets the holster next to her heart again. Holds up a $100 dollar bill. "My first big tip. Going to keep it as a souvenir."

"Money ain't made to be souvenired...made to be spent."

"You have souvenirs. Or so you told me."

The tip was bullshit, the money was hers. Open that fucking safe, she thinks. Let me see all your hidden souvenirs from all your dead women.

"Not goddamn money. But yeah, every one'a those girls had a talent and I got something to remember all those talents."

"Well, I want to keep this bill...for a little while, anyway, I don't know why...I just...I don't know—"

"You wanna reveal."

"What?"

"Reveal...in the glory. You wanna reveal in the glory of a C-note."

Stupid fuck. Yeah, I want to reveal in the glory. Or maybe revel.

Grins. "Anything you need, babe."

Follows him to his office. Sparse. A surprise given his ego. No prints or paintings, no expensive lamps or chairs. No glass-top desk. Liquor cabinet liberally stocked with alcohol, pills, and heroin. Empty glassine packets strewn everywhere, along with a pile of bloody syringes.

But—

Pictures.

Every chick who's ever belonged to him. Not the strippers, too many of those, but those who had padded his bed, let him ruin them, wet them, beat them.

In the middle row, third from left, a brunette with brown eyes and a sharp nose.

Bridgette says, "All these women. How can I ever measure up?"

"Don't even try. You got your thing, they got theirs."

Bridgette points at her mother. "What was hers?"

"Blowjobs, I think." He thrusts his pelvis toward the picture. "I like 'em fast and hard. A couple minutes and—boom—cum everywhere. She went down pretty hard, I remember right. Name of Jess, I think."

Name of Lynn, asshole.

He opens the safe while she stares at Mama. The hurt is already there, deep in every line and crevice in the woman's face, deep in her eyes. On her lips.

Puts the money in the safe. "Thought you kept souvenirs."

"Not in the safe." Snaps it closed. Unzips, shoves his pants to his knees. "You wanna kiss the snake?"

She holds back her gorge. "Do you want lips? Or hips?"

Leans back against the desk. "Both."

Goes to her knees. Stares at Mama's picture, lost in its deep-set frame.

Touches the holster.

§

"And tonight...what?" Nocturna asks, her leather tight around her body.

Bridgette stopped in a shitty gas station bathroom, furiously cleaned Seanny out of her. His smell is still thick and heavy. Tears burn like acid poured in her eyes.

"What manner of pain and self-loathing?"

Henryk Gorecki's 'Symphony of Sorrowful Song' floats, soft as Nocturna's skin. She is a beautiful woman. Languid. A sleek physicality. But a towering six feet tall in heels. When she wears them, Bridgette is intimidated, awed, protected.

Swallowing hard, Bridgette pulls a leash from her purse.

"Ah...tonight you are my dog. Dogs frequently get beaten, my young miss, for misbehaving."

"Yes."

Nocturna's hand flashes. Leaves a sting on Bridgette's cheek. "Mouthy already? It will be a long night for you, won't it?"

"I am sorry, Mistress."

"Yes, you are."

Attaches the leash to the dog collar Bridgette already wears. Shoves Bridgette to her knees.

"I let him fuck me tonight, Mistress."

"An animal in rut. How long will you allow that?"

Bridgette grinds her teeth. "Until I kill him."

Another slap, sharp and painful and so comforting.

"Until I kill him, Mistress."

Nocturna snorts. "You are worse than an animal."

"Worse, Mistress?"

Nocturna stands in front of Bridgette. "Animals have no choice. It's instinct." Shoves Bridgette's head to her boots. Bridgette licks. "You choose to allow it."

"I have to so I can get—"

Nocturna's crop snaps against Bridgette's bare ass.

It stings. It hurts.

And it is the only thing that keeps her from crying. It is relief and it is degradation and it will go on all night.

§

Winks at the audience. "And I said to him, 'Absolutely, honey, I'll try anything once.'"

Piano player stumbles like a pummeled boxer across a riot of notes.

"Twice if I like it."

A few laughs.

Seanny and the new girl are at the bar. The new girl, Seanny squeezing her breasts, stares at Bridgette. Learning me like I learned Mama, Bridgette thinks. She'll take my place because she wants that weak spotlight on her own face.

Bridgette purrs, comes off-stage to nuzzle a customer's ear. "Sometimes three times...just to make sure."

Shitty music and house lights up. Act is over. Scattered,

lethargic applause.

Then Seanny is next to her. "Don't know how the fuck you do it. No skin and still they buy shitloads of booze." Nods toward the new girl. "Been telling her. You the best. If she wanna learn, she need't'a watch you."

"You make it look so easy." New girl offers her hand. Smells of Seanny's cock. "Desiree. I'm not a stripper, either, I'm a performer."

"Of course, you are. We all are. I make it look easy because I've been working burlesque for a while. You'll get there someday."

Desiree frowns. "Burlesque?"

"The act," Seanny says.

"Oh." Desiree nods. "How come you ain't got no picture? In the office. I was looking at 'em." Face goes red. "I dropped one, too. I'm sorry, Seanny."

Seanny shrugs.

"The frame broke." She frowns. "A chink chick. There were metal balls inside the frame."

Bridgette says, "What?"

"Yeah," Seanny says. "Ben-Wa balls. It was her souvenir. Man, she was incredible. Loved ass play."

Bridgette feels stupid. Inside the frames. Of course. Big, heavy, thick frames and she'd had no idea.

I could have been finished this shit last night.

"How long we been together, Bridgette?"

"Two...three months?" Answers casually. A bullshit answer. Knows—to the minute—how long.

Since Mama was hooked on his candy. Since his name had tumbled from Mama's heroin-thin lips, syringe hanging out of her arm. Since Bridgette had hit the circuit looking for him. Since she'd found him and he'd pushed the candy on her.

"Been a good run, right?" Seanny asks. "Trusted me and we made a shitpile of money."

"Absolutely, Seanny."

"Think maybe the solo thing's empty? Houses ain't good anymore. Maybe time for a change."

"Add some bigger tits? Maybe a big ass and big hair?"

Seanny grins. "What I'm thinking."

Eyes on Desiree, Bridgette jams her sweaty bra and panties in Seanny's hand. The gleam is in his eyes so she goes down. He's unbuttoned and ready. She engulfs him and Desiree watches, wide-eyed, a tiny trickle of blood leaking from her arm.

§

Tonight, Nocturna plays Verdi's 'Requiem.'

Violent music. Sweeps Bridgette away. Whip cracks her ass while the bass drum booms and the trumpets explode. Her blood warms and her sex grows moist. Knows she's escalating. The shackles around her ankles tell her. The cuffs holding her face down and splayed out on Nocturna's St. Andrews Cross tell her.

The more she allows Seanny inside her—body and soul—the harsher penance she needs.

Whip comes down. Bridgette bites a wail.

The sin was of the flesh. The penance must be of the flesh, too.

Seanny slaps her when he fucks her. He shoves his hand deep in her backside. Leave himself on her face while he counts his money.

Sins all.

Nocturna steps on Bridgette's toes, grinds them. Bridgette stifles a scream. "Thank you, Mistress."

"The sin isn't of the flesh," Nocturna says. "It is in allowing your own humiliation."

She allows Seanny to slap her and fist her, to leave her stained with him.

Whip snaps. Again and again. Both women breathe hard. Back splits open like a vulva opening for a lover. The whip again and now blood spatters the wall. Drips down the wall; reminds Bridgette of Desiree's arm.

Bridgette moans; whip chews her behind. Touches the holster inside her bra.

§

A terrible crowd. They want skin. No dance. No seduction. No mystery.

Stands on stage, a length of rope in her hand. "A dame who knows the ropes...isn't likely to get tied up." Holds up a pair of cuffs. "Unless she wants to be."

Seanny and the new slit are nowhere. Bridgette knows the score. They're in the office, shooting it hard. Or about to.

"Let's see some pussy!"

Eyes snap to the old man. Clapping and whistling, beer spilled on his shirt.

Spreads her legs but shows nothing. "When it comes to choosing between two evils, I like the one I've never tried."

Ends quickly to a chorus of hisses. Piano player is startled. Next dancer is surprised and not quite in her Bat Woman cape. Darts on to the stage as Bridgette exits.

Office is cluttered with clothes and pills. Blood dots the floor. Vomit. Spilled alcohol. Desiree unconscious under Seanny's desk. White stains dried on her face and lips. Syringe hangs in her arm, trace of blood still in it.

Follows the stink of Seanny's musk. He's beneath the pictures of his women, pants open. Flaccid cock reminds her of a swollen slug.

"Bridgette?" His voice floats on a cloud of heroin. "That my Bridgette?"

Kneels and whispers, "It is."

"Did'ja come to eat the snake?"

"To kill the snake."

Laughing at his confusion, breaks Mama's shadowbox frame open.

Breath catches, heart races. Skin is warm, hands shake.

It's all been for this. The souvenir of Mama's blowjobs.

Two-shot pistol, .25 caliber pistol, chrome. A gift from Daddy. Dying of cancer, knew he wouldn't be around to protect his girls.

"This is mine." Tucks it into the empty holster between her breasts. Mama's holster, where she wore it.

"'Cuz that bitch could suck the chrome off a...." Seanny grins, a swollen thing. "What...what'r'yoo doing? Come on, kiss the snake."

Purple scarves from her act. One by one, binds Seanny. Hands together, feet together, those scarves tied together by another. Another secures him to the desk.

Eyes loll toward her. "A party?" Drool on his chin.

Opens her purse. "In your honor." Draws eight sealed vials and a syringe.

Won't shoot him. Two puny bullets might not do it. Or might do it too quickly.

Instead—

Mama's blood.

From the moment of her death. Stored carefully—lovingly—in tubes from a nurse friend of hers. Stored all these months since

Mama died. Stabs a syringe into the vial. Taps Seanny for a vein.

"Wha...."

"Shhhh, it'll only hurt for a second."

Later, it'll hurt much worse.

So many gifts...from contaminated needles and contaminated men; sex for drugs, drugs for sex. Which gift will Seanny get? AIDS? Hep C? One of the others?

"You hooked her. You raped her. You killed her."

She finds a vein. Stabs his flesh.

Bucks against the scarves. Eyes finally focus on Bridgette. "What're you doing?"

"Killing you."

"Wha...."

"Lynn was my Mama." Pushes the plunger, empties the vial. Replaces it with a full one. Empties that. Another and another.

"Getting hot." His blinks are a machine gun shooting.

"Hemolytic reaction. Uncross-matched blood. That might kill you first. Before the AIDS. I hope not."

Eyes bulge. "AIDS? Fuck're you talking about?" Struggles to sit. Candy with Desiree earlier left him confused, uncoordinated. Kicks at her.

She drives a fist into his face, feels nothing when his nose explodes.

"Bitch. You cain't do this." Voice high, piercing. "Just a shitty stripper. You ain't nothing."

"Did you hear the line tonight? About two evils?" Gathers the empty vials, stuffs them in her purse. "I've never tried murder."

"Bitch. Get back here. You can't do this to me...."

§

Crappy diner. Stench of eggs, bacon; shot through with grease and industrial cleaner. Bridgette grew up in places like this. Her and Daddy and Mama. Rode high and fine with him in his semi-rig across the country. Before his cancer. Before Mama tried to pay the bills.

"So he's dead."

"Will be."

Nocturna dressed in street clothes. Hair lost under a beret. Shakes her head. "Didn't think you'd do it."

"You don't know me very well."

Nocturna smiles. "True enough."

Pulls the gun from the holster in her bra. "She gave it to Seanny. He wanted a souvenir. She was rocked on the candy. Forgot Daddy gave it to her."

"Now you have it back."

"Yeah."

"And he'll be dead."

"Yeah."

"So all is right with the world. Except that whole exploitation thing."

Nods. Allowed Seanny to do everything to her. Didn't matter how vile or disgusting. For the gun. Revenge.

For Mama.

"Mutual exploitation. He did it to me. I did it to myself."

"Using what you need to get what you need," Nocturna says.

"What?"

Nocturna slathers jelly on toast. "Pain is how you find your lost moral center."

"They teach you that in college?"

"3.82 at City College. Accounting with a philosophy minor."

"I think people do what they do. They make up a reason why after they've done it." Breathes deep. Looks hard at Nocturna. "I'm sorry. For using you like he used me."

Nocturna chews. "Everybody's working out something. It's fine." Sighs. "But I will miss manipulating your body. It's beautiful and pliable and sensual and I love it."

Bridgette grins. "Finish your food. Seanny is dead. Anything I do now, I do because I want to."

"And what do you want to do?"

From her purse, Bridgette pulls the leash and collar.

One Corpse, Two Assholes

Eric Beetner

It was a great idea, even if Ricky didn't see it right away.

"You want us to kidnap a dead body?" he said, looking at me in that way of his I'd come to know so well through all our years of petty criminal enterprise and recreational drug use.

"Yeah," I said, trying to get my enthusiasm to rub off on him. "It's perfect."

"What the hell is perfect about it?" Ricky tipped the last of his beer from the bottom of the bottle into his mouth. I held my half-full Bud in my hand to use for extra-emphasis hand gesturing.

"Okay, what's the worst part of a kidnapping?"

"I don't know. Never done one."

I rolled my eyes at him. No vision, this dumbass. No aspirations for anything bigger in life. Me? I want to supersize it. Everything. More money, more drugs, more ... well, shit, more everything.

"It's the kidnapee, stupid. That's the biggest ass-ache." I scooted to the edge of the couch and made with the hand gestures like some fast-talking New York lawyer. A Jewish one, even. "See, the person can run, can scream, needs food and water, can I.D. you when it's over, might pick up on a name here or there. All that shit."

Ricky nodded like he sort of maybe kinda understood. At least it wasn't the dumbfounded look. I get the dumbfounded look a lot.

"With a dead person," I explained, "We got none of those problems. Quiet as a mouse. Don't need to feed him. Won't ever run away. Easy."

I leaned back into the couch cushions and drew on the rest of my beer with a satisfied grin.

Okay, come to think of it, I don't really want more of everything. That's stupid. I want more of a lot and less of a lot too. Less parole officers. Less ex wives. Less car repairs.

"You got a dead guy in mind?" Ricky asked.

"I do at that," I said. "Grab me another beer."

§

Parker Jeffries II was a rich son-of-a-bitch. When he died not more than a week and a half ago, where did all that money go? Did it vanish into the fog? No siree. It's still there, each dollar clinging like barnacles to trust funds, endowments, foundations and the like. Sheltered like a kitten in the rain from dear old Uncle Sam and his tax collectors. His heirs, all six living kids, wives and one brother, caring for Parker's memory by keeping his money warm at night.

"I still don't get why they're gonna pay a ransom when the guy's already dead," Ricky said as he unloaded two shovels and a flashlight from the back of my pickup.

"Who wants the family patriarch desecrated after death? They'd pay to stop that from happening, wouldn't they?" I hoisted the length of rope over my shoulder in a loop. "They got enough damn money."

"I don't even know half the words you just said."

"Desecrated. It means violated. When we get in touch with them we'll tell them all the things we're gonna do to him if they don't pay, like fuck him in the ass and stuff."

"Jesus, Kipp, leave me out of that shit."

I slapped Ricky with my hat, then returned it to my head. Even in the momentary exposure the sweat in my thinning hair took up a chill from the night air. Always seemed colder near the graveyard.

"We're not actually gonna do that shit to him. We just have to make them think we are. And we'll tell them we're gonna post pictures of it on the internet or something."

"Like when somebody passes out drunk and you take a picture with your balls on their chin or something."

"Exactly." For Ricky, this was total comprehension, or as close to it as he came.

Getting over the high iron fence was no easy feat, but we made it. Breaking and entering was our specialty so no two-bit cemetery bars were gonna keep us out. The gaps were so big I thought about shoving Ricky through the bars. Probably he could have made it, boy's so skinny these days. I wasn't so sure I could and I didn't want him going around thinking I'd gone fat and soft. So up and over it was.

Just like it should in a graveyard, the moon overhead peek-a-booed with the clouds and I could feel the moisture in the air and knew that a fog would be coming up any minute. Perfect weather for grave robbing.

Now, I've stolen a lot of things in my life, mostly with Ricky in tow. But, stealing a body was something new. We weren't quite prepared for how hard it was.

We found the grave, soil still brown and freshly turned. You could see the seeds in the soil like someone spilled a carton of takeout rice over the dirt, some of them already sprouting tiny tendrils that pointed straight up.

We started digging. We didn't say much at first. When we did talk it was mostly to complain about how hard the digging was going and by then we'd both started panting like sled dogs and talking only took more air, so we shut up and quit bitching pretty quick and got down to the job.

My plan was to ask for fifty grand, but that number went up by a thousand with every new shovelful. We were engaged in way more than fifty K worth of hard labor.

We made it about two feet down and had ourselves a wide open pit when we took our first break. We sat on the edge of our sad little hole and blew clouds of condensation into the air. If the fog wasn't going to come any sooner, we'd make our own.

The sweat chilled our skin. I watched wisps of steam rise off Ricky's forehead and from the collar of his shirt.

"Still a long way down," he said.

"Yeah."

"We still going through with it?"

"We came this far, didn't we?"

"Yeah, but," Ricky looked into the hole, measuring the distance of solid ground between us and our prize. "Still a long way down."

"You said that already."

I looked around at the headstones, my breath slowing a bit. Everyone in our vicinity was a Jeffries. Their own little gated community. I bet they liked that.

Last thing you want to hear in a graveyard late at night is a voice you weren't expecting. I jumped. Ricky jumped. No shame in it, you would too.

"Well, well. Looky here. Two assholes, no waiting." Then a chuckle. Not a devilish, maniacal laugh, just a self-amused little chuckle. But coming from the darkness behind us at ten past midnight, it scared the shit out of me.

Then I saw the barrel of the shotgun come into the pool of light from our upturned Maglight.

The caretaker, manager, what have you—the guy in charge. He didn't look like he took kindly to anyone disturbing his graves. His gun didn't look any too pleased either.

"Stand up slow, now. Raise them hands," he said. He wore dirty overalls, a hat held together by years of dried up sweat, and a stubbly face from high on his cheeks all the way down his neck and into the collar of his stained white t-shirt, the whiskers as long as the baby blades of grass on the new graves.

Ricky looked at me for direction. Always. Every goddamn time. Why did I have to have all the answers?

"Maybe y'all didn't hear me?" the caretaker said, then he pulled back the hammer on his gun. We heard that.

Ricky and I both stood, but neither of us dropped our shovels. We may be dumb, but we ain't stupid. I tried to go for disarmingly charming.

"No need for the gun, hoss. We're just looking for something we dropped out here a while ago."

"Bullshit." He looked like he wanted to spit a wad of chewing tobacco, but his mouth was dry. He stood firm, gun steady in his two hands, waiting for something to happen. He wasn't forcing us out or making us fill the hole back in. Maybe he was waiting for backup, but he never told us as much, so we all just stood there clouding the air.

"I tell ya'," I said. "I got respect for what you all do around here. That ain't easy work, all that digging."

"We use the backhoe, dumbass. Ain't nobody digs a grave by hand no more."

"Well, I can see why."

I looked at Ricky, gave him a nod. He got whatever signal I put out there – even I don't know exactly what I wanted him to do. Be ready, I guess. He took it upon himself to choke up on the handle of his shovel in a two-fisted grip.

"I guess we best be on our way," I said.

"Not till you fill in that goddamn hole, you little corpse fuckers."

I had to wonder if it was any reassurance to Ricky of the solidity of our plan that even this guy's first inkling was that we planned on violating the dead body sexually. When we put that front and center of our ransom demands, nobody would think it strange. They'd all be thinking it before we even said it.

"I suspect that's the least we can do for y'all," I said. I turned to my partner with another expectant get-the-message look in my wide eyes. "Ricky, you want to get started here?"

Took a second, but he caught on. "Oh, yeah. Sure, sure."

I moved like I was about to get me up a shovelful of dirt and Ricky took a few steps across to the other side of the shallow hole, then swung out with his shovel and caught the old timer on his right elbow. I heard the crack and he let out a moan that sounded like one of the dead had come back to life. The shotgun hit the dirt and he went after it, his arm bent at a funny angle, though I suspect it wasn't so funny to him.

Ricky looked at me. "What now, Kipp?"

"Whack him again, he's still moving."

Ricky gave an "Oh, yeah" shake of his head and brought back the shovel in a baseball stance and swung hard with the flat end of the blade. The caretaker's greasy hat flew off his head as the shovel hit. The sound of metal meeting skull echoed off all the tombstones.

Ol' Whiskers stopped moving.

I picked up the shotgun, jammed it down barrel-first into the dirt, clogging the thing with soil like a tightly packed musket. I tossed it aside, turned to Ricky. "Go through his pockets and find them keys to the backhoe. This digging shit is wearing me out."

§

The last scoop of the backhoe bucket took the whole top of the casket off with it. We saw Parker Jeffries II for the first time. He looked damn good for a dead guy. Sure, he was old, but they smoothed out most of his wrinkles, gave him color in his cheeks. His suit probably cost more than my truck, and they friggin' buried him in it. What a waste.

He didn't even smell that bad. All them preservatives, I guess.

I unspooled the rope and tossed the loose end to Ricky. "Go

get that around his middle, up under his armpits, and we'll lift him out."

Ricky looked like he was about to protest, but Ol' Mr. Whiskers groaned again.

"I got it," I said. Ricky jumped in the hole while I picked up the shotgun and turned the barrel in my hand until I held it like a golf club, the stock of the gun my driving wedge. I put a boot into his chest to turn him right, then swung and caught him on the jaw. Another crunch and I started to feel guilty about all the crunching we were doing to this guy. But he went out again, or at least he was smart enough to fake it.

Ricky needed a hand getting out of the hole, then we started lifting old man Jeffries back above ground. Wasn't easy.

Ricky forgot to bring gloves so he went into Whiskers back pocket and got out a red handkerchief to wrap his hands with. All I know is I'm damn glad I didn't have to put whatever nastiness lived in that kerchief onto my hands. And keep in mind, we were in the business of moving a corpse.

When Mr. Jeffries head first come up over the lip of the hole I almost dropped the rope to whack Ricky with my hat again. He'd looped the rope around the old man's neck, not his chest like I told him to.

"The fuck, Ricky?"

"I couldn't sit him up down there. This was easier. Besides, I didn't like being down there and, y'know, touchin' him and shit."

I shook my head and kept lifting. He came up out of the hole with his makeshift noose and flopped, stiffly onto the adjoining grave. We got Mr. Jeffries up out of there and left Whiskers to sleep it off using fresh grave dirt as a pillow.

I went first up and over the iron gate again, got to the top and had Ricky toss me the slack end of the rope. I climbed down to the ground on the outside of the gate and dropped our other supplies while Ricky climbed up to meet me, then we began hauling.

Using the top of the gate as a pulley, we lifted Mr. Jeffries to his feet, then to a dangling dance. One last hurrah from beyond the grave. I felt like an idiot that I hadn't readjusted the rope to under his pits like I wanted, but it wasn't like I was worried about returning him in pristine condition. Wasn't any deposit down on him or nothing. Once I had my cash, they could take him as is.

Being out of the hole and us moving him so much, he started

to loosen up and look almost lifelike. More passed out drunk than dead, so that you'd think for sure he'd sleep it off and come to in the morning with a hangover instead of a eulogy. But the weight of him hanging, the rope tugging at the top of the pulley system, his week old deadness – it all conspired to make him a little loose in the joints or whatever other connecting stuff holds things together. Like heads. On shoulders.

Pop. Off it went. His body dropped, the head came over to our side along with the rope. A clean sever. No blood. Just a seven pound bowling ball at our feet, and a headless body on the other side of the gate.

"Shit," I said. Ricky didn't say a word.

We climbed again and tied the rope to his feet this time and got him over.

His suit was torn, but not as bad as his neck. Without much else we could do, we tossed both pieces of Parker Jeffries II in the back of my pickup, covered him over with a tarp, and drove back over the river to my home.

§

"Does that have to be here?" Ricky asked, pointing to the expensive suit draped over the arm of my couch.

I'd taken it off Jeffries when we got back to my house. I could get the tears fixed and get it dry cleaned. No way I was letting a three thousand dollar suit get planted in the ground.

"It bug you?" I asked.

"Little bit."

I moved the suit to my closet, away from Ricky's delicate sensibilities. Time for the phone call.

The empty coffin was all the proof we needed. No point to cutting off a finger and sending it to them. Besides, we had Mr. Whiskers testimony to our seriousness as badass criminal types willing to do anything.

When I called to make our ransom demands, they believed me a hundred percent.

"A hundred and fifty grand by tomorrow midnight or we get all up in his sweet dead asshole. I know some websites that would pay big time for pictures of that shit. Big time."

The man I spoke to (one of the sons? I didn't know) stayed

calm. "There's no need to do anything rash. You'll get your money. We just want our father returned in one piece."

I almost laughed at his figure of speech.

"You just get the money together."

"We'll need to see proof that you will honor your end of things. We'll need to see..." he couldn't bring himself to say it. When he did he spit it out like he had a hair in his mouth. "The body."

"Yeah, yeah, of course, of course."

"So we're agreed? No body, no money."

"Hey," I said. "I'm a businessman. I understand the terms of the deal."

"Okay then," he said, calmly. "A hundred and fifty thousand. Small bills."

"I don't know, man. Maybe two hundred grand. His mouth looks pretty sweet too."

I smiled at Ricky, but he looked stricken. Even the thought of necrophilia gave him the spins. He stared at the floor the same way he did in high school when we all got a great big kick out of watching that fat girl porno movie. He failed to see the humor in it then, and he definitely didn't see any now.

"Is it one fifty or two hundred?" the calm man asked.

"Make it two hundred," I said. "Thanks for asking."

"Tomorrow night then," he said, rushing off the phone before the number went any higher.

"Better be."

I hung up and clapped my hands together, rubbing them so fast and hard I could have started a fire.

"You hear that?" I said to Ricky.

"I heard it." Sounded like he was trying to forget it.

"Two hundred grand. Hot damn." I stood and went to the fridge, grabbed two beers. "And we don't have to worry about a thing. We don't have to take shifts watching him. Don't have to feed him or let him take a piss. Easy money."

I handed Ricky his beer. We twisted the caps in tandem and I held out my longneck bottle to toast. Ricky looked up at me under worried brows. "Easy money," he said and we clinked bottles.

I have the perfect house for this sort of thing. I'm five miles off the major road, two miles from the nearest neighbor and he's deaf as a post and half dead. Many times Ricky has tried to convince me to set up a meth lab out here. It was really the only idea he's ever brought to our relationship and he won't give it up, even after I've told him "fuck, no" ten times.

I'm not saying it's not a great location for a lab, I'm saying I don't want a fucking meth lab in my house. I don't know how to cook, have no interest in learning and don't really want to partner with anyone who does know.

Over the years I've come to resent, a little, Ricky's lack of ideas and contributions to our partnership. Not like we have a contract together or nothing. It'd just be nice to get a little input now and again.

He'd passed out on my couch. I was about to do the same in my bed, when I heard noise outside.

Not unusual. Way out here in the woods I get a lot of critters. Raccoons by the scores, mule deer, coyotes, foxes, rabbits, of course. I'm right on the edge of where the woods go deep, where civilization, such as it is, ends.

I honestly felt no danger of being discovered, or of being followed by the cops or Mr. Whiskers from the graveyard. I wouldn't have given the noise a second thought unless I realized Mr. Jeffries was still out in the flatbed of my truck.

Now, don't go thinking I thought I had a zombie problem or anything. I just didn't want a rogue possum to go sniffing around the body and getting any ideas.

I went to the window, the one next to my gun rack. I parted the curtains with one hand while I lifted down my .22 with the other. My scare-away-critters gun.

The shadow I saw made me feel a little colder, and made me reach for the 30-30. My get-the-fuck-off-my-lawn gun.

I could have kicked Ricky awake, but all he'd do is ask me for instructions, so I let him lie. I squinted into the dark to see if I could see the shadow again. It'd been big. More than enough for man sized. Sure as shit it wasn't no possum.

The dead leaves crunched, twigs snapped. Whoever it was, wasn't trying very hard not to be found out. I slid to the other side of the window frame, keeping my body away from the exposed glass panes. I lifted the curtain away with one finger and had a good view of the back end of my pickup.

I shit you not—it was a bear.

We get them too. Not often, but we get them. Black bears. Small enough not to panic and sell the house, but big enough not to go outside when one is around.

He was nosing in the flatbed of my truck. He smelled meat. I wouldn't guess an embalmed body would hold much appeal to a bear, or any other carnivore for that matter, but I guess if you're hungry enough...

I watched him, slack jawed and frozen in place with surprise, as he dragged ol' Mr. Jeffries out and took him into the woods. I wished like I hell I was Ricky and I had someone I could look to for answers, for what the hell I should do now.

I couldn't very well return just a head.

§

I blanked on ideas the whole day. Could have been that I never got to sleep, but I was tapped. Nothing in the well.

"Shit, really? A bear?" Ricky said when he woke up and I told him about it.

"We're fucked."

Ricky had no ideas either. He'd used his one up for the year.

At ten o'clock I called again. "You got the money?"

"Yes," said the calm man. "I have it."

"Okay, let's do this."

"You have my father?"

"The fuck you think?"

"Sorry, I—"

"Just be there."

I hung up and ran a hand over my head, put my hat back in place, then wiped my hand on my jeans. The hair grease from two days without a shower and all that sweating at the cemetery made my palm slick.

An idea. An idea. An idea. Everyone knows, the worst thing you can do to think of an idea is to force yourself to think of an idea. I had two hours to figure something out. Really, though, what were they gonna do, not pay? Even a head is better than nothing, right?

Ricky sat on the couch awaiting instructions. A fucking robot, a jackbooted soldier sitting tight until his orders came through.

I tried to clear my mind like Ricky. To let everything go and wait for a brilliant idea to fill the empty void in my brain.

Sixty seconds like that, with nothing going on upstairs, and I had it.

I needed an extra body. Something to pair up with the head long enough to get my money and go. I had the suit already.

Ricky sat there, looking at me expectantly. I looked back at him the way a hungry man looks at a steak. You get rid of his head, and what are you missing really? He sure as shit ain't using it.

"What's up, Kipp?," he asked. "You got an idea?"

"Yeah, Ricky. I sure do."

What Goes Around

Terence Butler

Big Pat put down his magazine and looked around the scuzzy residence hotel room. A rust stained sink and a cracked mirror above it. A crooked-sashed, filthy window and a dead potted geranium on its sill. The broken TV; picture only, no sound.

"Fucking BORED!"

He grabbed the geranium, ready to toss it somewhere, and his eye fell on four Latino gangbangers from the projects across the street arguing on the sidewalk one story below his window.

He dropped the pot into the group and pulled back out of their view. A skinny, tattooed thug looked up just as the heavy plant hit him full in the face.

"Fuck, yeah!" Pat said, uppercutting the air at belly level. He grabbed his leather coat and headed for the back stairs.

At the end of the alley he heard a cable car bell and ran for it. The car would just be leaving the turntable and he could jump on the back steps and ride a few blocks free as the conductor collected fares up front and inside the cabin.

But this time it was that hippie fucker who hated him so much he'd rather let the tourists ride free than a San Francisco native like Pat.

Pat waited until the conductor muscled his way through the packed car to where he could yell at him to get off, and then he swung gracefully down onto the pavement native style, flipping the conductor off two-handed and yelling, "Fuck you asshole!" as he trotted away down the hill toward Broadway.

Under the tattered awning of a Chinatown grocery he grabbed an apple, took a bite and threw the rest at a rat scurrying near an overflowing dumpster. He leaned against a window full of hanging roasted ducks and congratulated himself on not being bored anymore.

Maybe now some lunch and a piece of pussy.

He snatched a pack of cigarettes from an old Chinese guy's hand and set off up the hill toward Dulce's apartment, laughing at the fearful crowd yelling at his back.

"Go back to China, you fucking communist bastards", he raged over his shoulder. Big Pat might be a criminal but he was patriotic.

He thought about fine, sweet Dulce and her big brown nipples as he trudged up the hill. Their thing was problematic. She acted like she didn't like him but she always let him in. He wanted her to like him, but if she didn't,—well who knows what goes on in a bitch's mind?

§

Dulce's old man was in Pelican Bay for gang related murder. His homeboys had immediately forgotten she was their sister when it looked like he'd never get out. In Soledad he'd kept right on killing guys to order. Sentences were stacked up for a couple of hundred years.

All Dulce had of value was her pussy. Her kid wasn't worth anything, being on track for Stockton Youth and Folsom, the same crime schools his daddy had attended. She loved him but he was already a hard ass.

She didn't mind the guys coming around and hanging out. Dockworkers, cable car drivers, cabbies. She'd fix them a sandwich and let them rub on her and later if they had some money she'd blow them. Or if the price was right, something more.

What she didn't like was when they thought they owned her.

Like Big Pat. He was a bully and a pervert, and the only reason she let him in was because he always paid for the full ride. He was a big part of her non-welfare funding and at this point she had to keep him happy.

She laughed when she thought of his broken nosed face, fake Irish tears in the corners of his eyes, his gap-toothed mouth talking about being "in love" with her. Yeah, he was in love all right. In love with a certain part of her he'd never touched and wasn't about to.

She rubber banded her curly hair back and checked her makeup as she heard his familiar ponderous steps climbing the steel staircase outside her door.

"Smile, Dulce," she whispered as she waited for his knock. A grimace came and she stuck it on her mouth.

A couple of thuds and a rattle of the handle. A pause, another louder thud, plus a kick.

"Dulce?!"

She opened the door on the chain. He was wearing his goofy grin so that meant he was in a good mood. Not that it guaranteed he wouldn't do something outrageous.

Slipping the chain she let him push open the door and come in while she coasted into the kitchen and got him a beer. He was absently going through her mail when she came back.

He dropped the mail on the floor and grabbed the beer with one hand and her ass with the other. Pulling her tight he growled his greeting.

"C'm'ere, you fine piece of ass."

He held her by her butt as she struggled. She still tried to smile while he chugged the beer in one swift pour. A loud belch, the clank of the beer bottle as it hit the coffee table and rolled across the rug, a beer smelling, sloppy attempt to kiss by crushing his whiskery mug onto hers.

She had had all she could handle. She popped him in the nose with her hard little fist.

"Stop it Pat, god damn it!"

He let go and gazed at her in amazement.

"You can't just come in here and start manhandling me, you dumb bastard! I'm a married woman and if I do you a favor every now and then, that doesn't mean you fuckin' own me, OK?"

"Ahh shit baby. I didn't mean nothing. I just get excited. I love ya, know what I mean?"

"You wouldn't know love if it bit you on your dick you big stupid white boy! Now get the fuck out of here."

"But hold on..."

"No! Not today, OK? I'm just not up for it. If you can treat me nice, well maybe tonight."

If 200 pounds of Neanderthal looking thug could seem like a bad little boy who has just been spanked and is not happy about it, that was Big Pat Sheehan right then.

He looked at Dulce a long moment and she saw emotion turning inward in his eyes. One dark look back from the doorway, the door closing softly, and then he was gone. She rushed to lock it.

Dulce started to shake and cry. If that tantrum hadn't worked out he might have beat her to death. Relief and dread chased each other around in her suddenly very tired brain.

She'd just slumped onto the couch and pulled a shawl around her when the door knob rattled. Dulce held her breath.

"Mama!" Tapping and rattling.

"Mijo?"

"Let me in Mama."

Up again and rushing to the door, she peeked and saw her son, threw the door wide.

"My god Enrique, your face!"

Dulce tried to hold her son and look at him but he sidestepped her and inspected the kitchen and both bedrooms. Looking for someone.

He was angrier than she'd ever seen him. White gauze wrapped around his head and down over his right eye, covering it completely. A large band aid was pasted on his cheek and his upper lip swelled twice normal.

"Henry, what happened?"

"You better ask that fucking white boy you're fucking, Moms." Pissed off sarcasm dripped from his words.

"Big Pat did this to you?"

Enrique's voice rose to a threatening shout; "Where's Papi's gun? I want it right now and I don't want no words from you about it."

Dulce peered at him, looking for the sweet boy she'd birthed and raised over these few quick years, but he wasn't there. Her baby was gone and she'd never see him again. He had become his father's son completely.

Her shoulders sagged and she felt old in her heart. When you're born poor this is the life you get. As hard as it is for women, it's these boys and men who carry the burden and the curse of ignorance to each new generation.

Her baby was trapped by the code and she couldn't abandon him now.

§

Pat was on the fifth floor roof of the Vallejo Street parking ramp watching his spit float down onto Northern Station cop cars parked in the alley below. This was his mountain top. He came here to plan or be alone.

Postcard San Francisco spread out below, not the grimy death trap he prowled day and night. To him the tourist sights were all fantasy. Coit Tower looked like a dungeon keep from here, and the houses crowding Russian Hill like cages piled on each other.

Dulce was right, he didn't know what love was because he'd never had any. Big fucking deal. You can't miss what you ain't never had. But just because she was right didn't mean she could disrespect him.

His biker old man told him that fear and indecision make you weak. Punks and bitches only understand power, and power has to be shown. When you crash you get back on the hog and ride.

He had hated his old man but respected him. When they found his body under a Bay Bridge approach there were chains wrapped around him. Brothers said this meant he went down fighting.

Pat knew if Dulce was going to be his old lady, she had to see him in charge right away. If he let her get away with this now, he knew she'd just have to tell everyone. He'd lose respect.

He'd have to take the law of the street to her.

Now he felt good, had a plan. He pushed the button for the elevator and keyed both sides of a Benz while he waited.

On Stockton Street he ran to the back door of a number 30 bus and elbowed his way aboard. Three blocks later he stepped down in front of the same Chinese grocery from that morning.

Skinny Chinese gang kids dressed skater style stood in a clump with a Latino gangster in their midst. Jacking him up, Pat supposed.

Until they all turned to look at him.

Pat didn't like the feeling in his stomach, so he toughed it out. He coughed up an oyster and shot it to the side, not caring where it landed, turned his back on them and strode up the hill.

The bangers followed.

§

When the door closed on Henry's back Dulce rushed to her sewing kit to get the bullets for the snubnose .38 she kept separate in case he stumbled across it.

She'd sent him to find .38 slugs, telling him she didn't have any, a trick to get him out of the apartment. It would take a while and she hoped in the meantime Pat would come back. This was the first time she'd ever hoped for that to happen but now she was almost praying for it.

She knew she shouldn't ask God to send her a murder victim, but she also knew that Jesus would understand.

It was that sort of prayer she sent out in a fury of concentration then. She shoved fat bullets into the chambers, each one granted a special touch.

"Here you go shiny bullet. Get in there you beautiful thing you."

Would it be this one that exploded in Big Pat's brain or that one burning through his heart?

Dulce cradled the snubnose like a new still blind puppy and smiled down at it. She pictured herself and Alvaro at the quarry where he'd given her the gun and taught her to fire it three days after Enrique was born.

They sat in his car out of the wind, Henry snuggled in her arms, strong, brown and barechested Alvaro spinning the chamber and breaking the brand new gun down for her, later holding the baby while she fired over and over to get used to the kick of the little revolver.

"Baby, you know I might not always be around to take care of my family and shit. Guys like me don't last long on the street, know what I'm sayin'?

She remembered how the tears had started then and how Al had gently but sternly admonished her.

"Hey, no tears. It is what it is. Men have obligations. When I'm gone you'll have to step up and protect my son so my name don't die, know what I'm sayin'?"

She'd never shirked her duty. There'd been many times she'd had to take care of Henry's various missteps and she'd never failed him. Now this bigger test seemed to logically follow.

She turned her recliner chair to face the door, sat down and steadied herself. She asked Jesus to help her remain calm, help her hold fire long enough so Pat would see what was about to happen to him, and to let her empty the chamber of bullets she'd blessed with mother's love into Pat's big pale body.

§

The main guy of the Chinese gangsters was Bobby Lee. Henry knew him since grade school and they were cool. Latinos and Chinese were loosely allied against whites and blacks through school and on into street life. They didn't party, but they didn't war either.

"'Sup Mexican?" Tommy said, keeping his hands in his pockets, tilting his head to the side, no smile there.

"Ain't nothing. Looking to get me some help right quick though." Henry showed the folded money at the top of his pants pocket.

"Where your homies at?"

"Down at the Wharf. You know. Busy with tourists and shit."

"What you need?"

"You know that white boy call Big Pat?"

"We looking for his ass right now. Motherfucker disrespected my uncle, man."

"Yeah, well he's the one did this to my face."

"For reals?" Bobby checked the damage closely, respectfully.

"I need some .38 bullets."

"I got some. Not with me."

The Chinese kid named Soldier spoke; "There the motherfucker is right now," and pointed his chin at the number 30 bus stopped in the loading zone.

§

Pat felt a slight movement of air just before the rock-hard melon hit him between his shoulder blades.

He stifled an outcry of pain and turned slowly to see who'd thrown it. The Chinese gang bangers were moving menacingly toward him. He had to make a choice quickly; deal with disrespect from his old lady or from these punk ass chinks.

These little assholes were available almost anytime and Dulce needed her lesson now, so the decision was made easily.

He started to walk away.

But one guy caught his attention. Standing out in front of the others, the fool who seemed most likely to have thrown the melon, the Latino kid with a bandaged head seemed familiar.

Big Pat pointed at him from the shoulder, his hand turned sideways as if he had a gun. He pulled the trigger and said, "Mas tarde, pendejo", and moved up the hill.

The bangers followed, keeping up. Pat acted unconcerned, but quickened his pace unconsciously.

The group of six behind him doubled their speed and got within hearing distance. Their rubber soled Vans slid and squeaked along the concrete. Sounds of cursing and name calling wrapped around him and made Big Pat nervous.

He was going to have to deal with this now.

He stopped, looked up at the sky, made himself look bigger like a cornered pit bull does, and turned around. The kids were much closer than he'd thought. Pat was blinking but he didn't know it.

Henry did. He moved.

Pat started to say something, a challenge, and the whole group was on him, Henry first with a tape-wrapped bar of iron in his gloved fist.

Big Pat went down quickly, and a steady kicking and stomping got started. Vans can hurt when there's a dozen of them all at once and dudes are leaping and dancing on a victim.

In a minute Henry called the bangers off and went to work on Pat by himself. The nose went first in a fountain of blood, the cheekbones and eye sockets deformed easily under the iron fist, teeth fell from Pat's mouth. He wasn't awake for much of it.

Henry sat on Pat's chest catching his breath, sporadically directing an exhausted punch to his head.

"Man, you gon' kill the dude man," Bobby said.

Henry laughed and stood, then bent to haul Pat to his feet, but he was limp, dead weight, and Henry looked to Bobby for help.

"I don't know, man. He's your problem." Then, reconsidering, "Where you going with him?"

"I'm taking him to my mom's, so she can see what I done to him. Then I'll finish his ass."

Bobby saw this for what it was. Henry had to restore respect to his family. Bobby and his home boys had been paid only to help bring Big Pat down and that was all. But Bobby could see the need in Henry's eyes. He needed help—and more importantly, a witness to his retribution.

Bobby bent and grabbed Big Pat's work-booted right foot.

"Aw'ight. Let's take this fool to your moms's crib then", he said.

Henry saw Bobby for a man now, not just a kid he'd gone to school with. He nodded, stooped to snag the other leg and the two dragged Big Pat along the sidewalk towards Dulce's crib.

§

Dulce had drifted off to sleep while daydreaming in her big soft chair about how it might be if Al ever came home. Noises in the street had wakened her but she couldn't shake loose of the dream.

The apartment seemed dim even though the sun shone through the sliding door that led to the tiny balcony. She heard the wavering hum and the clicking off and shudder of the refrigerator motor and thought how strangely quiet it was in the apartment.

A tiny sound came from the bedroom, a rattling like wind in partly open blinds.

"Al?" Dulce whispered, her breathing stopping there on the raw rush of the word. Her fingers pulsed as she gripped the arms of the chair.

"Al?" Louder now and struggling to sit up, she fought her way to her feet.

The fall of the gun to the floor reminded her of what she had been waiting to do. She retrieved it, pointed it down in both hands at the end of her reach. Now her fingers pulsed on the steel and wood of the grips, the curl of the trigger.

Still drawn to the bedroom, she turned that way in the beginning of motion toward a thing she knew was impossible but had to prove to herself.

Footsteps boomed on the steel staircase, a slow and steady climbing.

The sound sent a shock of fear through her. She thought to run, to hide under the bed or in the closet. Instead, frozen in place, she turned back toward the sound on the stairs.

When the steps outside stopped, she fired five times through the door.

§

On the sidewalk Bobby stood a few feet away from the heap of bloody clothes that was Big Pat, watching Henry pull himself tiredly up the stairs. Bobby was anxious to get his money and split. His homies were talking to him about cops.

When the shots cracked out above the gang ran. Bobby stayed, saw Henry fly backwards and slide down the stairs, his head coming apart, his shirt front completely red, dead without even a cry of wonder.

Five shots might mean that the shooter was done, but Bobby waited to make sure.

Henry's mom opened the door on the chain and peered out. Her eyes were the brightest thing in the gloom, her face a gargoyle's. She screamed when she saw Henry's body sprawled half way down the staircase. She staggered to the landing, the empty gun tumbling through the railing and falling near Bobby's feet She collapsed to her knees and crawled down the steps, reaching.

Bobby didn't think. He leapt to Henry and dug the money from his pocket, picked up the snub nose and ran.

Behind him he could hear the chaos of voices shouting, a siren whooping. He didn't look back.

How to Clean a Gun

Joe Clifford

"You're back?" Maggie said. It wasn't really a question. More like an accusation.

Billy cradled the phone and continued to scrub the bore with the cleaning rod. "This afternoon."

"I keep calling..." Maggie trailed off. Billy listened to her strained breathing. Several years ago on a bender, Maggie fell down a flight of stairs and smashed her nose. Deviated septum and permanent congestion. Even without a word Billy knew when his sister was on the line. "I don't know why you don't get a cell—"

"I don't like them."

Match struck, cigarette lit, deep, agitated inhale. "Sonofabitch took Brittney," Maggie finally said.

He applied a few drops of solvent to the cotton mop, inserted the patch through the barrel, carefully brushing each chamber for fouling; contact points had to be clear of debris to avoid a misfire.

"He had her for the weekend," Maggie said. "Called and said he wasn't giving her back, said she was his daughter too and that I was an unfit mother. You believe that shit?"

Yeah, Billy believed it.

He waited while his baby sister tabbed another beer and gulped. His sister drank beer like soda pop. "Caught that bastard with his dick in some high school bitch's mouth, and *I'm* unfit?" Maggie said, speech slurring. "Last time that asshole gave me money was her tenth birthday. Paid for a trampoline. Brittney wanted one so she called her father—you were gone—as usual—practically had to *beg* him for it. Oh, he's got money. Rubs it in my face every day, sitting in his ivory tower with his plastic Barbie doll wife. He got the trampoline—the cheap fuck *rented* it." Billy wondered what else she was on beside her usual diet of pills and booze.

Billy finished polishing the piece with a flannel cloth, shining grip and barrel like a pair of wingtips fresh off the shine box. He grabbed the next gun from the canvas sack. He had a lot of guns to clean. "What do you want me to do?"

"What you think?" Maggie barked. "Get my daughter back."

§

His sister hadn't always been like this. Billy and Maggie didn't have the same mother. He was eight when his old man met Camille and moved them both out of the Caddy and into her little shack by the river. A year later Maggie was born. Six months after that, the old man split and left Billy behind. Being abandoned didn't affect him. Billy was a special kid, tougher than other boys his age. No one pushed Billy Lugli around. Maggie may've shared the same blood. But none of these traits.

Maggie's ex, Cooper, lived with his new wife across town in one of the cookie-cutter McMansions. A light was on upstairs, bottom floor lit up, porch blazing as if expecting company.

Before Billy reached the top step, the door flung open and a pair of twisted, angry faces greeted him, ready for a fight. When they saw it was Billy, their demeanor instantly changed and they retreated inside.

"Sorry, Billy," Cooper said. "Thought you were your sister."

"We didn't know you were back from Florida," his wife said. "Maggie told us you'd be there a while."

"Where's Brittney?"

The three stood silently, Cooper and his wife exchanging nervous glances.

Then Cooper said, "You want a beer, Billy?" He gestured to his wife. "Grab us two beers from the fridge? Billy and I are going down to the basement." He turned to Billy. "That OK? You have a minute to talk and have a beer?"

It was late. Billy was tired from the flight and didn't feel like talking over a beer with his ex-brother-in-law. He wanted to finish cleaning his guns and go to bed. He hated grown men pleading. Whether on their knees in the Florida swamps, or groveling in their own kitchen, it wasn't a good look.

"Please?"

Cooper had renovated the basement. Mounted plasma flat-screen. Padded leather sofa. A man cave. But there was an entire area devoted to flowery, sparkly stuff, too. Dolls, clothes, nail polish on little dressers. A poster of that vampire movie all the tween girls go crazy for tacked to the wall.

"Brittney's at an age where she needs her privacy," Cooper said. "We have a big house—" He paused. "I wanted to talk about this first. I didn't know how to reach you."

"Nothing to talk about."

Cooper shuffled his feet, antsy, like a whimpering pooch eager for a walk. "I should've been given custody. I can provide more stability for my daughter."

"Take it up with the judge," Billy said.

"You know I can't."

"Then you shouldn't have let the babysitter blow you."

Billy had nothing against his ex-brother-in-law, he'd made a dumb decision, and getting a BJ didn't mean he wasn't the better parent. But blood's blood.

"I did everything I could," Copper said, "paid for rehab after rehab—"

"Just pay your child support."

"I do pay my support! Has Maggie been saying I don't? You can look at my canceled checks, Billy—"

Billy held up a hand. Did Cooper really think Billy wouldn't have addressed a deadbeat situation by now?

"I don't mean any disrespect," Cooper said. "But even you have to see what's going on with your sister."

Of course Billy saw. It's why he didn't buy Maggie a new car, get her a nicer place. He'd done those things before and gotten burned. Giving Maggie money was like flushing it down the slot machine.

"You know why I called Maggie?" Cooper said. "*Brittney* asked me to! She doesn't want to go back there. Maggie is mixed up with some bad people. Maybe you don't know how bad because you've been gone so long, but it's no way for a kid to live." Cooper stared with urgency. "Please, Billy, help make this right."

While other boys were picking out corsages and making up stories about getting jacked off behind the bleachers, Billy Lugli was digging holes in Upstate New York. At seventeen, he got in with the Sullivan Brothers, Cullen and Declan. He moved quickly through the ranks. Billy possessed an even-handed temperament, an ability to get around moral quandaries that stymied others, was merciless in his execution, which earned the Sullivan Brothers' trust and landed him some of the biggest contracts, coast to coast.

Billy made sure to check in as often as he could. Each time Maggie seemed a little further gone. Cuts, bruises, dead eyes and strange men walking around the house drunk in their underwear. Billy could handle the men, but Camille was too much of a headcase to be reasoned with, too far gone to be afraid. Billy could never hurt a woman, even if the best outcome for Maggie meant her mother going away for good.

Heading down the hills into the flats, Billy studied his niece, who was the spitting image of Maggie at that age, same stringy blonde hair and knocked knees. But innocence was fading. Brittney appeared gaunter, more withdrawn than the last time he'd seen her.

"You have a nice visit with your father?" It was all Billy could think to ask.

Brittney stared out the windows, at the passing fence posts and short stone walls, into the darkness.

Billy reached into his wallet, extracted a pair of bills and passed them along.

"What's that for?"

"You," Billy said. "Just you."

Brittney waited a moment, then flashed a sweet, cock-eyed grin and tucked the money in her sock.

The quaintly lit suburb roads snaked through the brighter town center, past the bars and restaurants, and into the darker reaches of the poorer sections. The railroad tracks, factory warehouses and muddy banks, where packed duplexes and studio apartments clustered between service stations and bilge pumps.

Billy pulled up a narrow drive, into a cramped tenement turnabout with so many grounded vehicles it left little room to turn around.

"Uncle Billy?" The girl nibbled her lip. "Maybe I could visit you some time?"

The back door flew wide and Maggie ran down the stairs. Despite cold winds whipping off the water, his sister wore only cutoffs and a tank top. Far from the wispy girl he knew as a kid, Maggie was hardened now with the coarse, ruddy face of a heavy drinker.

"My baby, my baby," she said, rushing to the passenger's side, jerking the door, stumbling in the loose dirt. Billy could smell the booze from his seat.

"You take care of that sonofabitch?" Maggie snapped at him.

"Watch your mouth," Billy said. "That's the girl's father."

Maggie glowered, then tried to drag Brittney from the car by the arm. Brittney resisted. Maggie lost her traction and fell on her behind.

"This is all *your* fault!" she screamed at her brother from the ground. "If you'd make sure that *asshole* paid the money he owes me—" The "asshole" dragged out with a long hiss. Billy could see why: his sister was missing her two front teeth.

Brittney bent down and helped her mother up. Maggie stink-eyed Billy, then schlepped toward the door with the exaggerated limp of the war-wounded, leaning on her daughter, dragging her along.

Billy slammed it in park and jumped out.

"What do you want?" Maggie said. "Haven't you done enough?"

"I'm coming in."

"Since when do you want to see inside *my* house?"

In the floodlight shining down, his sister looked even worse, bleached, brittle hair as dry as straw in a heat wave. He stared at the little red x's running through the crook of her elbows.

"It's not...a good idea," Maggie said, crossing her arms.

"Why not?"

His sister scratched nervously. "The place is a mess," she said, suddenly sounding sober and nicer. "It's embarrassing. I haven't had a chance to clean..." Maggie gestured with her eyes toward Brittney, like that would mean something.

He reached for the handle. "I've seen worse."

Two men sat on the arms of a pullout sofa with sheets hanging out the cushions. Hoodrats. Thugs. New school punks, whatever you wanted to call them. Gold chains, capped teeth, pants hanging off their asses like toddlers carrying a load. In the corner, Billy found a third man. Fat, bald, sweating. The fat man seemed blissfully unaware of Billy's presence, eyes pinned behind thick glasses, gazing goofily at invisible stars.

A ribbon of marijuana smoke suspended like low-lying cirrus clouds. Billy spied the stacks of delinquent bills and drug paraphernalia, his sister looming behind him. He heard Brittney scurry down the hall, slamming shut a door. Billy kicked aside the garbage on the floor and tugged open the refrigerator. A two-liter Pepsi bottle filled with tap water and a carton of leftover Chinese. Billy sniffed the takeout, then chucked it in the trash.

One of the hoodrats rose and fronted, eyes blazed.

"Get those clowns out of here," Billy said to his sister.

"Who you callin' a clown, bro," said the hoodrat, who stepped up and lifted his tank to reveal the grip of a Glock.

Billy turned but before he got very far, the other punk had run to his buddy's side, whispering in his ear.

Billy heard his own name repeated. The hoodrat lowered his shirt, eyes spooked. Like two school kids caught chucking snowballs at cars and granted a one-time reprieve, the boys gathered their cells and keys, collared the fat man, and bolted out the door.

"You get a kick out of that, don't you?" Maggie said after they were gone. "You're a bully."

Billy roved his eyes over the filthy room, the bloodstained, stretched underpants strewn over chairs, every furnishing like it had been fished from an IKEA dumpster. Tin containers perched on sills with plastic forks poking out of them. Place stank like piss in a parking garage.

"Yeah, it's a fucking dump," Maggie said, collecting trash as if she intended to clean up, but instead she stopped and began flinging the crushed donuts boxes and empty cans at him, pitching a tantrum like a little girl.

When she was finished, Maggie dropped her knees, sobbing. "I hate you for leaving, Billy."

§

Billy had been gone a couple years when he stopped by his sister's middle school to surprise her. He planned to take her out early for some ice cream. At the school, a teacher explained Maggie hadn't been to class for a while. He stopped by Camille's. No one there. It took Billy most the afternoon to find his baby sister. He eventually did, in the woods behind the park on Evermore. Deep in the brush, on her back, little sundress bunched up and underpants pulled down. His sister squirmed as she guzzled from a handle of Peach Schnapps, giggling. An older high school boy thrashed wildly on top of her. Three more lined up and laughing, cheering, dollar bills and bags of candy clutched in sweaty, eager palms.

It didn't matter if he put those boys in the hospital or a hole; there were too many of them—too many boys and too many high schools, too many men in too many towns. He couldn't fight them all.

So he focused on his work, and his sister slipped further away. When Camille's liver finally gave out, Billy hoped things would get better. By then Maggie was almost nineteen, an age when he had a place of his own, a path in the world. As soon as he saw his sister at the service, he knew it was hopeless. How do you give up on your own sister and say goodbye?

§

Back at his condo, well after midnight, Billy carefully inspected the forcing cone, scouring for any buildup. Then repeated the process for the cylinder ratchet. He checked under the ejector star of his double-action revolver, dabbed some solvent, wiped it clean. He was reaching for the lubricant when his cell buzzed. Kieran Sullivan. Sully. His father and uncle, Cullen and Declan, dead for years, Sully was the only Sullivan left. He rarely made calls himself.

"We got a little problem, Billy," Sully said.

Out the windows, Billy watched a pair of headlights slowly pull into his complex. "What kind of problem?"

"You see your sister tonight?"

Billy parted the curtains. "If you're asking, you know I did." Billy couldn't see into the idling car, lot lights too dim, headlights too bright and aimed right at his place. He let the curtains close and pulled out his revolver.

"Heard you had a run in with a couple street toughs."

"Wouldn't exactly call it a run in. Wouldn't exactly call them 'street toughs,' either."

"A third man?"

"Yes."

Sully was holding back.

"It's OK," Billy said.

"The kids work for Rory Ross. Your sister's in to Ross. Big time. Fat man's Jasper Gibbons. He was there to take it out in trade."

Billy heard car doors slam.

"How much?" Billy asked.

"Sixty-eight."

"How much trade is my sister worth?"

"Not that much. Gibbons did ten in Riker's for sex with minors."

"How young?"

"Young."

"How'd my sister get in that big a hole?" Billy waited, listening for sounds outside. "Use my name as collateral?"

"No. This is the first Ross heard she was your sister. His boys don't spend much time up here, y'know? Isn't their territory. Out of respect, Ross called me himself. Give you a chance...to make it right."

"And if I don't?"

"Billy. This is business. Maggie fucked up. Bad."

"Come on out here!" a voice shouted in the darkness. "I'm not scared of you!"

It was his ex-brother-in-law.

"Thanks," Billy said into the receiver. "I'll call you back."

Billy tucked his gun behind his pants and headed outside.

Cooper was drunk. He had a friend with him. Tweed and eyeglasses. Another insurance broker. Billy didn't know him. But he clearly knew who Billy was.

"Are you out of your mother-flipping mind?" the man said to Cooper. "Your brother-in-law is *Billy Lugli*?"

"Yeah," slurred Cooper. "Big, bad, Billy Lugli. That's my brother-in-law."

"Go home, Cooper," Billy said.

"Why don't *you* go home!"

The friend tugged at Cooper's sleeve.

"You don't scare me," Cooper said, shaking his friend off. "I'm a good father!" He was crying now. "The school's already suspended Brittney once—for drinking and smoking pot—bet you didn't know that, did you? Maggie doesn't care—"

The friend smothered Cooper to his chest, and guided Billy's sobbing ex-brother-in-law back to the waiting car.

Normally, Billy Lugli didn't touch anything stronger than aspirin. But the night had him wound pretty tight. Even with a couple sleeping pills, Billy had a helluva time falling asleep. When he finally did, it was a light sleep, the kind where you're not awake but you're not entirely under either, still aware of the world around you, its sights, sounds, the emotions you can't escape. He could hear the hum of appliances and water flushed through pipes. A meaningless dream looped endlessly, a random misfiring of synapses. Billy used to take Maggie to the train museum when she was little. Her favorite thing to do was ride the miniature steam engines. She never wanted to get off. In his dream, Billy was old, like he was now, but Maggie was still a young girl. They rode through cornfields and farms, up mountains and over the sea, and she giggled like she did when she was little, clutching him close and laughing so hard her belly hurt.

The phone woke Billy. He'd fallen asleep in a chair. This is why he never touched drugs, messed with your mind. He plucked the receiver off the wall and sat back at the kitchen table to reassemble the parts he'd left out to dry, working a Q-Tip between nooks and crannies.

"Two hundred dollars?" Maggie screamed. "You give a thirteen-year-old *two hundred dollars*, but you won't give your sister a dime?"

"Hold on." Billy set the phone down, walked to the sink, splashed some water on his face. When he picked up the receiver, she was still screaming.

"I have bills to pay! Groceries to buy! I need fucking money!"

"Then get a fucking job!" Billy shouted back, so loudly his whole body shook.

His sister started sniffling. "I can't work, Billy," she whined. "I just...can't."

Billy took a deep breath. "You take the money?"

"Goddamn right I did!"

"It was for Brittney."

"Now? *Now* you want to help out your niece? You haven't given a shit about her for thirteen years."

The line went silent for a moment.

"I'm in trouble," Maggie said softly.

"I know," said Billy.

"I screwed up. Bad this time. I made...a mistake. I'm in a lot of trouble."

"It's OK," Billy said. "I'll take care of it."

He heard her wiping snot and tear. "What would I do without you?"

Billy listened as his sister cracked another beer, lit something on fire and sucked in fumes.

"You're right," he said. "I haven't spent enough time with Brittney. What's she doing right now?"

"Sleeping. She doesn't have school today."

"It's Tuesday," Billy said.

Maggie stammered. "Parent/teacher...conferences."

"Get her up and dressed. I'm coming over now."

"Now?"

"I'll be there in twenty."

"OK, Billy."

When he hung up the phone, Billy fished his cell and punched in Sully's number.

"Tell Ross I'm not covering the debt," he said.

"If you don't have it, I can cover you—"

"Of course I have it."

A long pause.

"You know what this means, right?" said Sully. "They were extending a courtesy. Ross is within his rights. I can't have any retaliation. I don't need a war."

"There won't be retaliation."

"OK, Billy, if that's what you want."

"One last thing."

"What's that?"

"I want it taken care of today."

§

It was a little past nine when Billy knocked on his sister's door, the sun refracting a kaleidoscope through the junkyard metals and factory smoke. Maggie was already drunk, reeking of last night's vomit. But her make-up was freshly applied.

Brittney sat over a bowl of dry cereal at the small kitchen table, pushing her spoon around but not eating anything.

"Come on, kid," Billy said, trying to smile. "I'll take you to breakfast. Grab your things."

"How long you gonna keep her?" Maggie asked. "I have to go... to those teacher conferences. Remember?"

Brittney came to her uncle's side, and he put his arm around her.

Maggie had already begun buzzing around the room, cleaning up now in earnest, stuffing dirty laundry in plastic bags and dusting like a maid on a mission.

"Expecting company?" Billy asked.

Maggie ignored the question, suddenly pleasant as punch. "Keep her all day if you want," she said. "Y'know, dinner, too. Those conferences...run late."

She darted off into the back room, blasting the radio, singing along.

"Goodbye, sis," he said softly, but he knew she couldn't hear him.

Rollin' Mona and the Tijauna Slide

Garnett Elliott

La Araña, the girls call her. "The Spider." Not because of her gangly limbs, or her slender fingers flashing as she cuts hair with a straight-razor. Not because of her long black locks, hanging straight and limp, or the black strapless dresses she wears over her gaunt figure.

They call her the Spider because of her venom.

She's just finished with her one o'clock, a sweaty-necked homeboy. Instead of hustling him towards the register she shoos him through the back door, out to the stoop where the girls take smoke breaks. Leticia and Marta exchange knowing looks. The *vato* re-enters a minute later, red-eyed, swiping at his nose.

"Go easy on that," the Spider says. But he's already out the door, making for a low-pro mini with golden rims. Reggaeton bass slams the front windows of Señor Snips as the truck peels away.

"That's the most expensive fade he's ever had," Leticia says.

This gets her a look from the Spider. She's cleaning the razor by swiping it against the gauzy black scarf knotted around her throat. "You didn't see anything."

"No." Leticia shakes her head, making the wattles under her chin ripple.

"I can't speak for management, Letty, but don't you think it's time you dropped some weight?" The Spider folds her razor shut with a click. "Señor Snips is supposed to be about projecting an image. Barrio Chic. Not *arroz con pollo*. Not *tres leches*."

She makes her point by jabbing the razor's handle into Letty's ample waistline, causing her to flinch.

"Discipline," the Spider says. "Discipline is key. Think it's easy staying a size six when you're six feet tall like me? Two full hours of

Zumba, every day—"

"Christ, leave her alone already."

Breaths suck in and heads swivel to the rearmost chair, where Mona reclines, feet propped up on a vanity and face hidden behind a *Derby Times* 'zine. Her muscular legs are aswirl with stylized flames and angry golden carp, beneath black fishnets.

The Spider folds her arms. "You're addressing me?"

"You're the one talking all the goddamn time, aren't you?" The magazine lowers, revealing first a forelock streaked bright green, then a round face heavy with eye makeup. "I can't hear myself fucking think around here."

The Spider's skin starts to flush, but it's Letty who replies. "You can't talk to her like that. She's just trying to help me."

"Yeah," says Marta.

Mona snorts. "Stockholm Syndrome. You get tired of kissing that bony ass, let me know." The magazine slides back up.

But the Spider isn't letting it go. She sways over to Mona's chair, razor still in hand. A slap sends the *Derby Times* flying. Mona gets up, hands already clenched, and the Spider scuttles back quick as her namesake.

"Careful, Mona," she says, waving a slender finger. "Your P.O. wouldn't like it, you got into a fight at your new job."

Mona wishes to God she had a few of the Dust Devil Dolls with her now. For moral support, at least. She takes deep breaths through her nose. Her eyes track the Spider as she steps over to the closest vanity, double-checks the empty waiting area, and removes a tinfoil bindle from her dress. She twists it open and dumps the contents onto a hand mirror: a little white mound of the soft. Letty and Marta hurry close, eager as kittens. They bend their heads over the mirror, snuffling.

"Like to have a taste, wouldn't you?" the Spider asks Mona. She strokes the nape of Letty's neck. "That's what they popped you for, isn't it? Drugs? Gotta be."

Mona turns to her own vanity. Next to the combs suspended in disinfectant goop is a pair of Riedell skates, red leather with black stripes, and a framed photograph of her daughter taken just after she was born.

She counts to a hundred.

§

Mona's probation officer is a forty-something named Swinburne. He insists on meeting in her apartment. Does the piss-test right there, makes calls on her phone, uses her bathroom. He always carries a clipboard.

Mona blows him as a matter of course. The humiliation's not as bad as it used to be, but still.

"There's some, ah, trouble at your workplace," he says, as she's spitting out the taste of him in the trash below the sink. "What's it called? Senior Snips?"

"*Señor* Snips."

"Owner says you're not getting along so well with the other girls."

"They're bitches."

"Ah."

"The lead bitch is a tranny called the Spider. She deals coke out of her chair."

Swinburne massages the bridge of his nose. "We've discussed this before, okay? You're a probationer. Not an undercover cop. There's only so many businesses willing to work with someone like you."

"Get me another job, then."

"It's not that simple."

"I'll go back to dog grooming. I'll be good this time, I swear."

"Mona—"

"I just sucked you off."

"Don't cloud the issue." Swinburne gestures at the helmet and mouth guard on the battered coffee table. "It's a shame you can't make money with that skating group of yours. What do you call them again?"

"Dust Devil Dolls."

"Uh-huh. I'd love to watch you guys sometime."

"I get you tickets, you get me another job?"

He doesn't seem to hear her offer. "I understand roller derby is mostly just a bunch of lesbians looking to hook-up. Not that I've got a problem with that."

"It's a form of expression."

"Right."

She imagines Swinburne, with his paunch and cheap Target slacks, wobbling around a track on skates.

He checks his watch. "I've got a pedophile on house arrest in twenty. You need to make this haircutting gig work, Mona. Show some consistency. It's the only way your daughter's coming out of foster care."

Always, always he makes his Big Point using her daughter. As if the blowjob wasn't painful enough.

§

Just before noon on a busy Thursday, and Mona finishes a pair of blond fauxhawks. The boys' mom skimps on the tip. Mona watches her in the parking lot, a pixie-cut with a five-figure rack, as she stows the kids aboard a giant SUV. Some people have everything.

"That's what you rate, huh?" Letty says. She smirks, scoping the miniscule amount scrawled at the receipt's bottom.

"Cheap bitch."

"You gotta know how to play them. Like the Spider—"

"I'm taking a smoke break."

Letty's eyes go wide. She slips her bulk between Mona and the back door. "Not now. We need you up front."

"For what? Waiting room's empty

"You've taken too many breaks already." Her voice sounds urgent.

Something's up. Letty's trying to run interference, but Mona's had a lot of experience getting around people. She steps right, then shoots left past Letty before she can shift her balance. Shoulders the back door. Outside is a cement stoop overlooking a dumpster and the employee parking lot.

The Spider's in the lot. She's bent over the driver-side door of Mona's old Saturn, hands working furiously.

"She's out," Letty calls from behind Mona. The Spider whirls, a bent coat-hanger in hand.

Mona heads towards her. "Trying to get in there," she says, nodding at the car. "Gonna plant something on me, weren't you?"

The Spider says nothing. Backs away. She raises the hooked coat-hanger like an afterthought.

"Gonna put some of your product in there. Call my P.O." Mona's hands are reaching out. She can see the Spider's scared face at the end of a long tunnel.

"I'm calling 9-1-1," Letty screams behind her. "You touch her, I swear I'll do it."

Mona steps in close and snatches away the black scarf. A big Adam's apple quivers on the Spider's neck. "Fucking tranny," Mona says. "Afraid of a real woman."

"You do not talk to me like that."

"I bet you're hung like a donkey. What a fucking waste."

The Spider's thin lips compress. "Your ass is out of here by the end of shift. You're quitting."

"That a threat?"

"You're still hanging around, two of my boys will break your legs and all your fingers. You won't be able to skate. You won't be able to cut hair."

"Big talk."

"Miguelito and Ramon." The Spider's fingers curl into an arcane gang-sign. "Neighborhood boys. Where do you think I get my product?"

Mona squares her shoulders. Back inside the shop, she locks herself in the bathroom and makes a series of phone calls.

§

Five o'clock rolls around and Mona's still at her chair. As promised, a midnight blue Lincoln Continental pulls in at ten past. Out steps a pair of modern Aztec warriors. The Spider lets them in, locks the front door and flips the 'Open' sign to 'Closed.' Letty and Marta beat it out the back door.

"Last chance," the Spider says, folding thin arms over her chest.

Mona glances at the two men. She guesses Miguelito's the shorter one, in the wife-beater and Atzlan tattoos. Ramon's face registers no expression beneath a huge pair of Oakley's.

"Either of you packing?" Mona says. She takes a step back from her chair.

Ramon makes a spitting noise. "We don't need guns for this, bitch."

"Just checking."

"Take off now," the Spider says, eyes half-lidded. "I don't like violence. I really don't."

Mona turns like she's going to bolt for the back door. Neither man moves to stop her. The last moment, she whirls back around, throws the door open so hard it slams against the interior wall. Two women in elbow and knee pads step through.

First up is the Great Wall of Dinah, a Blocker. She's got about an inch on Miguelito and shoulders broad as Ramon's, wearing a black tank with the Dust Devil Dolls insignia on the front, her blond hair shorn up one side in a punk bi-level. The shop's fluorescents gleam off a checkerboard of gold teeth.

Next comes Polly You're-a-Thang, one of the team's Pivots. She's long and lanky underneath black leather, with a spit-curl pompadour and a chrome-studded forearm guard. "You fucking with our Jammer?" she says, draping a protective arm over Mona.

The gangster brothers can only stare. "What is this shit?" Ramon says at last.

"Solidarity," Mona says.

The Spider laughs. "It's just a couple bull-dykes. Kick their asses."

But the Dust Devil Dolls are already moving. Dinah lunges for Ramon, while Mona and Polly team against Miguelito. His chin goes down and his hands come up in a boxer's stance. He bounces a stiff right off Polly's forehead, slowing her. Mona aims a Doc Martin at his crotch. He sidesteps, and the kick lands on the inside of his thigh. He grunts, snaps a jab at Mona. Bright dots swirl across her vision, but it isn't as bad as taking a gainer on the track. Polly, meanwhile, has recovered enough to throw a looping elbow. Miguel's head slews sideways with the impact, the hard plastic of the elbow-pad cutting his cheek. Polly snakes behind him.

"Hold him still," Mona yells. She kicks again.

This time her foot strikes true. Miguel's face contorts like a raisin. Polly lets him go and he drops soundlessly, hitting the floor in the fetal position.

A glance shows Dinah's in real trouble: Ramon's got her down, both legs wrapped around her lower torso while he jacks short punches into her face. His Oakley's are hanging off one ear, and blood's trickling from bite-marks along the lobe.

Without thought, Mona snatches a pair of shears from the vanity and plunges them handles-deep into Ramon's thigh. He howls, rolling off Dinah.

But the Spider's grabbed up a stainless steel bowl, and tosses the contents in a watery arc. Permanent solution. She catches Polly flush. Mona ducks quick enough that only her left eye gets it, but the contact feels like liquid Hell. Polly's screaming contralto, clawing at her face.

Mona closes on the Spider, her eye already tearing shut as the caustic liquid attacks her nerves. "Don't come near me," the Spider shrieks, flicking open that fucking razor of hers. "You stay the fuck back."

Mona's not stopping: she drops into a sliding tackle that would earn her a major penalty on the track. Both legs scissor around the Spider's front foot and the willowy bitch goes down, razor flashing out to one side. Mona's up, atop her back. She slams the Spider's face against the linoleum, once, and yanks the razor from her unresisting fingers. Presses the blade right up under that throbbing Adam's apple.

"Call your boys off or I cut you," she says.

But the boys are indisposed. Miguelito's propped himself up onto a chair, looking ready to spew. Ramon's got a blood-soaked towel jammed tight around the protruding shears. Dinah, her face already one giant spreading bruise, is holding the still-screaming Polly over a sink, trying to wash the permanent solution out of her eyes.

"You should've just left," the Spider says. "Now your ass is going to prison."

"Woulda, coulda, shoulda," Mona says.

§

From the Pima County Adult Probation proceedings, State vs. Monique Kolodny, Tucson City Court:

Assault and Battery (two counts).

Assault with a Deadly Weapon.

Violation of Probation in connection with above charges.

RECOMMENDATION: Three to five years, Marana Medium Security Correctional Facility. Due consideration given to probationer's charges of sexual misconduct involving her surveillance officer, Thomas Swinburne.

§

Two weeks later Mona's talking to Dinah in a cinderblock room with low metal tables, normally used for family visitation. Mona's wearing a pale orange smock with numbers stenciled across the breast pocket. Dinah's got a neck-brace on. The bridge of her nose seems to be healing well.

"I'm almost afraid to ask," Mona says, "but how is Polly doing?"

"Fine. Washed most of that shit out. How's your eye?"

"Vision's still a little cloudy, but better."

Dinah takes a deep breath. "They, ah, tell you anything about your daughter?"

"She's gonna be ten by the time I get out. Foster parents say she likes school." Mona checks her hair in the table's blurred reflection; the green dye's completely gone. "She's probably better off. I don't think I'd ever make a good mom."

She doesn't cry, because that's not her way. And Dinah doesn't disagree with her.

"You know what I'm missing already?" Mona says. "Fucking mocha drinks. Prison coffee's for shit. Your cousin works here, right? Can she smuggle in something decent?"

"I've got a better idea. My cousin says there's a lot of tension at this facility. Racial shit, bangers. She says the girls almost had a riot last year, when the cable went out."

"Yeah?"

"And there's this recreation building. Big, got an open flat area that would make a perfect track, once it's taped off. What I'm thinking, my cousin goes to the warden, gets permission to bring in some skates and helmets—"

"—we could start a whole new fucking league," Mona says, "just for incarcerated chicks. 'The Rolling Cons' or some shit like that."

"'Avengers in Orange.'"

"Nah..."

They argue names for the rest of the visit.

A Blow to the Head

Rob W. Hart

The hallway is thick with the smell of food I can't pronounce. Richie presses himself against the wall and puts a finger to his lips. He reaches with his other hand to knock on the black metal door.

I stare at the pea-green paint on the wall across from me, squeeze the grip on the shiny snubnose pistol. Breathe in, slow and even. The gun isn't loaded. Richie doesn't trust me to carry a loaded gun. But, like he says, a gun doesn't have to be loaded for it to work.

Footsteps shuffle and stop behind the door. The guy is probably looking through the peephole, even though Richie stuck chewing gum onto it. He pretends it was an original idea but I know he stole it from *The Professional*.

A man's voice, muffled through the door. "Who's there?"

Richie says, "Electrician. Lights are out. I need to get in there and check some wiring."

"My lights are fine."

"That's good. But it would be a big help if I could come in. It'll be just be a second."

Pause. "It's one in the morning."

"We're very sorry to disturb you so late."

A longer pause. "There's no junction box or anything in here."

"Are you an electrician?"

"Well, no."

"Then no offense, but maybe don't tell me how to do my job?"

Richie looks at me, smiles, and winks. The door opens a few inches, stopping on the chain. Richie leans back and kicks the door the rest of the way open, leads with his shotgun. I follow and pull the door closed.

The guy is small and thin, with glasses and wispy hair combed over his balding head. I don't know what he does but he looks like an accountant. He's wearing a fuzzy baby-blue bathrobe, hanging open over an undershirt and blue boxers.

He doesn't seem upset or confused or afraid of the shotgun stuck in his face. He doesn't seem happy either. I can't figure out how he feels.

Richie says, "You're coming with us."

The guy shrugs. "What if I don't want to?"

Richie isn't prepared for this. He sputters a little, probably assuming the shotgun was the only convincing the guy would need. He steps forward, the barrel hovering a few inches in front of the guy's eyes. "Because Ginny wants to see you. And when Ginny wants to see you, you come with."

"Fuck Ginny."

"Fine, have it your way." Richie turns to me. "Good thing we brought the car, little brother. We're going to have to carry the prick."

Richie tosses the shotgun so it spins around. He catches it in mid-air and smashes the butt into the guy's forehead.

The sound is wet and hollow. I don't like it.

The guy goes down to his knees, but he doesn't go down quiet. He clutches his head, blood gushing from between his fingers. He mutters curses through the blood. Richie looks at me, confused. "I was trying to knock him out."

"I don't know if it works like that," I tell him.

The guy falls onto all fours, blood dripping onto the floor. Richie scratches his black, slicked hair. "It works in the movies and stuff. You hit the guy with the gun, knock him out, right?"

"Movies aren't always accurate, Richie. The guy might be really hurt."

"Maybe I didn't hit him hard enough."

The guy struggles to stand. Richie takes the shotgun by the barrel, raises it over his head, and brings it down on the guy's head like he's chopping wood. This time it sounds sharp, like he hit concrete.

The guy flattens into the floor, still moaning, softer this time. The butt of the shotgun has something fuzzy, chunky, and red on it.

Richie shrugs. "Well, that didn't work."

"You think?"

He looks at me, his eyes cobalt. "Don't talk to me like that, little brother. Don't forget who runs the show."

"Sorry."

Richie shakes his head, walks in a circle around the guy, who's moving his arms like he's trying to swim away. There's a puddle of blood on the floor under his face, and more leaking down the side of his head. Richie jerks his thumb over his shoulder. I check the apartment.

There's no one else there. Not much to search, either. Just a tidy bedroom and bathroom, and a kitchen even smaller than ours.

When I come back to the front door the guy is still moaning, and he's trying to say something but I can't make it out. Richie says, "We have to shut him up. Get a sock or something."

I head to the bedroom, find the dresser. The top drawer is overflowing with rubber dildos. This is awkward. One looks like a Stormtrooper from *Star Wars*. I go to touch it, out of curiosity, then pull my hand back when I realize I probably shouldn't touch something like that. I close the drawer and find socks in the one below it.

Back in the foyer, Richie has the guy sitting, leaned up against the wall, his legs spread out in front of him. The guy is staring across the room but his eyes are dazed, like he can't focus on anything. His face is red and wet. Richie reaches out his hand to me and snaps his fingers. I place the sock in his hand, and he crams it down the guy's throat.

The guy doesn't resist. His head rolls to the side and he closes his eyes.

Richie exhales. "Fucking finally. Thought he'd never pass out." He stands up. "First thing, we need to get the car around. So I think you should go down, park in front of the hydrant. Put on the flashers. It's late so the cops won't give a shit. Then we'll get the guy down the stairs. We should be able to do this quick."

The guy suddenly leans forward, a choking sound in his throat, and he heaves. The sock explodes out of his mouth, pink vomit screaming across his lap, mixing with the blood on the floor. He pukes three times before he stops, tries to say words that come out as grunts.

Richie says, "Fuck!" He pulls a plaid shirt off the coatrack on the wall and uses it to wipe the spray off his pants, while pulling out his cell phone. "Fuck."

"This isn't good," I tell him.

"I know it's not fucking good. I'm calling for help."

"Who are you calling?"

Richie looks away from me, turns on the speaker, and places the phone on the wooden breakfront. The room is filled with a high, tinny ringing.

I ask, "Who are you calling?"

The phone picks up. The voice is deep and dark, even over the static-y speaker. It says, "What."

Samson.

Shit. Shit shit shit. Fucking Samson. I clamp my hand over my mouth so I won't say his name, or curse, or cry. Richie wipes puke off his boot and says, "Samson, bro, need a little help. Some advice, you know?"

Pause. "What."

Richie's voice is shaking and cracking. He tries to hide it. It makes the shaking and cracking sound worse. "Listen, you know that guy Ginny asked us to grab? Well, we have a problem. He didn't want to come so I hit him in the head, and now he's all dazed and puking and shit. And I thought since you hit a lot of people, you might have some insight here. Is this something, you know, we should be worried about?"

"What did you hit him with?"

"Shotgun."

"You hit him with a fucking shotgun? Hard?"

Richie winces. "Well, pretty hard. Harder the second time, I think."

Dead air. Richie leans over to the phone to make sure the call is still connected, and lunges away from it when Samson screams, "Why the fuck would you hit him twice with a shotgun?"

"Knock him out, you know? I figured I'd knock him out and carry him downstairs. He didn't want to come Samson. What was I supposed to do?"

"You were *not* supposed to hit him in the fucking head with a shotgun."

"Samson, c'mon, I..."

"Shut the fuck up. Listen. You cannot knock someone out with a blow to the head. That's stupid movie bullshit. He probably has a concussion. Like, he needs to see a doctor or he's going to have a cerebral hemorrhage and then he's going to die and then Ginny is going to make me kill you. Do you want me to kill you?"

Richie looks at me like I can help. I don't want to take the hand off my mouth so I shrug. The guy moans on the floor, says something that sounds like 'please', but I can't be sure. Richie chokes on his words and speaks quietly, like a scolded child. "No, I would not like that."

Samson exhales into the phone. A blast of static on our end. He asks, "How does the guy look?"

We both lean down. The wound on his head has stopped bleeding, but his eyes look like a light on a dimmer switch that's slowly being turned down. Richie says, "He's seen better days."

"Do not fucking joke with me."

"Sorry, sorry."

"There's a doctor on East Fourth, by KGB. Do you know it?"

"Yea, he patched me up that time..."

"Don't tell me a fucking story. Just get this guy there toot fucking sweet. He knows shit. It's shit Ginny needs to know. If you scrambled his brain, then Ginny won't find out the shit she needs to find out. Then I have to hear about it. Then I'll make sure you hear about it. Do you understand?"

"Yes."

"Tell me you understand."

"I understand."

"And what am I going to do if this goes south?"

"Kill me."

"And?"

"And what?"

"And I'm going to kill your dumbfuck brother."

My shoulders tense and my face burns. I push Richie. Richie pushes me back. He says, "Billy isn't on this with me."

"Don't lie to me. You two can't take a piss apart. Far as I'm concerned you're both responsible. Now, doctor. Go. Fuck you."

Click.

Richie picks up the phone and looks at the screen, his face white as freshly-fallen snow, then places it in his pocket. He doesn't look at me, or at the guy on the floor, or anything in the apartment. He just looks. I ask, "Richie?"

"Not now."

"We need to figure this out."

"I'm thinking."

"We have to do this and we have to do it now. I'll get the car.

Park in front of the hydrant. I'll come back up. We'll carry him down."

Richie pokes his boot into the guy's leg. "Quicker than that. Get the car, be outside in five. Wait. He's small. I can carry him."

I don't want to argue.

I don't want Samson to kill me either, so I run out the door.

§

I tap tap tap my fingers on the dash. Look at the front of the building and expect to see Richie come out, carrying the guy over his shoulder.

I twist in the drivers' seat and expect see Samson standing behind the car, tapping the face of his watch.

I don't see either. I don't know which makes me more nervous.

The street is quiet. Nine cabs and one person went by. Nobody stopped to look at me, sitting in the car, the flashers blinking, tapping on the dash.

It's cold but I'm sweating.

Richie is taking too long. He shouldn't be taking too long. All I can think about is Samson, and that smile he gets on his face when he's about to hurt someone. He likes his job way too much. Richie should have never hit the guy. I don't want to get killed because Richie doesn't know what he's talking about.

I get out, check the car's distance from the hydrant. There's just enough room that a cop in a good mood might give it a pass. I leave the blinkers on and walk across to the building.

Then back to the car. He told me to wait.

I check my cell. Nothing.

Back to the building.

What if something happened?

I look around. There's no one coming. I push in, through the unlocked vestibule door, which they really ought to think about locking, and hit the stairs. A door on the landing above me slams. I follow the sound.

The second floor hallway is empty. A television is blaring somewhere. The light is harsh white and buzzing, like I'm trapped in a horror movie. That's exactly what it feels like.

I check the third floor hallway. The guy's door is closed. I peek into the apartment and it's empty, so I head back down to the second floor because that slamming door is bothering me. I walk down the hall, whispering Richie's name.

Around the corner and at the end of the hallway, there's still no Richie. I weigh the risk and slightly louder say, "Bro."

A door opens behind me. I'm pulled into a dark, cramped, moist place. There's a hand over my mouth. I struggle to get away but then I see the clover tattooed on the wrist and I realize it's Richie. He pushes me against the wall, whispers, "Quiet."

I hold my breath. I have to hold my breath. We're in the room with the garbage chute. It smells like death's rotting corpse was dumped in a sauna. My eyes adjust. Richie is twisted against the wall, the guy at his feet, whimpering. I think he's shaking his head at us. He makes a gagging sound, like he's going to puke again. We both try to twist away but we can't because the space is too small.

We wait. I don't know how long. Too long. Finally Richie takes his hand off my mouth and says, "Took me a few minutes to get clear of the apartment. Then I heard someone in the stairwell."

"I think that was me."

His scrunched his eyebrow and hits me in the chest. "Are you fucking kidding me?"

"Dude, shut up. The car is parked outside. I'll check and see if the coast is clear."

He grabs at me but I don't want to wait; I want to not get murdered by an angry hitman. I duck out and the hallway is clear. Walk to the other end and Richie peeks out. I wave him over and he hoists the guy onto his shoulder, bringing him toward me.

Just as we're about to get to the stairwell an apartment door opens. We both freeze. The guy takes this as an opportunity to puke down Richie's back.

Still pink. What did he eat?

The guy swings a weak punch into Richie's back, and says something that sounds like 'cunt'.

Richie pushes me toward the other end of the hallway. I put myself between him and the little old lady who comes out, blocking her view so he can get through the stairwell door without her seeing him.

The lady is short. Like if you shaved off another three inches she'd be considered a midget. Her hair is so white it's almost blue and she's swaddled in a giant yellow-and-white polka dot muumuu. She looks up at me with suspicious eyes behind thick glasses. She has a garbage bag in her hand so I reach for it. "Let me take that for you, miss."

She pulls it away from me. "Who are you?"

"I live upstairs. Just moved in. Nice to meet you. Let me take that trash for you."

She thinks for a moment. "If you live on the third floor and you come in on the first floor, why are you on the second floor?"

"I...thought I heard a noise."

"What apartment do you live in?" She says it like she's testing me.

Fuck. Is it numbers or letters? I can't look up at her apartment door. She'll call me on it. I think about it for a second, remember the combination on the mark's door.

"3D," I tell her.

She nods and hands me the garbage. I walk it over, toss it into the chute, and head back for the stairs, relieved that I managed to talk my way out of this one.

She waves. "Thank you, son. Now I'm going to call the police, because Mister Hunter lives in 3D, not you." She slams the door and a cavalcade of locks click into place, one after another.

Not good. I hope Richie is in the car because we need to be gone.

But he's not. He's standing in the vestibule, the guy who I now know as Mr. Hunter propped up against the wall. He looks up at Richie with wavy eyes and takes a weak swing at his legs. Richie jumps out of the way and looks at me and says, "Where's the car?"

I look out the window of the front door and the car is gone.

Richie asks, "Where's the car, Billy?"

I don't answer. Richie waves his hands in the air. Mr. Hunter leans forward, says something that sounds like 'imbeciles'.

Richie says, "Billy, if the car was parked right out front, and the car is gone, what the fuck then? Huh? What the fuck is going on? Did you leave the keys in it? I swear if you left the keys in it..."

I hold up the key ring. Tell him, "I wasn't that close to the hydrant. I locked the doors."

Richie smacks his forehead. "It's the last day of the month."

"What does that mean?"

"The cops have ticketing quotas. They're probably cruising around looking for people to tow."

"I didn't think of that."

Richie shakes his head, too frustrated to be angry. "Fuck it, doesn't matter. We need wheels."

"There were a bunch of cabs out before."

"That works. Let's boost a cab. Use the snub."

I'm not thrilled with the way this sounds but I'll risk jail over Samson. I push open the door a little, wait for Richie to get behind me with Mr. Hunter on his shoulder, then push through to the street.

We get to the curb.

And nothing.

There was a parade of cabs while I was waiting. Now there isn't a single one. I look down the street. There's a streetlight right over us. It feels more like a spotlight. Me with the gun out. Richie with Mr. Hunter over his shoulder. I head toward the corner to see if I can catch a cab headed down the avenue, but Richie yells after me, "Don't go that way. Fourth goes east. Go down to Third. We have to be going west."

"It doesn't make a fucking difference because we're on a one-way street."

Richie cries out in pain.

I turn to find Mr. Hunter on the ground, getting to his feet on loose limbs. Richie is holding both of his arms behind his back, reaching into his pants. He screams, "Dude bit my ass!"

Mr. Hunter steadies himself and takes off down the block, in the opposite direction of us. But he's not running so good, weaving back and forth, like he's on the tail end of a bender.

Or took a blow to the head, I guess.

He yells, "Help!"

Richie waves at me. "Go fucking get him. I'll get the cab."

A cab turns the corner and rolls toward us. I step into the street and get behind a parked car so the driver won't see me. I wave at Richie. "I'm closer. You go get him."

Richie yells, "Fine."

Mr. Hunter makes it easy. He doesn't get far before he weaves into a lamppost. It makes a 'clang' sound, like a cartoon sound effect, and he falls onto his back.

I listen for the engine of the cab and when it gets close, I pop out with the gun.

Too late—I see two guys riding up front.

Cabs don't carry passengers up front.

The only cabs with two guys riding up front are undercover

police cars.

I drop the gun. Richie asks, "What the fuck are you doing you..."

He's cut off when the cab screeches to a stop and the two plainclothes cops leap out, guns up, screaming at us to put our hands in the air. We both do. Richie drops Mr. Hunter again, who lands on the ground with a thump.

The four of us watch as he tries to crawl away.

And then the cops are on us.

§

The rest of the night is a familiar blur. We're shoved into the back of a cop car, taken to central booking, and split up.

A cop comes in and screams at me that my brother is ratting me out and he can help me if I cooperate. I tell him I want a lawyer. He keeps screaming and I keep saying I want a lawyer, until he gives up and sticks me with a kid in a suit that's two sizes too big. He tells me some stuff but I barely listen because I know the drill.

I sleep a little through the night and I don't see Richie again until we're both in an assembly-line courtroom standing before the judge. We listen as another guy in a suit reads off the charges. Breaking and entering, assault. The gun stuff is complicated because both the snub and the shotgun were unloaded, so the charges are slightly less serious.

The people in suits talk some more and we say we're not guilty and even on my feet I'm drifting, but then the judge bangs his gavel and I'm awake and he sets the bail at $10,000 apiece.

Me and Richie look at each other and shrug.

He's thinking the same thing I am: What a relief.

Spending a couple of nights in jail is fine. Samson can't get to us in here, and that gives us time for things to cool down, or at least for us to come up with a plan to flee the country.

The bailiff drags us to the back and pushes us into a cell, and we sit there on wooden benches across from each other, surrounded by people who look like jailhouse extras from an episode of *Law & Order: SVU*.

I sleep for a little. I don't know how long. Then Richie is poking me in the ribs. He says, "Let's go, little brother. Time to go to Rikers. Does it make me a bad person that I'm a little excited? Like maybe we'll see some of the old crew floating around?"

"Fuck you, Richie," I tell him.

Usually he would yell at me for talking to him like that but there are too many people around. He shakes his head and we go to the bars and stand and wait. An overweight Italian cop with a porn mustache walks us down a hallway.

I ask, "How's the guy?"

The cop asks, "What guy?"

"The guy. From our thing. With the head injury."

Richie says, "*Alleged* head injury."

I tell Richie, "It's not an alleged injury. It's a real injury. The only thing alleged is our involvement. Do you really not know how this works by now?"

Richie puts up his hands and smiles, like that's supposed to be an answer.

The cop says, "The guy will be fine. Whoever put the hurt on him is an asshole though. Nothing alleged about that."

I punch Richie in the ribs before he can say anything. He winces as the cop hands us each a plastic bag with the personal items they took off us in booking.

Richie asks, "What's this?"

The cop says, "You made bail."

Richie turns to me. "Did you call anyone?"

I shake my head as my stomach drops out from under me. The cop leads us down the hallway to a big, heavy door, where we have to wait for someone to buzz us through.

On the other side is Samson. All three hundred granite pounds of him, in a black leather duster. A yellow spot gleaming on his bald head, cast by the overhead lights. The walls of the small room seem to tilt inward, crushing us, like he's a center of gravity.

He smiles from behind the wraparound sunglasses he never takes off, says, "Let's go, boys."

Richie turns to the cop. "Can we go back inside?"

The door locks behind us.

When Monte Comes Calling
Andy Henion

When Monte comes calling, and pray he never does, pray to whatever god you hold sacred, you've got to lock the place down tight. We missed this, Sheila and I, because who thinks to check the dining room window when a known maniac is strolling up the driveway? I mean, of course you bolt the door with trembling fingers and grab the nearest utensil and stand your ground, hoping Monte won't have the plums to break in as the autumn sun disappears behind the evergreens. So what he does, he saunters away from the door, slits the screen with his legendary scalpel and then reaches in and slides the window open.

And says, as he climbs through, "Beautiful sunset, hey guys?"

I focus on the glinting blade in his fist while Sheila, all five feet, one hundred pounds of her, takes the gentle yet scolding tone one might with a child. "Mon*teee*," she says, drawing out that last syllable like maybe she used to do when he threatened to whack a winking deliveryman or pushed for relations on a Wednesday night, I really wouldn't know. I haven't asked about their domestic particulars and she hasn't offered.

I've known Sheila a shade over five weeks. Twenty-seven incredible days, to be exact. It's the first relationship of any substance since my divorce nearly six years ago, not counting the manic-depressive florist from Fowlerville who liked to laugh hysterically during sex. And cry after.

Monte ignores Sheila and stares a hole through me, the scar above his lip twitching like a pink grub. His unblinking gray eyes remind me of my old varsity basketball coach who would eschew halftime pep talks in favor of staring each of us down, in turn, as if he could send the needed motivation telepathically. Only Coach

Ryan, to my knowledge, wasn't homicidal.

A clock ticks on the wall. The sweat on my forehead is hot lead. My hammering heart threatens to detonate.

Finally I can take it no longer.

"I'm all in here," I say, jabbing the corkscrew at his stone countenance. "*All. Motherfucking. In.*"

Monte makes a face somewhere between amused and mystified, having a little fun with it, I can tell. He doesn't know me from Adam, but he can tell this isn't my scene. I write press releases for a living, wear khakis, run on a treadmill. He wiggles his eyebrows. I dab at sweat. But then his smile turns genuine and he slips the scalpel into his back pocket, blade up.

"I can tell," he says, spreading his arms wide. "You're gonna be magic together."

I turn to Sheila. She sighs. The thing about Monte, he's an odd hombre. You'd think with his line of work he'd be all Clint Eastwood stoic, but half the time you're not even sure if he's serious. Rumor has it he likes to toy with his marks, mixing in a healthy dose of hijinks with his scalpel work.

"I'm just going to grab a few things," he says, and heads off toward the back of the house.

Sheila slides a hand up between my shoulder blades and leans close.

"He's toying with us," she whispers, breath sweet on my face. "This will never be over."

And I can picture it, waking up one morning with an angry scorpion on my forehead. Or maybe my brakes fail. Coffee cup laced with ricin. They say Monte's professional creativity knows no bounds.

"*Well*?" she says, eyes wide.

"Well *what*?" But I think I know what she wants and I'm having trouble processing. I set the corkscrew on the counter so there's no confusion about my intentions. Sheila corkscrews up her face and marches to the den and I follow behind, transfixed by the bounce of her chestnut pony and knowing I should be walking straight out the door.

"I want you to leave," she says. "I can send your crap."

"Almost done," Monte says, placing notebooks in a duffle. He's bent over with his back to us, the scalpel tip pointing at the ceiling.

"He's taking your words," I say, but Sheila's eyes dart away from mine suspiciously. Monte stops what he's doing and says, without rising, "Is that what you told him? *Your* words?"

"Just *leave!*" she nearly screeches, and snatches the scalpel. He fails to react and my first thought is she's going to do it—drive the blade into his exposed spine—but then she steps back and simply holds it at her side, sneering, and I realize that perhaps my girlfriend still has feelings for this slate-eyed killer.

Monte turns, finally, and lowers himself to the floor, fluid as a sensei. Cross-legged he sits with one of the notebooks in his lap. Motions for us to join him. He has that easy, carefree way about him I've always admired in people. I take a seat on the carpet, folding my legs under me stiffly. Sheila looks down at my awkward pose and shakes her head as Monte reads aloud from the notebook.

"*Night is a famished beast,*" he says. Looks up. "I wrote that line."

Eyes back to the page—"*Devouring my soul*"—and then to me, shining with pride. "And Sheila wrote that one. Every other line, just like that."

Christ, I think, that took the both of you? But I keep it to myself and opt for a more appropriate nod and a "hmm."

Monte turns his attention to Sheila. "Gramma Norma's gone," he says, and if I didn't know better I would say he was tearing up.

Sheila's sneer disappears and her grip loosens on the scalpel.

"Aw, babe," she says. "I heard."

Babe?

"She was my mother, that woman. And I couldn't even go to her funeral."

Sheila bends down and thumbs the tears from his cheeks.

"She's in a better place, Monte-bear." Her touch lingers and he brings his hand up to hers, presses it against his face. This is the woman I've come to know in our short time together, the caring, passionate Sheila. Only I'm not used to seeing that passion applied to another man, grieving or not.

I clear my throat. When this fails to get their attention, I say, "So, Monte-bear, why couldn't you go to the funeral?"

They turn and look at me as if I just asked why opossums don't fly. I shrug. Whatever.

"How's the restaurant?" says Monte, still holding my girlfriend's hand, and she goes on to provide an update on the soap opera that is Astro's, a burger-and-chicken joint she manages and hopes one day to own. I ate there for the first time five weeks ago, the day Sheila was filling in for a sick waitress and delivered my chickpea chicken salad with a smile that made me forget my hunger.

When she finishes, Monte nods and wraps both hands gently around hers, the way someone might for a marriage proposal.

"I quit the business, Sheila. I'm out."

She goes still. Then pulls her hand free and steps back.

"I *beg* your pardon?"

"After we separated, after Gramma, I just ..." He looks to the ceiling to compose himself, sniffing in tears, and I smile inwardly at his angst. So much for Mr. Carefree Hitman. Here's the full Monte, indeed. But then I wonder how many other men have found themselves groveling at Sheila's feet, and when my turn might come.

Sheila puts her hands on her hips, a bad sign for the ex.

"I spend three years pleading with you to get out, wondering every night if you were even coming home."

"I came back to tell you, but each time PR-guy here was sleeping in my bed."

"It's not PR—"

"So you were spying on us? And you think this is a healthy behavior?"

"—it's media relations, actually."

Their heads turn in unison. "A common mistake," I add, and wave it off. Sheila's mouth pops open incredulously, a what-the-hell-is-wrong-with-you look if I've ever seen one, but Monte is grinning.

"I like him," he says. "The deadpan thing. He might—"

With that, his pants begin to vibrate. He pulls out a cell and squints at the incoming message for a good fifteen seconds. Shoves the phone back in his pocket and stands up.

"They're coming to kill me," he says.

"*What*?" says Sheila. "*Here*?"

His answer is to reach behind the bookcase and detach a large silver handgun. As he pulls off the duct tape and checks the chamber, I climb to my feet and step over to Sheila. I move to put an arm around her, to comfort her amid this craziness, but a quick, barely perceptible shake of her head stops me short.

"My source says they're on their way," says Monte. "Three of them."

Sheila thrusts the scalpel at the door. "Get *out*," she says.

He nods.

"That's the plan. But understand this: These people know everything about me—right down to my cholesterol level—and that means they know about you too. Both of you."

Monte eases the curtain aside with the barrel and peers into the fast-spreading darkness.

"They're gonna burn this place to the ground," he says. "Whether I'm here or not. At this point, they're cleaning up—Monte and everybody Monte is close to."

"God*damn* you for this," cries Sheila, and lunges at him with the scalpel.

In a flash, Monte half-turns, grabs her wrist and spins her like a ballerina so he's bear-hugging her from behind, arms bracing hers, lips an inch from her ear. It happens so fast it seems choreographed.

"I know," he says gently. "Not fair."

Sheila doesn't struggle and I get the sense they've done this dance before. There's a scowl on her face but a spark in her eye, and I wonder, as I watch them together: Is she turned on? Just how hard was she trying to kill him anyway?

"Okay then," Monte says. He releases his grip and Sheila retreats slowly to the corner where she slides down the wall to her rump, deflated. Drops the scalpel to the carpet.

"Follow my lead and I put your odds at sixty-forty."

"I think you're selling yourself short," I tell him, and he shrugs in mock modesty. "So why not just kill us and flee?"

"*Flee*?" he says. "No one says *flee* anymore. Take a floor, PR-guy, so you're out of the line of fire."

I do as I'm told, letting the PR thing go this time. Monte opens the window and pulls up a chair. Takes a seat and rests the barrel on the sill. Reaches over and kills the light.

"A good cleaner needs to see in the dark. Take a few minutes and let your eyes adjust."

"Wait. You're teaching us the trade?"

"You'll need one if you make it out of this alive. Your days in the public eye are over."

Sheila laughs bitterly. "Funny story," she says, voice small and detached. "I quit my job yesterday and signed up for classes." She goes on, in that hollow tone, to explain that in the past few months she's developed a burning desire to do something worthwhile, something meaningful, so she was going to become a teacher, work with disadvantaged urban kids, living off her restaurant savings in the meantime, and that she was going to do it alone, she was finally going solo, because ever since she was eighteen, hell sixteen, she'd been with a man, man after man after man, as if her life was defined by the Y chromosome in the bed next to her.

It's at this point I realize what she's saying. My stomach turns.

"I was going to tell you tonight," she says. "I was actually in the process when the *cleaner* here crawled through the window."

Silence follows. Crazy-loud silence. But Monte's not feeling my pain. He says, "You gonna teach those little buggers English? Some poetry perhaps? You've got a real voice."

"That's your deal," says Sheila. Then, with ample bitterness: "Poetry fuckin' *sucks*."

More silence. Brutally tense silence. The hitman has been rebuked—what now? Will he do us both? But suddenly a snort escapes, and then another, and I'm laughing despite myself, waiting for the dreaded blast from the silver handgun, but then Monte joins in, and he's got quite the old lady cackle, not that I would ever tell him that, and this makes me laugh even harder, *uncontrollably* would be the word, and before it's all said and done the three of us are sharing this moment of levity as we sit and wait to be possibly cleaned ourselves.

"This," says Monte, once the mirth has died down, "is refreshing. All these life transitions happening at once. Everyone baring their soul. So what do you have, PR-guy?"

"His name's Aaron," says Sheila, and these three words give me a glimmer of hope.

"That's Aaron in *media* relations," adds Monte.

What do I have? I reach in my pocket and pull it out, rub it between thumb and forefinger. I too have dipped into my savings account. Depleted it, actually.

"Sheila," I say, kneeling before her in the dark, "will you marry me?"

"No fucking way," says Monte.

Sheila's eyes must have adjusted, for she reaches out and feels the ring. Doesn't take it, just confirms its presence. Her soft little hand stays with me, and so does the hope.

"Oh, wow," she says. "This is why you were acting so jittery tonight."

"You make me jittery," I tell her. "You make my stomach queasy, like a schoolboy. Just being around you."

"You sure that's not the lactose talking?" says Monte, rude but, occasionally true.

"How could you possibly—"

"You're the schlub sleeping with my girl. I know it all."

"She's not *your* girl. Give up the dream, *Monte-bear*."

"Boys, boys," says Sheila. At this point she pats my hand and I know what's coming.

"Aaron," she says. "Such a beautiful gesture. A beautiful thought."

"Shh," says Monte.

"Damn it, Monte, stay out of this."

"*Shh*," he repeats. "They're here."

We freeze to the sound of tires crunching pine needles. They drive up with their lights off, which I suppose hitmen are wont to do, and I forget about marriage proposals and digestive issues and decide quite suddenly that I don't want to die. I begin a rambling prayer in my head to a god I scarcely know, promising that if he gets me out of this I will lead a better life, be a better man, do something purposeful like Sheila, maybe build houses for the destitute or be a big brother to would-be gangstas or even move in with my widowed mother and strain her pears and light her nasty cigarettes, the ultimate sacrifice ...

"Shit," whispers Monte. "No shot from here. I'm gonna take 'em by storm. You two stay put."

And he crouch-walks swiftly out of the room.

"*Wait wait wait*," I say, to no avail, and suddenly Sheila and I are left listening to the front door banging open and Monte ninja-screaming across the yard.

But no gunshots.

A car door opens. A woman's voice. Laughter.

"...gullible shits..." I hear Monte say. "Like I'd shoot them in the house."

The door shuts and the car drives away.

I purge a quart of air. Thank God repeatedly under my breath. I'm unclenching my fingers from around the diamond when Sheila grabs my elbow and I start, dropping the ring. It bounces once, twice, then clatters down the air register.

"You don't know him," she says quietly.

She's crying now, though I doubt it's over the ring. I reach out for her but she knocks my hand away. I tell her I will find a way to protect her and her cries turn to laughter. She mocks my sanity, my manhood, but that's only the fear talking, surely. I say we can disappear together: Canada, Mexico, what the hell, New Zealand, but this brings a squeal of fury and a fist glancing off my cheek.

"You don't get it," she shrieks. "He finds people. That's what he does."

Now she's up on her knees, flailing away. I cover up and absorb the blows, wincing from the sting of her slender fists but feeling grateful, above all, to be the target of her passion. Let her swing it out. As I said before, I'm all in.

No Place Like Home

John Kenyon

Jake stood over the bed, the gun in his outstretched hand. A sliver of moonlight through the curtains revealed the outline of a man lying on his back. His deep, steady breathing was just this side of a snore. The gun shook a little, not because of the weight, but because Jake had never done anything like this. He was a crook, not a killer. Parnell had promised a decent payoff, and maybe that would be enough to stake him somewhere else. One and done. He sure didn't want to stick around.

The man in the bed snorted. He opened his eyes for a moment, then closed them, then popped them open wide. "Stinson? What the —"

Jake silenced him with a blast from the barrel of his gun, a bullet straight into the mouth. The recoil surprised him. Hell, the shot itself surprised him, more reflex than intent. He squeezed the trigger twice more, putting two in the man's face. He staggered back into a dresser, turned with the gun out as if expecting to face someone, then relaxed when he realized his assailant was a piece of furniture.

He hastily wiped the pistol grip with the bed sheet and laid it on the man's chest. He walked out of the room and made his way to the back door. A sort of calm overtook him as he descended the stairs, his breath slowing with each step. Well, he thought, that was pretty easy.

Then he heard the siren.

§

The first time Parnell came around, Jake had only been out for four days, holed up in a dingy trailer behind a roadhouse. If he told it right, his situation sounded like a joke: what's the difference between this trailer and a prison cell? Thing is, Jake's punch line wasn't funny. One had carpet so dirty you couldn't tell the original color, the other was a square of concrete with iron bars for a window. One had been used at one time by the whores who worked the bar, the other, well, let's just say the more things were different, the more they seemed the same.

The place certainly was as depressing as the one he'd just left behind, but he didn't have many options. He'd had no fixed address when he'd been sent up; came into lockup like a homeless guy, wearing everything he owned. He felt pretty smart with that move, knowing they had to hold it all and give it back when he was sprung. Only trouble was the shirts were too tight thanks to his prison yard workouts, and the pants slipped off his skinny frame because he'd lost weight thanks to the shit they served in the cafeteria.

He was sitting on the bed—he'd flipped the mattress the first night, hoping the whores hadn't thought of it first—watching the eight-inch black and white, when someone knocked on his door. He figured it for the bartender, and called out that it was open. The latch pulled and he heard the door swing on its rusty hinges.

"Well, Jake Stinson. I finally found ya."

He looked up as an overweight man in sagging blue jeans and a sweat-stained T-shirt pulled himself up the steps and into the trailer.

"Pokey?" Jake said with surprise.

"Now, you know I don't like that nickname, Jake," said the man. "Out here, folks call me Parnell, just like my momma always did."

Pokey filled the doorway, a man whose excesses were draped over an already-stocky frame. He stood stock-still, as if waiting for an official invitation from Jake to move farther into the trailer. Jake motioned with his head for Pokey to do so.

"C'mon in," he said, not taking his eyes off of the TV. "Beer in the fridge."

Pokey looked left, saw, the fridge, and reached in to pull out a can. He popped the top, sucked foam loudly from the opening and moved toward the front of the trailer where Jake sat.

"That's two parole violations and I ain't been here but two minutes," Pokey said. "Livin' within one hundred feet of a bar and consuming alcoholic beverages. I could have you back inside by nightfall."

Jake slid to the front of the bed and dropped his feet to the floor, peering intently at Pokey.

"Whatcha playin' at here, Poke?" he said. "Why are you here?"

"I told you," Pokey said, pausing mid-sentence to take a slug of beer, "It's Parnell, OK? And I ain't playin' at nothin'. Just making conversation is all."

"That's what they call threatening a man now?" Jake said, his fists tightening. "I guess things changed more than I knew while I been inside."

Pokey help up his hands in mock defense.

"Now, now," he said. "Didn't mean to offend. Consider it advice from a friend. Not everyone on the outside has your best interests at heart. You cross the wrong person, won't take but a phone call to get you locked up again. What've you got left on your sentence? Couple years?"

"Something like that," Jake said, his muscles uncoiling a bit. He picked up his beer from the table and took a drink. "So, what do you want?"

Pokey took a long pull from his can. He shook it and looked in as if hoping to be surprised, then set the empty on the counter.

"Just wanted to say hi is all," he said. "Most fellas in there, I'm happy to see 'em leave, figure I'll be seein' 'em again all too soon. But you, well, we got along pretty good, huh? Figured once you were out and we were on equal footin', so to speak, we could probably be friends."

Pokey was the guard everyone gamed for favors. Tell him a joke, he'd give you a smoke. Tell him a sex story that seemed plausible and he'd give you the pack. They imagined him sitting alone at home in a ratty recliner watching porn with one hand in his pants. He seemed to spend a lot of time in front of Jake's cell, and the con figured they got along all right, all things considered. But he never would have guessed Pokey would be desperate enough for company that he'd look up an ex-con on the outside.

"Pull up a seat," Jake said, gesturing to the other end of the bed. He wasn't too jazzed about the guy sticking around, but the crack about parole violations had him on edge.

"What'cha watchin'?" Pokey asked.

Jake shrugged and tossed the remote in Pokey's direction. Pokey picked it up and flipped idly through the channels. He would stop on something for a moment, then skip to something else. After finishing a second beer, he stood.

"Good to hang out with you, Jake," he said. "Next time don't talk so much, OK?"

"What?"

"Just a joke son." He moved to the door, then turned. "Mind if I stop back sometime?"

Jake, who hadn't bothered to rise and see his guest out, shrugged again.

"Well, don't seem so enthusiastic about it!" Pokey said, leaning in to punch Jake lightly in the arm. "All right, I'll see you around."

He lumbered out onto the step, his weight pulling the entire trailer to that side an inch or two.

§

Jake slipped around the side of the house to the back, keeping tight up against the bushes to stay in the shadows. He had no idea if the sirens were for him, and he didn't want to take a chance. If he could make it to the alley, he figured he could be blocks away in a couple of minutes. There was a tall wooden fence at the back of the small yard, and he stood for a moment, listening. The sirens had stopped, so he figured they must have reached their destination. Relieved, he moved slowly to the gate, popped the latch and swung it open a few inches. He stuck his face through the gap for a look and was greeted by the barrel of a gun.

"Nice and slow, Stinson." He pulled back, but the gate was kicked in, knocking him to the ground. He was surrounded immediately by three officers in SWAT gear. One, who Jake recognized as a former prison guard named Hayden, keyed a mic on his shoulder.

"We have the suspect under control," he said. Then, turning to the other two officers, he said, "Go inside and check on Mason."

They ran off, leaving Jake on his back with a gun in his face.

"Hibbs?" said the cop.

Another person lumbered through the gate, his bulk obscuring the light from a streetlamp so that Jake could only see his outline.

"Yeah, Hayden," said the man.

"That's Sergeant Hayden, to you. Come on up here. Is this the man?"

The other guy stepped closer and looked down.

"Sure is. That's Jake Stinson." It was Parnell.

"All right, Pokey, that's all we need. Step back and let the pros handle it from here," Hayden said.

"Sergeant?" It was the two-way on the cop's shoulder. He tilted his head to speak.

"Hayden here."

"Mason's dead. Shot in his bed."

"Copy." He looked down at Jake. "Looks like we've got you for murder, friend. A whole world of shit is about to open up on your ass."

Parnell shifted, and Jake blinked against the now-visible streetlight. When he opened his eyes again, Jake could swear he saw Parnell smile.

§

The second time Pokey showed at the trailer, he brought his own beer and a bag of chips.

"Figured if you were providing the accommodations, least I could do is cater the party," he said as he stuck four of the beers in the fridge. He handed a can to Jake, then pulled the chips open and held out the bag in offering.

"You're a strange one Poke, I mean, Parnell," Jake said as he grabbed a handful.

"Ah, you remembered!" Pokey said. "That means a lot to me, Jake."

The big man sat down hard, nearly pulling Jake to the middle of the bed as it sagged. They watched TV again, Pokey occasionally making a comment about the football game. The tension Jake felt on the first visit eased a bit; it seemed the guard really did just want to be in the room with someone else, and Jake had to admit he didn't mind it. He'd be doing the same thing with or without Pokey, so why not have him around?

"You been lookin' for work, Jake?" Pokey said during a commercial. "You know, that's part of your parole. You gotta be looking for something."

Jake had, wandering around town, filling out applications that he was sure hit the trashcan before the door closed behind him. Pokey seemed to read his mind.

"Nothing out there, is there?" he said. "And even if there was, nobody's gonna hire a drifter with a felony on his record, am I right?"

Jake nodded. He'd heard that, in less-polite terms, from the few managers who actually bothered to speak with him.

"Maybe I can hook you up with something," Pokey said. "I'm pretty well connected around here, you know."

Jake stifled a laugh. Sure, Pokey was connected. So well connected that he hung out in a converted whore's trailer behind a bar on a weekend night with an ex-con. Then again, Jake was one to talk. He'd been out for three weeks, and had done little more than scan want ads and drink.

"What do you have in mind, Parnell?" he said.

"Oh, nothing specific," the guard said. "Just, you know. I'll keep my ears open."

He raised his can to take another drink but found it empty. He pulled himself up with some effort and went to the fridge.

"Beer?" he asked. Jake nodded. Pokey returned with two, cracked his and sucked the foam.

"What kind of job you lookin' for, Jake?" he said.

Jake had been wondering this same thing. He'd done a little of this, a little of that, but mostly what he had done was rob people or sell things that weren't his to sell. He said as much.

"I kinda figured that," Pokey said. "Well, I hear about a lot of that kind of stuff, too."

"Really?"

"I'm not a cop. Not yet, anyway. People talk," Pokey said.

§

Jake was outside at a picnic table in front of the trailer a few days later when Pokey arrived in a rusted pick-up. Jake had started out scanning the want ads in a day-old newspaper, but had worked his way to the sports section by the time Pokey walked up.

"How's it hangin', Jake?" he said.

"Heavy," Jake said. He was warming to the guy. He knew Pokey meant well, even if he was a little annoying and not exactly who Jake would pick for a friend if he had the choice. Thing was, he didn't.

Pokey walked up and placed a foot on the bench.

"Found a job for ya," he said.

"Oh yeah?" Jake said. "Doing what?"

"Want you to kill a guy."

"What? Not funny, Parnell."

"Not a joke. It's a job for me, actually. Remember Mason from the joint?"

"Sure. The supposed big shot mob guy. Loud mouth, right?"

"That's him," Parnell said. "He gets out this week. Cut some deal. He's getting out."

"So?" Jake said.

"So, I want you to kill him."

"Why would I do that?"

"Because I'm gonna pay you a thousand bucks."

Jake hadn't had that much money in a long time, and immediately thought of all the ways he could spend it.

"OK, I'm listening," he said. "The bigger question is why you want it. What's in it for you?"

"You know how he always rode me. Called me a fat ass. Expected me to be an errand boy for him just because he was some connected thug. I got tired of it real fast," he said. "But that's just a fringe benefit. Somebody wants him dead. I find the guy to do it and get a little taste for the effort."

"Why don't you kill him and take it all?" Jake said.

"Because they'd connect it right back to me. Everyone there knows I have a beef with the guy. I'd be in prison like that, maybe dead."

Jake stood up and walked around the table. He climbed up and sat on it next to Parnell.

"Why wouldn't it come back on me?"

"They're taking him to a safe house for a night before he talks. Didn't want to do it in the prison. Too many prying eyes and loose lips, I suppose. Plus, he said he wanted to sleep a night in a real bed before he spilled. Thing is, I know where he'll be, and there won't be anybody at the place until he arrives. By then you're already in, hiding. You cap him and slip out. I'll go to the bar and make a scene, make sure I have an alibi."

"If they look at you, why won't they look at me?"

"I haven't been trumpeting the fact that I'm buddies with an ex-con, if that's what you're gettin' at," Parnell said. I was embarrassed he could tell the remark hurt.

"It's for your protection as much as anything," he said quickly. "I know cons don't look favorably on us guards. Besides, if they started looking at every guy that ever jailed with that son of a bitch, it'd take 'em years to get to you."

§

Jake was in an interview room at the station. One hand was chained to a table that itself was bolted to the floor. This was different. He'd never been chatted up by the cops before. They'd collar him and throw him in lock-up. End of story. Then again, he'd never killed anyone before.

Two cops came in, both plainclothes. Hayden, the cop who led the arrest, was one. He pulled out a chair across from Jake and plopped down. The other walked behind Jake and leaned against the wall.

"Think you're pretty crafty, eh?" Hayden said. "Get tipped to where the Mason fella is holed up, think you'll sneak in and whack him. Collect a big payday. Be a hero."

"I'm not sure what you mean," Jake said.

"Look, this will be easier if you just tell us what we want to know. This is a black eye for the Marshal's Service, and they're gonna throw the book at you. You give us what we want before they get here and maybe we can put in a good word."

"The Marshals? As in U.S. Marshal's? What do they have to do with it?" Jake said.

"Don't play cute. Who did you think oversees witness protection? Mason was big-time, baby," Hayden said.

Jake sat fiddling with his fingers, sweat pouring off of him. He didn't know what he'd stepped in, but it was major.

"Look, I'm going to level with you," he said. "That guy? Mason? He was at Larchmont when I was. Everyone knew him. Guy was an asshole. One of the guards, Parnell, asked me to kill him."

The cop behind Jake began to laugh.

"Pokey? He's contracting hits now is he?" the cop said. "That's funny. Would this be the same Parnell Hibbs that led us right to you? If he's some criminal mastermind, he's sure piss poor at it."

"I know it seems funny to you, but it's true. I mean, I'm delivering up a bent cop, right? Isn't that worth something?" Jake said.

"Let's get one thing straight," said Hayden. He leaned in and poked Jake in the chest with a finger. "Pokey isn't a cop."

The other officer walked up behind Jake and placed a hand on his shoulder.

"Jake? This plays one of two ways. You get the needle, or you help us and we try to get you into federal Supermax. Tell us how in the hell you knew where a guy in witness protection was going to be in the transition day between his release from prison and being sent off on his new life, and maybe we can keep you alive. And tell us the truth this time."

There was a knock on the door, and the standing cop went over to answer it. Whoever was outside spoke animatedly. The cop came back inside with a paper in his hand. He looked at Hayden.

"We have a problem."

§

Jake watched as Parnell's truck bounced across the gravel lot behind the bar. The fat man rolled out of his seat and, without a word, waved Jake into the trailer. Once inside, he handed Jake a paper bag. Jake looked inside and found a handgun.

"It's loaded, clean and untraceable," Parnell said. "You're ready to go. You been casing the place?"

Parnell had given Jake the address a couple of days ago, and Jake had taken the bus by the house a couple of times. He got off once and walked the neighborhood a bit. If it was really as easy to get into as Pokey said, it should be pretty easy money. The police wouldn't bother guarding it until Mason was brought in. If Jake could get in beforehand and hide out, he'd be able to cap the con and slip out before anybody caught on.

"You gotta do it tonight," Parnell said. "He'll get there this evening after dark, and the place will be crawling with cops tomorrow. This is our shot."

"You mean my shot," Jake said.

"Well, sure. Technically," Parnell said, mimicking a shot with his hand. "But we're in this together, buddy. You help me, I help you."

Jake was trying hard to see the catch, but had to admit it seemed like a good deal.

"This isn't any way to live," Parnell continued, gesturing to the surroundings. "I'll get you where you need to be."

§

Jake wasn't sure if it was day or night. Twenty-three hours in a Supermax cell did that to you. Messed up your internal clock. In hindsight, he was glad he hadn't had what it took to make a deal. The big sleep was a better end than fading away in this concrete tomb, he thought.

He heard the metallic scrape as the lock mechanism slid back. The door opened, and there was Pokey.

"Howdy, Jake," he said. "Figured you could use a familiar face, so I pulled some strings and got a transfer to this facility."

Jake leaped at the guard, hoping to strike a blow before he was subdued. But Pokey showed surprising speed and hit Jake with a taser before the prisoner could cover the distance. Jake dropped, the painful voltage flowing through his body locking his limbs.

"Hey, no need for that, Jake," Parnell said. "Let's keep this friendly, all right?"

He grabbed one of Jake's arms and dragged him down the corridor and out into the ten-by-ten fenced scar in the ground that constituted a yard for those on death row. Parnell locked the gate and went to sit on a wooden bench next to the cage.

"I'm sorry to see a good man like you stuck in this situation," Parnell said. "This is really not going to end well for you, is it?"

Jake was still prone on the ground, waiting for his body to recalibrate after the jolt.

"Fact is, this didn't turn out well for anyone. Mason's dead, of course. And old Hayden, well, he'll be joining you here soon from what I hear," Parnell said. "Found his prints on the bullets you fired. Seems they think he hooked up with you when he was head guard at Larchmont, before he caught on with the force."

Parnell stood and walked over the fence. He laced his fingers through the chain link and looked down at Jake.

"Gotta admit, I'd love to see Hayden behind bars, but I won't be here," Parnell said. "With that egotistical son of a bitch off the force, there's an opening. Leading the police right to a cold-blooded murderer—no disrespect meant, of course—seems to have given me an inside track."

Jake reached an arm up to wipe the drool from his chin that had slipped from his slackened jaw, then looked at the gray sky.

"Least we got each other until then, right?" Pokey said. "I told you I'd get you home. Fella like you isn't any good on the outside. This is where you belong."

How I Spent My Summer Vacation

Nick Kolakowski

I

So this is what happened.

More or less, I mean.

The fire at the Ground Zero Café turned my friends into piles of ash and blackened bone. Their phones and car keys, melted into the tile floor. The backpack with my whole life in it, burnt to a lump of charcoal in a plastic evidence bag. Everything is gone, I guess, except for me.

My shrink, this court-appointed slob with a salt-and-pepper goatee and midlife spread drooping over his belt, is crazier than I am. "You know what I like in the morning?" he asks, eyes locked on mine. His fingers tap-tap-tap-tap the steel table between us. "An ice-cold shower. No heat. Fifteen minutes. It's so awful, the rest of your day feels like a vacation."

I guess that means it's time to open up. To share.

My shrink asks: "Do you ever feel paranoid?"

"Who doesn't, these days?"

Tap-tap-tap-tap. "How about depressed?"

I mime slitting my wrists.

Tap-tap-tap-tap. "What did you want to be when you grew up?"

I smile and tell him that I always wanted to be a suicide bomber, or a kamikaze pilot: "Not because you kill people, but because you believe in something so strongly you're happy to die for it. I wish I had belief like that."

He stops tapping.

II

At our next meeting, the shrink slides a glossy magazine across the table: my alumni quarterly, with an artful cover shot of the quad buried in autumn leaves. I think about my former classmates already well on their way to becoming the next generation of suburban ants, hot and bothered by the thought of 300-thread-count sheets and watching Sunday football games on a massive television in the den.

The magazine's back section features recent graduates gushing about their lives:

Jamie Herbert *is in graduate school at Harvard University doing endocrinology research and is also a math tutor for disadvantaged youth. She lives in a big apartment with a rubber ducky–themed bathroom, and studies physics in her spare time.*

For the love of everything holy, shoot me now. Here, share my pain:

Rick Koontz *has been in southern Argentina for the last two-and-a-half months, spreading the gospel of micro-loans to the villages there. He loves cooking under tarps, kayaking, and helping out local farmers.*

I wanted to write in. Just to flaunt how I had steered away from the One True Path:

Julia Nirdlinger *spent the past couple months lost in the deserts of the American southwest with her no-account boyfriend and his equally no-account uncle, who made a living out of ripping off drug dealers and other sketchy types. She's thinking of having a kid out of wedlock and getting really high on quality meth.*

I bet they wouldn't have found it funny.

III

The truck is so battered, so rusty and old, a photo of it deserves placement next to the dictionary entry for "wasted." The exhaust pipe farts like an old man after taco night at the retirement home as I shift into fourth gear. It's not the worst thing I've smelled today. Out here in the desert, the rest stops and barbeque joints all stink of gas and fried chicken and piss.

We roar past a wooden cross with plastic flowers piled at the base: yet another shrine to a highway crash victim. I snatch my phone off the dashboard and snap a photo, the latest in a long series of beautiful images:

–A dog splattered across a highway intersection.
–Two old gas pumps rusting away.
–A swarthy dude in a trucker cap flipping me the finger.

Kenny grinning at me, sunglasses perched on his sunburnt forehead, as he says: "Never had a college girl driving me around before."

I smirk, refusing to play his game. My lower back itches constantly, thanks to the fresh tattoo there, and it takes all my willpower not to scratch. Kenny drafted the design—an angel with fiery wings and a cherubic face—and once the ink settles he'll create a matching devil for my stomach. He fucks poorly but draws like Michelangelo and that, in my estimation, makes him worth keeping around.

"Don't test your luck, buddy," I tell him.

"I know," he says. "I'm lucky. Too lucky."

"Quit it."

"I'm lucky."

"Stop."

"I'm lucky."

"I'll hit you, I swear."

"I'm lucky."

I stomp on the gas. The truck shudders as the odometer's crooked needle inches toward maximum warp and Kenny grips his seatbelt in mock fear.

"Do you love me?" I ask him in my best loony-cartoon voice.

"Oh yes, yes, I do."

"How much do you love me?"

"Lots. Tons. Bunches."

"Cool it up there," Manny growls from the backseat, underlining the request by tipping back his battered cowboy hat to reveal eyes gray and cold as moon-rock. Poor man: one moment he's carrying equipment for Johnny Cash and boosting cars from parking lots on the side—not a bad life for a roadie—and the next he's in prison on a twenty-five-year bid, thanks to a bar fight that ended with him jamming a knife in some poor bastard's eye. Now he's back in the World, tough and rugged as battered steel but flat-out broke, dependent on his idiot nephew and a lunatic co-ed if he wants anything close to a decent retirement.

"Your wish is my command, sir," I say, and stomp the brake. The truck fishtails in its lane, my precious phone bouncing against the windshield with a disconcerting crack, before we drop back to rational speed.

I reach behind me and squeeze one of Manny's rough hands. "Sorry," I say. He squeezes back.

Kenny reaches down and retrieves his pistol from the pack at his feet, pulls back the slide to load a bullet in the chamber, and nods at something through the windshield. Ahead, the squat concrete box of the Ground Zero Café shimmers in the desert haze. In front of it stands a pale scarecrow of a man, left hand raised to shield his gaze from the blazing sun.

IV

This is what the cops found in my pockets, after the fact:

−Half a pack of menthol cigarettes.
−My silver skull ring.
−A butterfly knife.
−Three crumpled dollars and a handful of change.
−A Zippo lighter.
−My iPod

That stuff's already tagged and bagged for its inevitable appearance as People's Exhibits A-F, but I want the iPod back. Something about random strangers shuffling through my playlists, the Tom Waits albums and Jay-Z remixes, makes me feel violated in an odd way I can't quite explain.

The rest of my worldly possessions went up in smoke along with the café: *au revoir* to my big wad of cash, my spare clothes, and especially my notebook. Whenever I crave a cigarette, I think about the flames burning up Kenny and Manny, and that kills the urge. The shrink drones on and on, like my father whenever he'd downed enough drinks to make him feel like a star. I wonder if he'll stop if I just confess, before realizing that's probably his whole strategy.

V

Headline from three months ago: "Local College Girl Disappears."

That morning I locked myself in a mall bathroom and cut my hair and dyed it an ugly brown. Kenny already had the guns. We holed up in a motel room with a spectacular view of a truck depot and watched reality shows while we waited for Manny to show himself.

("Why did you do it?" The shrink asks.)

I don't know. I could tell you that school was boring, nothing more than books written by dead people, studied by people who seriously needed lives. Except that's not the whole truth. Sometimes when you test the ledge, you're seized by the unstoppable urge to leap off.

Headline yesterday: "Missing Girl Involved in Shoot-Out"

I was missing, at least from my family. I am a girl. That makes me a missing girl, I suppose. But that headline neglected to mention all my best parts: I am also tall. Blonde. A big fan of old-school hip-hop, singing along while dancing around all spastic, the beat filling me with wild joy. And a lover of chaos theory, where everything falls apart at the most random moments.

VI

The bony man standing in front of the Ground Zero Café is named Chuck Bauer and rumor has it he once bought his worst enemy a drink before making him eat the glass. One look into those dead eyes, and you'd wonder how much glass you could swallow before you started to bleed. He stands unmoving as we pull up in a big cloud of dust.

I have to tell you, for a long time I was stupid. I thought people would actually be interested in knowing about my life. That I could write something so compelling, the sheep would stampede for the nearest bookstore to buy it. Ha. After a little study, though, I realized that the public doesn't want your story unless it features some epic tragedy: you need a needle jammed in your arm, or your Daddy diddling you, or your best friend shot to death over a smoothie. Alas, my upbringing—filled with sunshine and puppies, literally and metaphorically speaking—featured none of that. I grab my backpack, slinging it over my shoulder as I open the driver's side door.

Manny is already out of the truck: "Chuck, how's it hanging?"

And then everything gets a little wonky. It starts with Kenny, who climbs out of the truck with a weird pimp lope and proceeds to give Bauer the hard stare.

"Who the fuck is this?" Bauer says, and his tone immediately makes me feel too big, too vulnerable, too stuck in the middle between all these morons.

"Call me Perro," my boyfriend says, opening his jacket to reveal the pistol jammed in his waistband. I glance at him and roll my eyes like, Really?

"Why they call you that?" Bauer asks.

"Because he bites," Manny chuckles, the old man trying to defuse the situation, having seen far too much of this shit in his life.

That makes Bauer grin a little. "Why they call you Manny?"

And Manny shrugs. "I don't know. Ask my momma."

Walking toward the café I shoot Kenny a look of death, which he ignores. Inside we pause for a moment, to adjust to the dark, and the first thing I see makes my skin crawl: a pyramid of rusty coffee cans stacked on what used to be the lunch counter, each plastered with a yellowing photo of a mutt. Bauer's shrine to his long-departed dogs, I guess. But that's not the worst of it. One look at this place would have made Martha Stewart's head explode: every inch of the dining area piled high with trash and dirty dishes and beer bottles full of frantic roaches, the rearmost booth stuffed with musty blankets for a bed. The walls lined with canvases splattered with paint. What's worse than a drug dealer who can't keep a clean home? One who thinks he's an artist.

Manny places his pistol on the counter and takes a seat, hands on thighs.

"Where's the shit?" Bauer asks.

"Close by," Manny says simply. This is a lie, but we need to play out the thread a little longer, and get Bauer into a better position, before we rob him blind. The good thing about ripping off dealers: they never call the police. The bad news: you need to get as far away from them as possible, after the fact.

Bauer's eyes creep over me. When he turns away for a moment, I zip the front of my nylon windbreaker to the very top. But Kenny sees how uncomfortable I am, and it flips that stupid gangster circuit in his head again. And that's when chaos theory really kicks in.

Kenny pulls his pistol and aims it square at Bauer's chest. "Hand over the money, man," he says.

"What the hell are you doing?" I yell at him.

"I'm doing this for you, baby. For us."

I almost snort. Men take up too much space. "Drop it," Manny says, soothing as a priest chanting Latin, as his hands glide toward his own pistol. Bauer smiles but one of his hands is drifting a little too far to the left, toward a stack of crushed cardboard boxes that none of us can see behind, and my sense of time and space is warping like plastic on fire, heart banging loud in my ears—

VII

What happened next, my court-appointed shrink asks. He's rapt, pencil in his hands frozen, obsessive-compulsive movements forgotten. Completely spellbound. My first reader, my first customer.

Oh, you know, I say.

Bang. Bang.

Bang.

Bang.

VIII

"Daddy!" I scream, adrenaline speedballing through my system. I scream it again, but of course Manny is not my Daddy, his only child was a towheaded boy named Tommy who grew up to become a major dope-fiend and just another waste of space, while my real Daddy sits in a downtown skyscraper typing court papers or screwing his personal assistant on his wide glass desk.

Manny leaning hard against the counter, choking on the bullet in his chest, his flailing hands knocking over that stupid dog shrine. He shudders a bit, gurgles, slumps.

Kenny is already dead, shot through the neck. I kneel beside him, checking his broken face for any hint of life. A busted tooth pokes from his bloody lip, his pupils fixed and already clouding over. My hands shake, my vision blurring.

"Amateur hour," Bauer groans from the floor where he fell after Kenny's bullet pierced his stomach.

The adrenaline in my veins flares into high-octane rage. I take Kenny's pistol and stand over Bauer and point the barrel at his head. Little Julia Nirdlinger, who once cried at the thought of kittens dying and grew up wanting only to write books and be left alone, cocks the hammer back.

My moment of moral decision: the big story climax. Bauer is facedown on his stomach, unaware of this incredible moment. It might sound a little sociopathic, but already in my mind I'm at the book reading, the television appearance, getting teary over how I went astray, feeling the love of millions of people as the sadness crumples my face in front of those high-definition cameras, and I'm missing this moment before it's even over. Can I do it? Can this tiny blood-soaked girl commit murder most foul?

But Bauer ruins it. He coughs once and spasms and that's it, *sayonara*, before I can decide one way or another.

I look out the dirty windows, at the faint contrail of a jet arcing over the distant mountains. Picturing myself in the climate-controlled cabin, surrounded by people dozing or reading away their utterly normal lives. It would be nice to be up there among them, cocooned in a metal tube rocketing at half the speed of a bullet, kept aloft by simple physics. I close my eyes. When I open them again, Manny has risen from the dead, Hallelujah.

He's upright and rocking slowly on his stool, his chest bleeding a flow so red it's nearly black. His shaking fingers dig in his breast pocket, retrieve a cigarette, and jam it between his slack lips.

"Little girl," he wheezes. "Why are you here?"

"Huh?" I drop the gun on my foot without feeling a thing.

"With us." He jabs his chin at what's left of his nephew.

"I don't know," I say. "I was bored, I guess." It sounds horrible but Manny seems to understand. He laughs a little, the hole in his chest hissing loudly.

"I should have stayed in school," he says, and then says nothing else, ever.

IX

Behind me, the diner goes up in a devil's belch of greasy flame. I wander down the highway, figuring that somebody will see the smoke and stop. I turn my ankle a bit with each step, so it looks like I have a limp. My shirt smells of gasoline and blood, and the sweat pouring down my spine makes my tattoo sting like a handful of bees crushed into the skin. A hundred yards down the road and it hits me: I'd dropped my backpack during all the excitement, forgot to pick it up again after striking the match. Damn, girl, get it *together*.

("Why did you do it?" my shrink asks.)

I think a better question is: Why do they do it? How can people fill each other with lead? The hesitation you might feel, pointing a gun at another human being, I think a certain kind of life beats that out of you one day at a time. Like those jackasses who take rubber hoses to dogs to make them mean. Even if Bauer hadn't died, I don't think I could have squeezed that trigger.

("They're calling your parents," my shrink says. "They'll be here in the morning. They've been worried sick.")

Tears roll down my cheeks, drying instantly in the desert heat.

X

I bet someday, an enterprising soul will demolish the Ground Zero Café and build something new in its place, a roadhouse or something, where people can come and drink and laugh and listen to music. That's life: built on the ashes of old mistakes.

So go ahead and pump me full of Xanax.

You can't help somebody who's begging to be nailed up on a cross.

"I want some paper and a pencil," I tell anyone who'll listen. Nobody tries putting handcuffs on me anymore, which is a good sign. I need to get the details down, while they're still fresh in my mind. I have a friend who has a friend who is a literary agent. I hope you'd approve, Kenny. I keep scratching my back, where your fiery angel smiles forever in the dark.

Buffalo Squeeze

Ed Kurtz

So: you're sitting at a small round table, front center stage, your chinos riding up and an Old Gold hanging from your bottom lip. All around the jerks are honking and whistling, something like a cross between heavy traffic and the baboons at the zoo, but all you do is watch the creamy stack of louvered double Ds on stage, twirling her tassels in perfect time and making that powder blue feather boa wriggle like a real live snake. The MC says her name is *Phoenix* and you somehow doubt it's her Christian name, but those fire-red curls spilling over her shoulders make the point moot. The band is terrible, the drummer looks like Krupa but sounds like shit, and the Dewar's in front of you has about the same percentage water as water. It's a Tuesday night, for Chrissakes—what did you expect?

But Phoneix, she's Saturday night quality. These boys will hoot for anything in a G-string, but there's a reason they holler louder when she steps out from the dusty lavender curtains. Faux-Krupa strikes up a clumsy tempo, kicking the bass to match her hips, and it's off to the races, old son. The colored guy at the next table launches to his feet and couldn't care less how the front of his pants poke out a mile—he's all teeth and slamming his palms together like he just won a grand at the track. The cat behind him shouts to *sit his ass down*, but nobody listens to him, and you think the colored guy paid the same bread to get in as anybody else and this sonofabitch ought to shut his goddamn trap. None of these boys are here to hear his bullshit; they're here to see something worth more than the two bucks they paid to see it, and that includes you.

So: here comes Phoenix, what a bird! Feet are stomping and booze sloshing and you crush the butt of that Old Gold under your heel as you stand up and sidle up to the stage. The band goes all boogie woogie and there's a crumpled bill in your fist, enough to get her attention. She wiggles over. Slow enough to make you sweat and not see two of her. Her ruby reds clack together at the heels and she bends over, a perfect right angle, until there's nothing left in the whole rotten world apart from the Jack Rabbit Twist and the buttery valley of Phoenix's cleavage not three inches from the tip of your bright red nose. Her pale arms hook underneath her breasts and she presses herself into a tight hug, spilling those puppies over until you think you haven't ever seen anything better in your life than that buffalo squeeze. Not Alma (wherever she was), not Maudie (God rest her soul), and not even ten grand you took off Dave DeFeo this morning after you jammed that blade between his ribs.

(Maudie *was* pretty good, though, before the dose wrecked her.)

Of course, you hadn't gone in with any intention to commit a murder/robbery, but then you never expected the dago bastard to be sitting on a mound of bread like that, either. All you'd wanted was an extension on that goddamned loan (*Another one?* DeFeo would have asked, had you ever actually said anything about it). Now you don't owe him jack and you got ten times what you were into him, anyway. And though you're well on your way to burning through a lot of it tonight on watered-down whiskey and the illusion of sex, there'll be plenty left come morning and it's all yours.

You pocket the lousy Lincoln and go rummaging for a Franklin instead, never moving your head, never taking your eyes off that magnificent bosom and its red glitter-capped peaks. You can afford it, and Christ knows Phoenix never saw a guy with that kind of scratch to stuff between her tits. Maybe it'll impress her, at least that's what you're thinking when you come back with the Hunsky and waggle it in front of her, as much a tease as she is. Her ruby mouth expands into a broad O and she winks one of her hooded eyes, shuttering the over-mascaraed lid like a corner bodega closing down for the night.

You say: *That's for you, baby.*

Phoenix just coos. (*What a bird!*)

Old Ben's face folds in on itself as you poke the bill down into the valley with your middle finger, watching it vanish into the milky abyss. Phoenix quivers all over, her body like jelly, and those big girls pummel your cheeks like Rocky Marciano. All the other boys love it, living vicariously through your generous excess, though you can barely hear their catcalls from the soundproof booth of the stripper's cleavage.

She grins, her pearlies dotted red from her lipstick, and twists away to plant a kiss on your face. Faux-Krupa marks the occasion with a rimshot as Phoenix rises back to her full Amazonian height. She's all red lips and red pasties and a molten waterfall of flame-red hair...

And you shudder despite the mounting pressure in your chinos, because you can't help but think about how all that red is a perfect match for the blood Dave DeFeo leaked out all over the carpet and that ugly chaise lounge. Phoenix shimmies up to another hard-dick on the other side of the stage and you go back to your table. You fire up another Old Gold and snap your fingers at the waitress, but you'll be goddamned if you aren't still thinking about all that blood.

If it had been a planned thing, you'd have gone about it differently. Knocked DeFeo over the head with a bat, or just shot the bastard (if you could've gotten a gun). The way it went, it was off the cuff. You half expected a beat-down yourself for coming up short again, but all those stacks, bound up so nicely with little paper bands—well, plans change, don't they? And you with a switch in your pocket, which you'd never used except to show it off to the guys, who you always told was how you killed a deputy in Arkansas for giving you the business about trespassing...

That shit never went down except in your dreams, but Dave DeFeo really did join the Great Majority and Christ did he *bleed*. Even the stacks you swiped ended up sticky with the stuff, a problem you plan on taking care of with your landlady's washing machine once you figure out how to get her out of the building first. That C-note between Phoenix's girls, though? Clean as crystal—or at least it didn't have any fucking blood on it. Neither do any of the other bills crumpled up in your pants pocket, come to think of it, so you gulp the Dewar's the waitress just brought and fish another hundred out for Round 2. Why the hell not?

This is a celebration, after all.

So: another girl has already come and gone in the time since you last advanced the stage—a curvy little trailer trash chick with a tattoo of melting cherries on her pubis and knockers like flapjacks—but it's Tuesday and the workforce is light, which means Phoenix is back in action (as the MC is all too excited to announce).

You've got the Hunksy in hand and Phoenix can smell it a mile away, so she comes sniffing right over as a grin spreads across your face and you pull out another one with your other hand. Hundreds in each paw, held up like penalty flags, and the girl is practically in love with you for that minute and that minute only. The band drops into Jelly Roll Morton's "Sidewalk Blues," just to ham it up, and by the time her thighs are close enough to see the peach fuzz you've got your fingers pinching at her garters to deposit the funds. She lands a wet one on the side of your neck and whispers *Thank you, handsome*. Your guts get a little gooey as she squats down for some face time with her principal assets, and this time she digs her plastic nails (red, natch) into the hair on the back of your head and jams your face straight into the Kingdom of Heaven.

Hallelujah!

She smells of roses and sweat, cigarette smoke and brandy. You let your face go slack and close your eyes, taking in the scent, knowing damn well she'll never be yours but reveling in the fantasy. Fantasy and friction, that's all this joint is, but you know that going in and still plan on walking out with a smile on your face—and about $9,500 in your trunk. The Chevy's parked right out front, probably not the wisest move considering, but nothing could be further from your mind while you experience everything Phoenix has to give to you: her smell, her softness, her sharp nails scraping your scalp.

That cut-rate Krupa is really going at it now when her hand explodes and an ice-cold spike travels through your skull. You bite down on her downy breast, not really meaning to, and start to drop when you see the red-black hole between those magnificent globes. You're looking up at her and she's looking somewhere behind you, and the band stops abruptly while the boys shout and scatter. Phoenix drops like a brick, flat on her back, and even dead she still looks pretty damn good. (*Tits up,* you can't help thinking!) As for you, you slide down to the grimy carpet at the foot of the stage where the shooter stands—a slick, Eye-Tie looking guy like good old Dave DeFeo—waiting for you to die. Everyone else has cleared out, so you shut your eyes and keep on thinking about her, about Phoenix the Fantasy, who really wasn't bad company to keep in the final moments of your rotten life.

Three Count

Frank Larnerd

Misty paraded across the stage, shaking her tits like a ground controller guiding in a crippled plane. The multicolored lights shimmered over her skin as she grabbed the pole and twirled around it. Moving with the music, she turned, letting the suckers get a good look at her tight waist, round ass, and the most perfect tits you'll ever see.

She called from the stage, "What do you think about that, Joe?" and gave her ass a smack.

I shot her a thumbs up from my spot by the door.

Now, I've seen my fair share of tits, but Misty's are something special. I'm pushing sixty, but watching Misty's melons jiggle still makes my fire hose flutter.

I used to be a wrestler for that big company in Connecticut. Was a time, every city in the country had tits waiting for me. They had me wrestle under all kinds of gimmicks; it didn't matter to the ring rats that I wasn't a superstar. I'd be Inquisitor #2 in Toledo, or Mack Truck in Huston; I didn't care as long as the tits and paychecks kept coming.

After a while, they both dried up. I was too old; my knee was shot from my cage match with Crazy Caliph, and I couldn't take the bumps like I used to.

So I left the business, came south to Knoxville, where it was warm and people still play decent music. My life ain't no golden parachute retirement, but it ain't that bad either. Bouncing drunks at the Stinky Pinky pays the rent on my trailer, plus, I get to watch titties jiggle for free.

I was trying to enjoy the last of my golden years, daydreaming about sticking my ugly bald head between Misty's creamy knockers, when a dumbass in the front row decided to climb the stage.

He was young and drunk with a popped collar on his blue polo shirt. Before he could put a hand in Misty's cookie jar, I was on him. I grabbed the back of his shirt and yanked him off the stage. He cursed as he tumbled backward, spilling drinks and crashing onto the speckled carpet.

He came up quick, angry and red faced. I felt his eyes on me, reading the word BOUNCER on my black t-shirt.

"What's the problem, man?" He said, his breath a mix of ash tray and Mexican beer.

I folded my arms across my chest. "You're gunna have to go. You can't get on stage with the ladies."

He put his finger in my face. "That's no lady. That's a whore."

I slammed my elbow into his teeth. The kid bounced off a table and crashed to the floor. I grabbed him, one hand full of hair, the other on his belt and lifted him up. The kid screamed and thrashed, but I got him through the club and to the front door.

I used the kid's head as a battering ram and shoved him out onto the gravel parking lot.

"Get your ass out of here," I growled and closed the door behind me.

Back inside, Misty was finishing her set. She crawled along the stage while the chumps slipped a few dollars into her garter. I sat down on my stool as Misty gave her boobs a final squeeze and disappeared behind the curtain.

An old George Thorogood song came on as Cherri Lee clomped onto the stage in her catholic school uniform and six inch heels. I was having a great time watching her cheeks jiggle when I felt a tap on my shoulder.

"You're fired."

I spun around on my stool. Behind the bar was Terry, hands on his hips. He's the owner of the Stinky Pinky and a short, nasally, backstabbing fuck, but a pretty decent boss considering strip club owners.

"What'd I do now?"

"What you do?" Terry said, vibrating with rage. "You roughed up another customer!"

"Terry, he was-"

"Shut up. I fucking told you a hundred fucking times, be cool, be like Patrick Swayze. But no, you've got to go fucking cromagnon on any asshole who looks at you the wrong way."

I put my hands up. "Terry, come on."

"No." Terry put a wad of tens in my hand. "You're done."

Terry walked away and I looked down at the bills in my hand. A hundred fucking bucks.

Shit, I thought, the dog needs food and the goddamn rent is due again. Better spend this wisely.

I motioned the bartender over. "Give me two shots and a brew, Jackie."

After I finished my shots, I took my beer and wandered into the crowd as a paying customer. I was halfway to the stage when three giant motherfuckers came in through the front. They were all huge, even the smallest guy was ripped like a Lou Ferrigno on horse steroids. I knew who they were instantly. Hell, any wrestling fan would.

The big guy with the afro and the diamond earrings is Devon Brody, aka "The Business." He's a 400 pound giant with a chest like a refrigerator. He and Lou Tessle were tag team champs last year. Now, he was doing the monster gimmick, squashing jobbers and building up heat.

Danny Zero came in behind him, a third generation highflier daredevil type—plays a babyface most of the time. Besides being reckless and handsome, Danny Zero is one of the best technical wrestlers you'll see on TV.

You might not know those guys, if you don't follow the shows, but everyone knows the Champ. He's held the belt six times, been an international movie star, and is one of the most recognizable men on the planet. He strolled in like a Greek god, the club lights shining off his gold-rimmed sunglasses and platinum rings.

I was even a little star stuck. They must be in town for the Pay-per-view, but what they were doing in a shithole like the Stinky Pinky I didn't know. Furthermore, I was no longer paid to care. Losers and dancers crowded around the trio to rub against success.

The Business picked up Cherri with one arm, cradling her ass with one giant hand. "Do you know what time it is?"

He tossed a stack of bills in the air. "It's business time!"

Pushing through the crowd, I found Misty at the back of the club, sitting with a punchy salesman with a face like a used truck tire. She had changed into an electric blue nighty with fluorescent pink undies.

I felt the front of my jeans jump. "Mind if I sit down?"

Misty's brown eyes got big. "Shit, Joe, don't let Terry catch you drinking."

"Don't worry, I'm off the clock. Terry fired me."

I slunk down into the chair next to her as tire-face got up to shake hands with the superstars.

She kissed my bald head. "I'm so sorry, baby."

"Ah, life's shit and then you're flushed," I said and took a swallow of my beer.

Misty wrapped her arms around me, purring in my ear, "Anything, I can do?"

I set what was left of the hundred bucks on the table. "How 'bout a lap dance?"

We made our way to the private booths as the rest of the club cheered on Danny Zero as he gyrated under a waterfall of champagne with Babydoll and Peaches.

I raised my beer to Terry as he scowled from behind the bar.

Once we were alone, Misty pulled the booth's curtain closed and selected some slow bluesy music. I propped up my knee and lay back on the big leather chair.

Misty swayed from side to side, inching the nighty off her shoulders to the music's rhythm. She pushed the material over her hips, letting it fall to the floor. Stepped out of the puddle of fabric, she turned and stood with her back to me. Then with a wink over her shoulder, she unclasped her bra.

When she turned around to face me, I didn't even try to pretend like I wasn't looking.

Misty crawled over me, brushing my chest with her perfect hooters. "I'm gunna miss you, Joe."

She grinded against me, the tips of her breasts brushing my face.

"Don't worry, I'll land on my feet," I gulped.

Misty leaned in closer, lips on my neck. "I feel like it's kind of my fault. How can I make it up to you?"

I was coming up with all kinds of good ideas when Terry busted through the curtain.

"Joe, get in here! They're tearing the place apart!"

Misty climbed off my lap and began gathering up her clothes.

Fuck.

I sat up. "I don't work here anymore, Terry. Now if you don't mind, I'd like to finish my private dance."

Outside, I could hear bottles breaking and shouting voices. Terry put his hands together. "I'll hire you back."

I rolled my eyes.

"With a raise," Terry moaned.

I forced myself out of the chair. "No more shit about how I handle security."

"Fine," Terry said. "Just get out there!"

Any stiffness in my pants left when I walked back into the club. It seemed like a hundred more people had come in, all of them buzzing and cheering. Danny Zero was behind the bar, pouring drinks for anyone who wanted one. On the stage, Cherri Lee screamed as the Business slurped champagne off her jugs. Unsupervised strippers were everywhere – dancing, screaming, humping, and drinking.

The Champ watched from the shadows of the corner table, flanked on either side by two of the dancers. Even with all the chaos, he seemed totally in control and totally cool.

I put on my serious face and elbowed my way to through the crowd.

As I climbed onto the stage, my knee popped, sending a flash of pain through me. I ignored it and walked up behind the Business. He had his head down, rooting around Cherri' tits. His diamond earrings flashed like warning beacons as he snorted and rutted away.

"Alright, fun is over." I grabbed him by the arm, hard.

The Business pried his face from Cherri's tits and looked at me like I was dog that ate Christmas dinner and shit it on the rug. "Fuck off."

He pulled his arm from my grip and buried his head back into Cherri's tits.

She screamed, "Do something, Joe!"

I let out a long sigh and twisted one of the big man's diamond earrings.

He screamed and I threw my punch.

The hit staggered him, backing him up a few steps. Cherri Lee ran clear, while I wriggled some life back into my fingers.

The Business rubbed his jaw. "You're about to get fucked up, old man."

We locked up on the center of the stage, grappling back and forth. He caught me with a head-butt, making black spots float through my vision. I stumbled, but I didn't let go. Instead, I pulled him back with me, snaking around him as we fell. He landed with a crunch, head first into the stage.

As I pushed myself to my feet, everyone in the bar surrounded the stage. They were all screaming and cheering. Shit, it was just as good as wrestling in Madison Square Garden on a Monday night.

I took a few steps back, lining up a kick that would punt the Business into the next county, when out of nowhere, Danny Zero slammed into me with a dropkick.

When I opened my eyes, I was hanging halfway off the stage and my back felt like it was snapped in two pieces.

Danny grabbed my legs and hauled me to the center of the stage. He held my legs out like a "V" and with a yell, drove a foot into my nuts. It felt like having a cinder block drop on your hard-boiled eggs. Before I could puke, or cry, Danny locked up my legs in a figure four. He crossed his legs inside mine and leaned back, applying pressure, so that my knee was pulled away from the socket.

I forgot about all my balls as my knee flared like a super nova of pain. The agony snaked through me, cutting through my hip and deep into my guts. A mix of pain, shame, and endless regrets.

I wasn't the fist time I felt that feeling; I had it on the day I hung up my wrestling boots. When life gives you the finisher, you lay there and you take it, no matter how much it hurts.

One—You're old, fat, and tired.

Two—You got as far as you're ever going to get.

Three—It's over. Now, powder out and hit the showers.

I raised my arm, ready to tap out, when I saw Misty at the edge of the stage. She was jumping up and down, her beautiful titties bouncing like a rodeo cowboy.

Fuck losing.

I grabbed Danny's foot and bit hard into his ankle. He screamed and kicked my face, but he let go.

He was up faster than me, smashing my face with two rapid kicks. I caught the third one and twisted his leg, dropping him to his knees. Before he could get up, I threw myself at him, catching his neck with a clothesline.

I paused to wipe the blood from my face. Misty was shouting something from the crowd, but I couldn't make it out.

The Business snaked his arms around me, squeezing me from behind. "You know what time it is?"

"Sure," I grunted with the last bit of air in my lungs. "It's business time."

I grabbed a handful of his crotch and twisted. Squealing, the Business let me loose. I dazed him with a right hand and wrapped an arm around his neck for a DDT. Dropped with all my weight, I drove his face into the stripper pole.

Before I was on my feet, Danny Zero came flying in with a kick that flattened my nose.

The hit blasted me backward, and made a lot of blood, but didn't knock me off my feet. Screaming, Danny threw himself at me like a kamikaze pilot on bath salts. Bracing myself, I grabbed him and pivoted, using his momentum to launch him off the stage. He hung in the air for a moment, then crashed onto a table, scattering strippers and empty bottles.

I lifted my fist, signaling to the crowed, and dove off the stage. I came down with an elbow, slamming into Danny and blasting the table under us into pieces.

I rose groggy, waiting for cheers. Instead, Misty screamed and I wheeled around. The Champ stood there, a finger pointed at my face.

"I know you."

I spit a wad of blood onto the floor. "Oh yeah?"

"Every wrestler knows the demonic elbow. You're Joe Jumper, the man who wrestled Crazy Caliph at the Cage of Rage 3. I've seen all your matches, you're a legend."

He held out his hand and I shook it.

After things settled down, I had a few beers with the guys. We laughed and horsed around 'til closing, telling stories of the good ol' days.

Terry was even smiling.

When they were ready to leave, The Champ pulled me aside. "I've got a new angle I'm working on for the pay-per-view. If you ever want to come back, call me."

He passed me a business card and the three of them shuffled out into the night.

I looked over the card and then tore it in two, letting the pieces flutter to the floor.

Misty put her arm around me. "Oh my God! Are you not gunna do it?"

I looked down at the perfect tits spilling out of her top. "Why would I? I've got the best job in the world."

Loose Change

Chris Leek

Dead people are all on the same level. It doesn't matter if you're a big noise with a cash machine job that spits out dollar bills, or if you scratch by on nothing more than your wits and a smile. When you're laid out on the slab, none of it counts for jack.

People spend their whole lives just trying to make money; they think that actually counts for something. It doesn't. You can forget what those TV preachers tell you; God ain't short of cash. Those who don't have it are just as bad as them that do. They sit around feeling sorry for themselves and get all het up about life dealing them a losing hand. But it's not the cards that count, or even how you play them. When you cut through all the bullshit and get right down to it, the end result is always the same. Dead is just dead. I tried to explain that to Wendy more than once, but she never took to it. That was sort of funny, because she was smarter than most and she had a great smile too. All I had was outstanding warrants.

§

The gas station was about an hour North of Elko on the 225 and about 30 years behind the rest of the world. I rolled in under a big porcelain sign, advertising oil from a company that went out of business when I was still blowing snot bubbles and hitching at my daddy's pants. I eased the Camaro to a stop alongside the only pump. A fire bucket sat next to it, all planted up with bright red flowers that had wilted in the afternoon heat. A 10c coke machine stood off to one side. I guess if my old man was still around to ask, he might tell you about the time when you could get soda for a dime. Places like this gas and go just didn't exist anymore, not in the real world anyway. Occasionally they still showed up on TV, but only in black and white.

I cut the motor and lit up two smokes, handing one to Wendy before leaning back and letting 200 miles of thrumming tires and static filled country songs ebb away. The empty landscape that had blurred past the windows at a steady 75 MPH was now back in focus, and suddenly being inside the car felt claustrophobic next to all that nothing. I got out and stretched while Wendy fixed her lipstick in the wing mirror. A hand written sign on the pump said, *Open 6 till noon and other times by coincidence*. I glanced at my watch, it was a little past two. Life was full of coincidences.

I started towards the little store, Wendy caught up to me by the entrance. Somehow she always managed to look hotter than a forest fire in nothing more than skinny jeans and a crop T. If you looked close up you could see the white trash bleeding through, just like the dark roots in her suicide blonde hair. I didn't mind. In fact if I had the choice, which of course I never did, I would take trash every time. You know where you stand with your own kind. You don't expect nothing and you're not disappointed when that's exactly what you get.

I opened the door and set the little bell above it to ringing. The clerk was leaning on the counter, reading. He was just a kid and judging by the bits of tissue paper stuck on his chin he was still new to shaving. He looked up from his comic book and blinked with surprise. It seemed that customers and Sundays came around with about the same frequency out here.

"Howdy folks," he said grinning, mainly at Wendy, his eyes fixing on her ample breasts.

"Hey there...Jimmy" Wendy said, squinting to make out the name embroidered on his work shirt. "Can I get $10 on the pump and a carton of Camel lights?"

"Surely ma'am, will that be all?" He asked her cleavage.

Wendy flashed her smile, and I could see ol' Jimmy boy wilting under its heat just like those flowers out front.

"Well, now that you mention it," she said leaning across the counter, giving him a better view. "I'll take everything in the register too."

Jimmy just stood there staring at her tits. It was a lot to take in, being robbed that is; although Wendy's tits were kind of breathtaking too. I thought I had better help him to understand the gravity of the situation.

"I guess you didn't hear the lady, Jimmy," I said stepping up and easing my shirt back so he could see the butt of the .44 sticking out of my jeans. He looked from Wendy to the gun, to me and back again. It was the sort of look that fell somewhere between dim witted and full on retarded.

"Don't get all bent out shape 'bout it sugar, its only money," Wendy said and cracked her gum loud enough to make him jump.

"Well, ma'am, I'd like to oblige, truly I would, but it ain't mine to give. This here money belongs to Mr. Poolman. He owns the place."

Jimmy was undoubtedly the politest boy I had ever run across and possibly the dumbest too. Raising your kids with good manners is to be commended; however a little common sense doesn't go a miss either.

"Jimmy, look we ain't asking, we're telling, capisce?" I said and drummed my fingers on the gun to make the point.

Jimmy did some thinking and by thinking I mean he went back to staring at Wendy's assets.

"Well... I. No, I'm right sorry mister, but I can't."

I couldn't believe this kid thought he had a choice. An armed robbery isn't a subject for debate, not unless you want a couple of extra holes in you. His arguing was burning up time and I was starting to think it might be easier just to shoot him and have done with it. I made to pull the gun; Wendy put her hand on mine to stop me. She always did have a liking for hapless fools and lost causes. I suppose that's why she stuck with me for as long as she did.

"Sugar, I can see you're a dedicated employee and your Mr. Poolman should be right proud of you." Jimmy seemed to grow about a foot taller at that. "We are all getting along so well that I'd hate for it to turn out bad. If'n you was to hand me that money, I'd sure be grateful," she said all coy as if butter wouldn't melt in her mouth, but something else might.

Wendy traced her fingers across her chest and hit him again with that smile of hers. It sealed the deal. Jimmy rung up a *No Sale* on that old brass National and dumped a dozen or so worn notes on the counter. I scooped them up and stuffed them in my pocket. I doubt they added up to more than half a bill all told.

"You're a real sweetie," Wendy said and stood on tip toe to plant a kiss square on him.

Her lips lingered on his and her tongue wormed its way into his mouth. Jimmy's eyes bugged out and his face turned a shade of pink that a paint company might have called bubble gum.

"Damn girl, give the boy some air, "I said pushing past them to liberate a couple of packs of smokes for the cause of freedom. Wendy pulled back, grinning and left Jimmy standing with his mouth hanging open in a slack jawed gawp.

"You think we should tie him up?" she asked fishing inside Jimmy's mouth and retrieving her gum.

"I'll do it, you go gas the car," I said.

I pulled Jimmy's hands in front of him and set to tying them with some bailing twine from a counter display, normally I would have saved myself the bother and just punched him out to see us clear down the road. I suppose I had a thing for hapless fools as well. Wendy patted him on the cheek and headed back outside.

"G' bye ma'am and thank you kindly," he called after her. She looked back over her shoulder, blowing him a pouty kiss and went out the door with a boop-boop-a-doop wiggle that was good enough to give a dog a bone.

I finished tying Jimmy and pulled the cord out of the phone. Then for good measure I ripped the receiver off it as well. You can't be too careful and a call to the sheriff in the next town is the kind of thing to put a real dent in your day. I crouched down and gave the shelf under the counter a quick once over for anything worth my time.

"You know Jimmy boy, you made a good decision today. Alive trumps dead every time and don't let no one tell you different. Now you just remember to forget what we looked like when you get asked and we'll call it square." I said, palming two dusty rolls of quarters from the back of the shelf. "You understand me Jimmy?"

The kid hadn't heard a damn word I said; he was too busy staring at something. The look on his face wasn't that vacant, glassy thing that I'd come to recognize as normal for him. It was square set concentration, like maybe he was taking a hard shit. Good sense told me I should stay down behind the counter, but I ignored it. Curiosity kills more than cats. It also poses a lot of dumb ass questions, such as: I wonder what would happen if I put my finger in the wall socket? Rarely does this sort of question require a practical test to answer it, but people do it just the same. I peeked over the counter, sticking my finger in that socket up to the knuckle, and found myself at the wrong end a big gauge side by side. Behind it was a fat man with a red face and a bad case of alopecia. There must have been a back way into the place, because I would have heard him come in the front.

"I got the triggers wired and I'm a might jumpy, so you best get up real slow," he said out of the side of his mouth as if he was chawing on something nasty. He talked the talk alright, but I saw something in his eyes I didn't much care for. It looked a lot like fear to me, and that will fill more body bags than curiosity or even good old fashioned bullets.

"Careful Mr. Poolman, he's got a gun," Jimmy piped up.

"What the fuck do you think this is dumb ass, a chair leg?"

"I was just sayin'."

Jimmy sounded a little hurt. That was nothing; he would ache a whole lot more after the ass whooping I just decided he had coming. Poolman ignored the kid and switched his big talk back to me.

"Do I stutter mister?"

I considered my options. It didn't take long, there wasn't too many of them and none involved a cold beer and a good steak. I stood up, keeping my arms out wide and my palms towards him. I stole a glance out the window and saw the Camaro was still parked by the pump, but there was no sign of Wendy.

"Jimmy, get your ass over here. You can stay put for now, mister."

Jimmy squeezed in front of me to get around the counter. It was a stupid move, but the kid didn't know any better. I did what I had to. Five minutes ago young Jimmy was getting his first tongue smooch and now he had a .44 jammed up under his chin. Life has a habit of doing that to you, just when you think you got your shit wired nice and tight, everything will suddenly turn on a dime, or stop on it. I edged sideways around the counter, holding Jimmy in front of me like he was made out of Kevlar.

"Now I don't want no trouble Poolman, and I ain't got none to give, so long as you put that old thumper down."

"And what if I don't?"

"Then I'll paint your place with the kid."

"Ha! You have at it mister, that idiot don't make no never mind to me."

I thought he was probably bluffing and deep down I knew I was. Either way it was too much for Jimmy. A warm stream of piss ran down his leg, turning his pants dark with fright. I can't say that I blamed him. Everyone is a hero in their own head; having a loaded gun shoved in your face will shatter a lot of illusions.

"Tell you what Poolman," I said changing the angles. "Seeing as you ain't so concerned about your workers, how do you feel about your own hide?" Keeping one arm tight around Jimmy's neck I swung the pistol up and drew a bead on Poolman's forehead. "Now maybe you get lucky and hit some of me along with the kid, but I guarantee if anyone is getting it today, it's you."

He stood there working out the odds; hoping I would blink and rightly guessing that I wouldn't. I'll admit I had a soft spot for the kid, but I didn't have whole lot of love for his boss. If it was him or me, he would come in a poor second. Poolman's aim started to waver and if I was a betting man I would have had a five spot on him throwing in this hand. Just then the bell over the front door sang out and saved me a Lincoln. Wendy stood there with the bucket of flowers in her hands.

"Time to go sugar," she said and hurled the thing at Poolman.

I shoved Jimmy out of the way; he fell backwards and sat down in a puddle of his own piss. The bucket struck Poolman in a shower of dirt and red petals. I don't know if he meant to fire or if it was just the impact that jarred his hand, but he gave me a barrel and turned my arm into ground beef. I spun to the ground like a bird with one wing; the gun gone from my hand.

The recoil slammed Poolman back into the wall; he shook himself and turned on Wendy. She was still standing in the doorway, framed by soft afternoon light that danced on her shoulders and seemed to shine through her as if she was made of glass. I shouted at her to get down, but the shotgun blast swallowed my words. And like a vision, Wendy vanished.

"You bastard!"

Jimmy's face was ugly with the kind of rage he never knew he had. He scooped up my .44 in both hands and ran at Poolman, pumping a hard six into the wide expanse of his gut. He dry fired on a few more before he realized the gun was empty. Poolman went down in installments, taking a stack of oil cans with him to the floor and a look of bald surprise to show to St. Peter.

§

I knelt by Wendy, her eyes were closed and if you ignored all the blood and the torn flesh, she looked real peaceful, just like she was sleeping.

My old man once told me he lived by three simple rules: never play poker with anybody who's first name was the same as a state, never pay for something you can get for free and never fall in love with a beautiful woman. He was bob useless at cards and they sent him to the chair for the second one, but I will stand by the last. I guess Jimmy would too.

"Can I come with you mister?"

Jimmy stood beside me, he had cut the twine around his wrists and he held the empty gun limply at his side. I got up and looked at him, piss stains drying on his pants, tears doing the same on his cheeks. I suppose even running down a dead end street can seem like a good idea after a lifetime of standing still. Jimmy was only a kid; maybe he still had a chance. I had used up all of mine long ago. Somewhere down the road, I knew it would be me lying gut shot and bled out over a tank of stolen gas and handful of loose change.

"Anyone would be proud to have a man like you for a partner, Jimmy," I said. He smiled at that, it was weak and sort of sickly, but it was still a smile. "But I need you to do me a favor. I need someone to make sure Wendy gets treated decent; you know, see that she's planted right and spoke over by a minister and all. Would you do that for me Jimmy, for Wendy?"

"It'd be my honor mister," he said and held the gun out to me.

I stuffed the .44 in my waistband, offered him my hand and we shook on it. I knew he'd be alright. No matter what story he told the law would stick Wendy and Poolman on me. That was okay; after all, when it came down to it, the three of us were all on the same level.

Loose Ends

Mike Loniewski

I've managed to see a lot of dead bodies working for Owen Madden. They get dragged in and out of his pub all hours of the night, and I have to follow right behind them mopping up the blood. Hell, I once seen the "Mad Dog" himself smash a guy up against a brick wall with his Lincoln Zephyr. Radiator was hissing steam all over the poor guy. I always wondered how Madden enjoyed it so much.

But, killing this guy right here, feeling his legs kick against the floor as I choke the life out of him, I can see why.

Sol gives off this wet, guttural release and I know he's dead. I let the rope go slack from around his throat, and he flops off of me, and I climb to my feet. I've got some scratches to my neck and hands from the struggle, but I barely notice them, what with the broken nose and stab wounds between my ribs I got earlier from Billy Bees. Or the glass in my hand I got smashing through the window to escape, or the busted knee from some car that hit me as I ran away.

These things happen when you get into debt with Owen Madden. He's the kind of guy that sends a psychotic like Billy Bees out to cut you open when you don't pay on time. And the reason I couldn't pay on time is dead on the floor.

I start to look over the room. Son of a bitch had his bags packed. I kick them open and toss out his clothes. Not a cent of the money. I find a key to the Waldorf Astoria and I think of Ellie. Another reminder of the fuck up I am.

The Third Avenue El is the quickest way to get there and I catch it a block down from Sol's place. My head is pounding and the damn thing makes so much noise, shaking and clacking across the rails, that high pitched metal on metal scrape as we hit all the stops.

Between all the noise and rattling I get flashes of the last twenty four hours. The card tourney in Atlantic City that changed my luck. The case full of cash that got swiped by my dear old pal and my beautiful wife. My wife. See, as my mistakes piled up, Ellie turned to Sol. In the end, they figured the money to save my ass was better suited for their new life together. By the time I knew what hit me the money was gone, and Billy Bees was throwing a sack over my head.

I start to realize a few people are staring at me now. I tug my fedora down over my eyes to hide my busted nose and face, but I hear these soft drips hitting my coat. Damn thing's bleeding again. I quickly wipe it away on my coat sleeve, and the old lady across from me sees the streak of blood and inches away. I stuff my hands in my pockets, and she jumps up as we hit the next stop. She shuffles out with a few others as a bunch more pack into the car. I try not to look up when some barrel-chested cop struts on in.

He's clanking his billy club across the handrails and stops in front of me. I keep my face buried in my chest, but my nose just won't stop bleeding. My lip and chin are covered in a warm, salty mess. I feel the billy club slide under my chin and lift up. I snort up the stream of blood, and he twists his face at the sight of me.

"Rough night."

"You got that right."

The train jolts and starts clattering along the rails again.

"So, what did it? Bar fight? Mugger?"

"Yeah."

"Which one?"

"I don't know"

Damn it, I can't even think up a story to save my ass.

"I got beat up."

"I see that."

The big cop sits down next to me. There's not enough room on the seats, and I feel his weight pushing on me, letting me know not to try anything or he'll mash my skull up. I don't have the strength to fight this guy. He taps my knee with the billy club.

"When we hit the next stop we're going to walk off together. Can't have you bleeding all over this train."

The brakes start shrieking again. I feel him put his paw under my arm, his grip like a vice, squeezing hard just to remind me once again how bad he could beat me if I tried anything. The train lurches to a stop, and he calls out in this booming voice.

"Stay in your seats, folks. Let us through."

He drags me up, and I try to keep pace with his stride. He yanks me over to the wrought iron stairs, and there's a sedan waiting at the bottom of it. That's no cop car.

The door flies open, and Billy Bees steps out, a goddamn Browning automatic in his hands. He sets it loose and slugs the size of shot glasses start slamming all around us. The cop takes a bunch to the chest and pulls me along with him over the railing. I smack down onto the pavement, and something else inside me breaks when we land.

The Browning automatic is still blasting away, hunks of pavement chewed up around us. I'm pinned under the cop's body trying to tug myself free. I feel his revolver, it's still in the holster. I can hear Billy's wingtips tacking across the pavement. I slip the revolver up under the cop's arm, gives me a bit of cover. Billy's around the corner now.

The revolver claps off three rounds, and Billy's feet go out from underneath him. I dig myself out from under the cop, and I hear the sedan speed off as sirens rise up from a few blocks over. I look over at Billy Bees, and he's not moving. Neither is the cop. I limp off.

Billy Bees. His handler happens to be Owen Madden. And when you owe Madden money he sends Billy Bees to get it back. I've been dodging the psychopath ever since I got back from the casino. The stab wounds and a busted face are there to prove it, and I just pumped three rounds into him.

There's no way I can give this money to Madden now, even if I had it. I give it to him, and I'll find myself at the bottom of the East River with a bunch of fish eating out of a hole in the back of my head.

I've got to get to Ellie. Got to get that money from her before she skips town. I look at the revolver and stick it in the waistband of my trousers and limp over to a handsome cab driver. His horse is a brute. It snorts at me and rears its head. The driver looks at my face and takes a few steps back.

"How much you make tonight?" I ask him.

"You want ride?"

"Yeah, I want ride. You want money? A lot of money?"

He looks me up and down.

"You have lot of money?"

"Lots. Take me over to the Waldorf Astoria and I'll get you a big fat wad of it, more than you'd make in a week."

He doesn't believe me. I step closer so he can get a good look.

"Look at my face. People who want my money did this. They didn't get it. You can."

Still nothing from the guy.

"All you gotta do is keep your mouth shut and have that horse of yours trot us on down to Park Ave."

The guy cocks his head to listen to the sounds of wailing sirens. He turns away and climbs into his cab.

"You want me to lift cover?"

"Yeah. Yeah, good thinking."

The horse starts with a jolt, and the next thing I know we're plodding along toward Park Avenue. The cover is high, and the seat is set deep. I lay my head back, but the blood starts running down my throat, and I sit back up and hack up a big spot of it. The night air is cool and it feels good on my face and takes away some of that pain rattling around in my head.

I start to relax a bit, what with the air and the soft city noise. I drift off for a bit and I see Ellie. I'm lying with my head in her lap, and she's brushing the hair from my forehead, running her fingers down the back of my head and neck. She whispers something to me, I can't tell what it is. I can smell her, and I think of how we used to make love, and how I thought she'd change my world. Instead she got sucked up into mine, and was fighting to get out. I was just too dumb to notice.

A truck's horn snaps me awake, and my heart's racing, and I remember the dream, and my head starts pounding all over again.

The clapping of the hooves start to slow down, and the driver turns back to me.

"We here."

I sniff up some blood.

"Wait for me up the block." I tell him. "I'll be back in fifteen."

The Waldorf Astoria is one hell of a place. I always talked of me and Ellie spending a night here after some fancy dinner and a big Broadway show. I guess she couldn't wait any longer. I tug my fedora down and head across the street, dodging the midtown traffic. I feel for the revolver in my waistband. Damn thing's so heavy I think my pants might come down.

I'm through the revolving doors and walk into another world. Everything has this shine to it, even the guests who seem to be above the rest of us bottom feeders. I look at the key and the tag reads 'Penthouse'. Jesus, I'll be lucky if there's a cent left at all. I walk toward the bank of elevators and hop into the first one that chimes.

The doors part, and I step off onto a swanky floor with a hall that seems to just stretch on and on. I start walking and after a bit I can see the double doors of the penthouse waiting for me at the end. I pick up speed, limping from the pain, and barrel my shoulder right into the door. It splinters at the lock, and I'm standing in the foyer of one hell of a nice room.

I hear the skipping of a record player as the needle keeps bouncing off the track. It gives off this soft beat beat beat as I move out of the foyer and into the main room and that's where I find her.

She's lying in a heap all bloodied up. Furniture is bashed around her, and I can hear this sound coming out of her and it hits me like a shot to the gut. My wife is dying.

I kneel down next to her and pull her close. I call her name. There's a rasp and she answers.

"Hal"

"I'm here, Ellie. Who was it?"

She struggles for air and then says his name. I brush back her hair, it won't be much longer, now.

"He take the money?"

There's a pause and then another rasp.

"Yes."

"Where is he now?"

Nothing.

"Ellie?"

A whisper leaves her body and then she's gone, and I hold my wife and everything goes numb. I kiss her battered face and leave her behind as I move out into the hall.

I'm limping out into the cool air of the night as cops start swarming into the hotel. I head up the street and find my cab waiting just where I told him. I climb in and he turns to look at me.

"Money?"

"Not yet. You're gonna take me to it."

"No money? I get cops. Lots of cops right here!"

I take out the revolver and pull back on the hammer and he stops dead in his tracks.

"Sit."

He does, never taking his eyes off me.

"Now, I don't lie. I'm not lying about the money, and I'm not lying that I will shoot you if you run off. "

The driver nods his head and we pull away. I look down at my hands and I see blood. Ellie's blood. Why do I care? She left me for Sol, cared more about money than what happened to me. But, she's dead. Dead cause of me and the mistakes I made as a man. I'm tired of the mistakes. Tired of who I am and what I didn't do. Tired of it all. I lean back in the cab and my eyes start to drift again.

I'm back with Ellie, this time her head in my lap. I wipe her bloody hair from her face. She whispers something again and this time I hear her.

"Did you love me?"

I'm awake again and there's only one place left to go.

Madden's Pub sits in the heart of Hell's Kitchen. "Mad Dog" lives upstairs, and on any given night you'll find him and his Irish crew drinking, counting money, and carving up bodies. And here I am, ready to pay my debts back. Every last one of them.

The driver lets me off, but he doesn't give a shit about the money anymore. He just cares about saving his ass, and he tears off down the street with his horse. I don't blame him. The next few minutes are gonna be ugly, and I don't want that pretty horse of his getting hurt. Don't want anyone getting hurt but the people responsible for this mess.

There's a Ford sitting right on the corner and it's running. It's the car from the train stop. Someone's at the wheel, I can see the red embers in the rearview glowing from the drags of a cigarette. I take off my trench coat and wrap it around the revolver in my hand and move alongside the heavy tank of a car and blast a hole in the driver's head. The sound is muffled into the coat, and the glass shatters like chimes.

I drag the oaf out onto the street and take out a handkerchief he's got in his pocket along with a hip flask. I take a swig and it burns the cuts in my mouth and I pour the rest out onto the handkerchief, soaking the thing right through. Then I stuff the rag as deep as I can into the gas tank and then light the damn thing.

I climb into the Ford, wiping away bits of meat off the wheel and put the brute in gear. The whole damn car is heavy. I can feel the weight behind me as I gun it toward Madden's, the rise of the engine like a charging beast. My headlights hit the window of the pub, and I can see old friends, friends that tried to kill me. Friends that murdered my wife. For once they look afraid. Good enough for me.

The thunder hits deep, slamming through my body. I rattle around the cab as glass rains across my face. I can feel the soft thuds of bodies against the fender. My teeth bite into the steering column and all sense leaves me. I lie still, and the horn blasts on into the night.

The fire hits the tank and there's a gust and a flash and then nothing but a blast of heat. The smoke is black and thick and the fire swallows in all around me. It rages on and burns my enemies, my failures, and the mistakes I've made. It burns us all to hell.

Ciudad de los Niños

Bracken MacLeod

The child leading Martín down the path looked over her shoulder at him and, despite the summer heat, he shivered. An oily drop of sweat trickled down her temple, streaking the painted flower design outlining the blackened pockets of her eyes. Martín couldn't tell if the girl was pretty through the la calavera catrina death mask, but the blankness of her stare was clear enough. Her eyes were solemn and old and she looked at him the way a butcher looks at a Corriente cow—with a little pity, but mostly boredom. She frightened him. He would have dropped her sweaty little hand if she'd let him, but the girl held on tightly. She guided him through the rows of half-sized candy skulls set along the narrow dirt road. The calaveras de azúcar were baking in the hot sun, scenting the air with caramel. "Is it far, niña?" The girl smiled cheerlessly. The teeth painted around her lips framed her own tiny white incisors. *She looks like a shark*, he thought. *Dia de los Muertos isn't for another five months.*

Farther up the path, he saw more children in unseasonable corpse paint. Martín had always assumed the name of the place she was taking him—Ciudad de los Niños—was poetic, not literal. He had yet to see a single adult, however. He got his own start as a twelve-year-old working the secuestro express in Mexico City steering gringo tourists toward his partners' taxicabs. Like the girl was doing to him, he'd drag turistas by the hand through a confusing maze of alleyways, warning them along the way that it was imperative to be careful choosing how to get around the city. The drivers would then take the marks to Tepito and demand that they withdraw as much money from an ATM as they could if they didn't want to be left in the barrio bravo. As he got older, Martín graduated to extorting supplemental money from the families of secuestro express marks before breaking out into his own business for an entirely other class of victim—the kind who came to a trade with a suitcase full of money instead of an ATM card. He considered himself a legitimate businessman now—a broker—willing to serve as a neutral party to bring family members home alive and untouched. For a fee. But he'd never been called to work the Ciudad de los Niños. That didn't happen. They didn't bargain. If you went missing there, you were simply one of los desaparecidos—The Disappeared. That's what he'd always heard. Then his daughter disappeared, and he heard differently.

An image of Luz's mother, Narcisa, flitted through Martín's mind as he made his way to trade a briefcase full of money for his daughter. He remembered her panicked voice, yelling about how *her* daughter had been taken to Ciudad de los Niños. She told him some bruja—some witch—was holding her hostage. His ex-wife wasn't the only woman trying to take what was rightfully his. *Narcisa was the one who let her get snatched in the first place. No. No more Narcisa in our lives!*

Martín and the painted girl walked past a small band of young boys lounging against the side of a red adobe building. Their faces were also ornately decorated with flowers and spider webs, black tears and spades transforming their round babyish features into leering reflections of death. The boys stood guard with Kalashnikov rifles, their eyes tracking Martín as the girl led him by. He felt sized-up and categorized like they were deciding between pasture or killing floor. They let him pass, clearly put into the category of not-a-threat by the casual indifference of hardened soldiers. Not one of whom was older than fourteen.

A blast of hot air buffeted him with sand, carrying away the caramel smell. In its place he smelled something else.

Rot.

Martín refused to look down again, not wanting to know why the skulls were getting larger or why they no longer smelled like caramelizing sugar. He stared instead at the back of the girl leading him over the next hillock. Her bare shoulders were brown from the sun and coated with pale dust kicked up from the dried river bed that encircled the encampment. She looked like she hadn't bathed in weeks and carried a heavy scent of corruption along with her which the unmerciful wind swirled around him. He marched forward, toward his meeting, clutching his suitcase reminding himself that it was only business.

Over the next rise appeared a small chapel. Two more boys with Kalashnikovs guarded the entrance while other children milled about in the street. So many. Drawing closer, the guards sized him up. This time, he did not feel dismissed. He felt cowed. Itching sweat ran down his body in constant rivulets like rain on a windshield. He wanted to rub at the moisture slicking the small of his back, but he kept his hands at his sides where the children could see them, knowing beyond certainty that the gesture would get him killed. Normally he would have his gun nestled behind him in his belt, but in his haste to get the ransom for Luz to the drop, he'd forgotten it in the car. *Everything's different when it's your own child.* The little girl had frisked him anyway.

The guard to his left looked no older than eleven; the one on the right, maybe thirteen. Both boys were slender and wiry, dirty like his guide, their round faces were padded with baby-fat and they were half his height. Still, they exuded the kind of menace that he had felt from dealing with cartel soldiers and guerillas—the willingness to commit an act of violence was just a single misstep away—except these kids seemed without the limitation of conscience. *Life isn't cheap to them. Cheap still has some value. Life here is worthless. Even if I had my gun, could I kill a child? These children. Yes, I think I could kill them if it came to it.*

Around a corner appeared a group of girls and boys playing with a black and red soccer ball. As a boy kicked the ball toward Martín, another intercepted it, punting it away. The ball careened into the side of an outbuilding, bounced back and sent one of the painted skulls lining the street lolling out into their path. The boys squealed with delight and abandoned the ball for the head. Another kicked it in front of Martín. The group stopped and waited, staring silently at the adult in their midst looking expectant like they wanted him to kick the new ball back into play. He looked down at what had been offered to him. The head was painted white in the same Dia de los Muertos style as the children's faces. It was not made of sugar, however. A roughly hewn neck, caked brown with dried blood and mud faced him. The ivory color of a budding vertebra peeked through behind the collapsed fold of a trachea. Martín's guide scowled disapprovingly and kicked the severed head back to the boys, barking in a little girl's squeak, "¡Ponla donde estaba!" They immediately did as they were told and put it back before returning to their game.

"Por aquí," the girl said. "La Bestia le espera adentro."

La Bestia! Martín wanted to ask if he couldn't just give the girl the money instead. But he kept it to himself. *¡Sé hombre!* he told himself. *Be a man! You'll pay, and you'll get Luz back and everything will be fine because you were a fucking man and you did what it takes to protect what's yours.* "Por aquí," his guide repeated, pointing with the machete she held in her other hand. *Jesus! Was she carrying that the whole time? Why didn't I see it?* She still hadn't let go of him, and Martín wondered whether he'd be able to break her tiny grip if she tried to pull him into a machete swing.

Willing his legs to work, he took a step forward. The girl nodded, commanding the boys standing guard outside the chapel to open the doors. Together they walked through the portal and up the aisle like a father leading his daughter to her waiting fiancée. Except, the girl was leading *him* toward a wooden throne atop the dais where, in any other church, there would be an altar. She was pulling him toward the woman who held his daughter captive. Delivering him to La Bestia.

The woman's head was framed in a garland of red roses woven into the thick black hair cascading down her bare shoulders and over her red ruffled bosom. Thorns scraped tiny crimson lines in the skin of her exposed alabaster cleavage. Martín's gaze would have lingered at the buxom chest that rose and fell softly with La Bestia's breath if it weren't for the fact that her tattooed face terrified him and kept him in thrall. Delicate white lines like the outlines of teeth were permanently drawn on her full lips. Her nose and eyes were tattooed black, while around them soft swirling lines drew attention to the intricate roses tattooed on her chin and at her forehead where her hair parted. Cold blue eyes stared out from the black holes.

"Bienvenidos." La Bestia held out a lace-gloved hand to Martín. The girl gave him away, placing his hand in hers. Martín did his best to hold the contents of his bladder at the rough scratch of the woman's grip. "Me complace que usted está aquí," she said. Behind the death mask, she actually did look happy to see him. *As happy as a wolf about to eat a jackrabbit.* Without releasing her hold on him La Bestia leaned back in her chair forcing him to half kneel on the step in front of her if he didn't want to sprawl across her lap. He definitely did not want to touch any more of the woman than he had to. His guide pried the suitcase from his other hand and stepped back to the first row of pews.

"Tengo t-tu dinero."

"Si. ¿Y por lo tanto...?" She challenged him to ask her for something. To beg.

"Please. I do not..."

"Do you know who we are?" she asked.

"You are The Beas—"

"Who *we* are." She tightened her grip, grinding his knuckles painfully against each other.

"Esta es la Ciudad de los Niños."

"And what is the City of Children to you?" she asked. Kneeling near her legs, Martín's senses were overwhelmed by the woman. She was all he could see. He smelled the roses in her hair—her sweat, her sex. He felt caught in a web next to a sac of eggs waiting to hatch.

"This is where the lost—"

"None of my bebés are lost," she said. "They are all seen and heard."

Martín wanted to fall back—to scramble away—but she held tight. He winced at the strength of her hot dry grip. "But this place..."

"Is the womb of a new nation. Every child here is a wanted child."

"The heads..."

"Each one is a birth from death." La Bestia gestured to her left at a painted head resting on a shelf beneath a reclining porcelain doll. "That is the head of Padre Marcial Evaristo. From that óvulo I gave birth to my sons, Raul, Ricardo, and Carlos. Evaristo was scheduled to be sent back to Rome, but instead, he resides here where he can watch my sons grow." She pointed at another skull on a shelf beneath Evaristo's. "This cabeza belonged to a pimp named Israel Fonseca Moreno. He gave me the girl who stands behind you now and a half a dozen others. All baptized in blood. All risen from the graves these men and women dug for them and reborn from my body. All of the men and women who decorate my city are paying the price for betraying la sangre de la Raza." She took a deep breath and cocked her head at an angle considering him for a small moment.

"Just like you," she said.

Martín's heart raced. A spike of pain shot through his left armpit. *Better to have a heart attack or my head chopped off?* "I haven't betrayed anyone," he protested. "I get people back to their families. I get them back alive. I'm a neutral broker."

"After you extort them for their life savings and leave them destitute. You think you are a predator. But you are just a parasite drinking la sangre de la nación."

"I brought you money."

"And for that you want what exactly?"

"The deal. To leave here. To take my daughter and leave."

"That she is the second thing you mention explains why you will never leave." La Bestia released Martín's hand and gestured toward the rear of the chapel. The guide who led him tossed aside the suitcase and opened the door. On the other side waited a congregation of children who filed into the building, taking seats in the pews. Martín considered making a run for it, pushing through, but he knew that the boys with the rifles waited just on the other side of the door.

"Are you ready to pay for your sins?" La Bestia asked.

"I brought you the money you demanded."

"And the tribute is apreciado. Your money will buy food for the children and ammunition for their weapons. But money is not the only debt you owe."

Martín looked over his shoulder at the child approaching him. He barely recognized his daughter dressed in a delicate white dress with her face painted in a death rictus like the other children. "¿Mi Luz?"

A pair of children marched behind her holding a white silk pillow upon which rested a gleaming new machete. La Bestia stood up and spread her arms wide in a gesture of welcome toward her soldiers. Martín tried to feint sideways, but three children from the front pew leapt up to stop him. He wondered how many kids it would take to hold him. He couldn't wait around to find out. He bucked off their small hands, grabbed Luz by the arm, and rushed toward the front doors plucking the machete off the pillow as he passed. A howl of anger went up among the children. He swung the machete menacingly, but none of them backed away. They could not be intimidated.

Glancing back over his shoulder, expecting La Bestia to be coming for him with her own blade, he saw her standing in place, smiling. Martín wished she would make some kind of threat, show that she was concerned that he would get away with his daughter. She didn't. That worried him more than the children with the rifles.

She already knew how this would end.

"I got your confession, puta! I know what you did. I'll bring the Policía Federal back here and show them the heads and they'll shut down your revolución before you can—"

La Bestia kicked a head from the top step of the dais down the aisle at Martín. "Tell this one. Él va a escuchar." Martín shuffled back away from the head that stopped in front of him face up. The man's badge glinted up from where it had been pinned to the skin of his forehead.

A shirtless boy with ribs protruding through his skin lunged forward with a knife, clumsily stabbing at Martín's guts. Dodging away, the knife stuck in his hip instead. He yelped in pain. Beneath the paint, a dark look of amusement showed on the boy's face as he drew back to stab again. Martín swung the machete, chopping into the skinny boy's shoulder. The child went from a hardened soldier with a death-dealer's stare to a shrieking infant in the time it took for the blade to open his arm up. Horrified, Martín's guts threatened revolt. *I can't fucking do it! She's using children because* no one *can do it. They'll do the terrible things she wants because they don't know any better, and she'll win because that sound... that sound!*

Luz struggled to break his grip on her arm. He swung his daughter up in front of him, betting that the cult wouldn't take the chance of hitting the girl. She howled in protest, kicking her feet, as he clutched her tightly around the waist. "Come at me and you'll hit her." Shoving through the children, he kicked at the doors, swinging them open, startling the guards outside.

Turning to take another look back, he saw La Bestia's placid countenance break. Her glare sent a shiver through Martín's body despite the summer heat. He began to run backward as best as he could hoping the first band of children he'd seen leaning against the stucco wall had chosen to attend the service instead of waiting for him over the rise. Relief danced at the edges of his panic as he crested the hill and they weren't there.

Hefting his daughter up over his shoulder, he turned and sprinted the rest of the way to the car. The stolen machete slipped from his sweaty grasp as he went. *Fuck it! I just need to get to the car. We'll get away in the car. We'll head toward Texas and we'll disappear. Just you and me, Luz.* He didn't feel the bite of the blade in the back of his leg at first—just warmth. It wasn't until the second, deeper cut that the pain reached his conscious mind and his brain replied with the command to fall. Martín crashed face first into the dirt, landing on his daughter. Her knees drove into his chest, pushing all the air from his body. He gasped, inhaling a lungful of dirt instead of air, drowning on dry land. She kicked at him and scrambled out from under his weight. "Luz," he choked, spitting mud. The car was only meters away. He could see freedom.

His daughter stood over him staring down with the same blank look that his guide had given him less than an hour earlier. She waited, loosely holding the wet blade at her side like a favorite blanket dragged everywhere. Martín started to pull himself toward the car. Luz stood still. The footsteps of the congregation soon followed as children came running over the hill, surrounding him. They encircled him wordlessly, each one sharing his daughter's quietly malicious gaze. When La Bestia walked into the ring, two boys jumped in after her and roughly flipped Martín over onto his back.

With the sun behind her, La Bestia's garland of roses framed her corpse-white face in a bloody red halo. She gently positioned Luz in front of Martín. The girl raised the machete over her head. She hesitated a moment, looking to the woman with an expression of concern. "Igual que con mamá, pero esta vez será más fácil," La Bestia reassured her. The girl smiled sweetly.

"No, Luz! I'm your papa! Don't do this. I don't care what she's made you do. I love you!"

"Niños, ¿Qué el amor?" La Bestia asked the children.

A chorus of voices answered, "¡Amor es lo que hacemos por los demás!"

"Muy bien. Love *is* what we do for others." She smiled and Martín lost hope.

"You're insane," he said.

La Bestia looked into Martín's eyes. "Don't despair," she said. "I only want your head. I'll leave your heart for Luz. Because she loves you."

Love Gone Bad

Julia Madeleine

There's an ancient Chinese proverb that says an invisible red thread connects those destined to be together despite the time, the place, and despite all circumstances. The thread can be tightened or tangled, but it will never be broken.

Jessie thought of how Frank had said that to her once, as she listened to the shower down the hall. And she thought of Frank in there, and the fact that he wasn't thinking of her anymore.

She smoothed a curl of blond hair behind an ear as she glanced around Frank's bedroom for anything that might belong to her; a random pair of panties perhaps. She found a barrette on the bedside table and draped over the arm of a chair, a pair of her stockings.

Her fingers skimmed across a shirt of his lying on the unmade bed. She had the urge to lift it to her face, breathe in his fragrance—that comforting mixture of hash and Robert Cavalli cologne. For one flickering moment she felt the foundation of her existence threatening to splinter, the consumptive hemorrhaging of her soul clawing away inside her chest. She held up a hand before her face, watched the way it trembled.

She had nothing left of him at her apartment. She'd gotten rid of it all. Every piece of jewellery. Pawned it. Every photograph. Burned them. All of it was gone, every memento. Not a random strand of his hair mixed in with any of her things remained. No torturous reminders of how her happiness had been sabotaged. He was completely departed from her. Purged physically and mentally. Severed from her being like a cancerous tumor. Although the longing, in so many ways, still remained.

It was with conscious effort that she made the choice to stop looking for fault within herself as to the why things had to end.

It was possible—no likely—that the issue lay completely inside of Frank, and had nothing at all to do with her.

Foolishly Jessie had thought things were going well with Frank. The passion between them was off the charts. The abrupt ending didn't make sense. It was like hitting a glass wall, breaking through, and the shards shredding you, carving the flesh from your bones.

"I met someone," he'd said, days earlier when she arrived at his townhouse unannounced, surprising him with a latte. "Sometimes love just happens like a car accident. It's not something I planned. Just fate I suppose." His lips stretched into a smile underneath his dark moustache, his eyes staring at something through the kitchen window. Then he shrugged coldly. Actually shrugged, like it was nothing.

Jessie stood there with her jaw hanging open as if he'd just doused her in gasoline, and she was waiting for the match. Four minutes of pure torture felt like it would go on forever as she listened to his lame excuse and even lamer apology.

Then her friend Amy swaggered down the stairs in his robe with her strawberry blond hair all disheveled, hugging herself tight, Frank's scent all over her.

"Oh sweetie, I'm so sorry," Amy said as if talking to a child, pressing her traitor's hands tenderly on Jessie's face. "I know this must be a shock for you. But one day you're going to find someone who really deserves you. You're an amazing woman."

Jessie stared in disbelief, still unable to find her voice, and then incredulously Amy said, "You know sweetie, when one door closes another opens, and at worst there's always a window you can jump out of."

Amy had nearly a disabling penchant for saying the most inappropriate things. She couldn't help it. She'd tried and failed often enough.

Funny word for Frank to use: fate. That sounded like something Amy would say. Amy was a big believer in things like destiny and omens and signs, as if everything and everyone but herself had control over the direction of her life. She had Tarot cards she consulted regularly. She did her own horoscope, mapping out complicated charts on pieces of lined schoolbook paper with sharpened pencils and geometry instruments. She always consulted the cycle of the moon before making any major decision. She was a conspiracy theorist and followed David Icke like he was the second coming of Christ. The other odd thing she'd seen Amy do on occasion was bite her hands whenever he got stressed. Short of wearing a tinfoil hat, Amy was a first class weirdo.

Jessie failed to see the attraction. Amy was pretty if you liked the red-headed freckled look. But she wasn't educated or even employed. She was living off an inheritance from her grandmother and the way she went through it, throwing her money away on designer clothes, that gold vein was sure to dry up in no time. She smoked a pack and a half of cigarettes a day and drank nearly a bottle of wine a night. As far as Jessie knew, she'd never stepped inside of a gym in her life.

Frank worked in finance as an executive on the forty-second floor of a gleaming steel and glass building in downtown Toronto on Bay Street. He went running every morning at six o'clock and drank kale and celery smoothies. If he knew his zodiac sign it was only by accident.

She was far better suited to Frank; had a Phd in education, a teaching career she loved. She did yoga and pilates religiously. It was true she had anger issues, impulse control issues, was on medication for depression and borderline personality disorder, and of course there were all those suicide attempts in college. Her own mother had personally considered killing her as a child with anti-psychotic medication, shamelessly admitted to it, generally after one too many glasses of wine, as if it was her one true regret in life. Still, all her issues were beside the point. Everyone had problems in varying degrees of one sort or another.

It must be the sex. There was no other explanation for him and Amy.

Jessie should have known, should have seen it coming a mile away. The signs were there—that broken false fingernail with its sparkly purple polish that she'd found in Frank's sheets. It had stabbed her in the back—an interesting metaphor now that she thought of it—while she lay beneath him one night. What was the excuse he'd used to explain its presence? Oh yes, he'd denied ever seeing it before and then when she pressed him on it, he'd said it probably belonged to one of the maids who cleaned his house. But she was certain they never made beds. In fact, she couldn't remember ever seeing his bed made. That was one thing about Frank, as much of a clean freak he was, he never made his bed.

Then there was his incessant flirting with her girlfriends,

especially Amy. She would catch glances between them across tables at parties. That should have been an obvious sign. But that's the thing with denial—an acronym for didn't even know I am lying—it's designed to protect as much as harm.

The only thing left to do was accept it, and get over it. Chalk it up to just another love gone bad. There was simply no figuring him out, or understanding him. Frank was a mystery better left unsolved. He refused to talk. He just shut down, shut her out, became angry. But she couldn't help feeling the horrid agony of that rejection—another rejection. Just what she did not need at the moment with her heart already so fragile. The thing was, Frank knew that. He knew what she'd been through with her last boyfriend. Knew how much she'd worked to put her life back together. So for him to go and do this to her was really beyond her ability to accept. How could she have laid her heart down to this man, dragging out his broken emotion with her love?

The truth, if she was really going to face it, was that Frank was a narcissist. She'd thought that the first day she met him. In spite of it, she'd fallen hard for him. The physical attraction had been all consuming—his tall, dark, bad-boy good looks and charm. She'd known he was completely wrong for her. And she'd wanted him anyway.

Jessie balled up the stockings and buried them deep in her handbag along with the barrette. In the spare room across the hall she sat down at his desk and sucked in air. She logged onto his laptop. There she found all the pictures he'd taken of her—pictures she'd asked him not to take but he did anyway like it was his right because he was having sex with her. She didn't bother looking at them, seeing herself bound and gagged like some kidnap victim in various positions. It depressed her now the way she'd allowed him to do whatever he wanted to her body. That special brand of insanity called love could make you do the craziest things.

She moved the pictures to the trash on the desktop and then emptied the trash. She went through the pictures on his digital camera and removed the ones there. It was time to leave now. She was done.

Jessie went into the bathroom and slipped a hand inside the shower, turning off the taps. One more kiss before she said goodbye. She swept the shower curtain aside and looked down at his pale naked body, the water still pooling pink underneath him. Closure was what mattered now.

"Goodbye, Frank," she whispered as she leaned over the tub and brushed her lips next to his cold ones. She was careful not to touch anything, or leave fingerprints in the spatter on the tiles.

Jessie wondered what the Chinese might have to say about a buck knife to the chest. She was certain those twenty-odd stab wounds had finally severed that invisible red thread between them.

Set Fire to the Trees

Brian Panowich

"You ever been stung by a hornet?" Hal said out of the blue. He didn't look at me when he spoke. It was pitch black out, and he kept his eyes on the dirt road ahead. He had one hand dangling lazily over the steering wheel, and the other gripped around a can of Stroh's in his lap—his third since we left the house.

"Sure I have," I said, "It stings like the dickens."

Hal narrowed his eyes at me then looked back out at the road. "Well, I don't think you have then, Clayton, 'cause if you did, you wouldn't say 'it stung like the dickens'. That just don't cover it. Those sum' bitches hurt like nothing else in this world. Pain you ain't never gonna forget. You get stung by one of those suckers, and it's enough to bring tears to your eyes. God forbid, you get stung by a bunch of 'em…" Hal paused to find the right wording. He blew out a long trumpeter's breath of air and shook his head. "You get hit by a bunch of 'em—buddy, you're going down."

"No, really," I insisted, "I did get stung once. It was only one and I killed it when I stepped on it, but I thought my foot was going to swell up like a watermelon."

Hal killed his beer and slung the can into the floorboards at my feet. "Did you know that hornets will attack you for no reason?" he said, "Not like a yellow jacket, or a bumble bee like the one you stepped on."

I didn't argue.

"Bees will mind their own business if you do the same by them, but a fuckin' hornet? You could just be walking by a nest and those on'ry bastards will chase you down. Did you know that?"

"Uh-uh," I said, and shook my head. I had no idea why my brother was talking about hornets, but I didn't much care either.

Hal never really talked to me at all, so I was enjoying having a little of his attention. We were born ten years apart with my brother Buckley born slap between us, so me and Hal didn't have a whole lot in common. Besides, he was normally too busy with all the crops higher up the mountain to be fooling with his kid brother. I understood that. Business first, it was the Burroughs family way. But even since I turned fourteen, and Deddy started letting me help out on runs, Hal still didn't really pay me no mind. This conversation was probably the most Hal ever said to me at one time. I wanted to think maybe it meant Hal was starting to see me as a man—as a brother. That thought made me sit about a foot taller in my seat.

Hal pulled the POS Ford pickup onto a side road anyone who wasn't from around here would have missed. It wasn't so much a road as it was two channels of dirt cut into the dander and weeds from the tires of trucks much like this one. I had to roll up my window to keep overgrown brush and tree limbs from whipping me in the face. Hal cut the truck's headlights down to the orange parking lights. I could barely make out the road in the moonlight, but that didn't slow Hal down a bit. He just hauled ass through the dark like he'd done it a thousand times before.

"You remember Big Merle?" Hal said.

"Sure," I said, holding onto the armrest for dear life. "He was that fat kid that used to come get schoolin' from Mama before she left."

"Yeah, not that it mattered, no amount of schoolin' would help that fat fuck. He was as dumb as a sack of hammers." Hal grabbed another beer from the six-pack on the seat between us and peeled the pop-top off with his teeth. "Anyway, he may have been a dumb-shit, but he was still a buddy. A *good* buddy. The fella' would do just about anything you asked without a bitch or complaint." Hal handed the open beer to me. I couldn't believe it. Hal was sharing his beer with me. I knew I looked a little too eager when I grabbed it with both hands. Hal let a brief smile escape before he reached down, and popped open another beer for himself.

"Anyways," he said, "when we was kids, a few of us were out by the southern ridge shooting at squirrels—Me, Buckley, Scabby Mike, and Big Merle. He was a fat shit even then. It was the year Deddy bought me that shitty .22 rifle. I think you got that gun now."

I told him I did. I didn't tell him that gun was my prize possession 'cause it used to be his. Instead I took a swig of warm beer and forced it down. It tasted like swamp water.

"We were having a pretty good time," Hal said," Just fuckin' around, and Big Merle says he needs to a take a piss, so he bolts into the woods. If it were me, I'da just whipped it out right there, but Merle was pee-shy. Little pecker, I guess. Anyway, a few minutes later, he comes barreling out of the woods, trying to yank his pants up, screaming like a banshee. Wailin' like I ain't never heard before." Hal paused and took a sip of his own beer. I could tell he was remembering back, watching the scene play out in his mind's eye.

"Hornets?" I said.

"Yeah, buddy. Hornets. A whole damn swarm of 'em. He only got a few feet out of the woods before he toppled over. There must have been hundreds of 'em on his ass."

"What'd y'all do?"

Hal looked at me like I just asked the dumbest question ever asked.

"We ran like hell, is what we did. I ran so goddamn fast I thought my heart was gonna explode and I didn't stop 'til I was inside the hunting cabin Deddy put up near Johnson's gap."

"Dang," I said, "That's far."

"I know, right?"

"What happened to Merle?"

"He managed to get his big ass off the ground and to his folk's house, but he was all fucked up. He had to be holed up at the hospital down in McFalls County for damn near two weeks. The poor bastard almost died. We didn't get to see him until way after, but even then, he still had tubes runnin' out of him to drain the puss, and his eyes were swollen shut. He never did talk right again. We felt bad, 'cause of runnin' and all, but damn, what were we supposed to do?"

"That's messed up." I said.

"Yeah well, we handled shit the next day. Once we found out Merle was in the hospital, we headed back up to the southern ridge to clear those fuckers out. I mean, that was our spot. We hung out there. A bunch of hornets weren't gonna just build a nest and sting up our friends. We were there first. You understand what I'm saying?"

Hal was looking dead at me now, and awareness spilled over me like a bucket of well water. I nodded. We weren't just talking about hornets.

"We marched our happy asses into the woods, and sure as shit, we found the nest hanging in a hollowed out pine tree probably right over where Big Merle tried to take a piss. We brought a can of gas to torch the thing, but it was way too high for any of us to reach, so Buckley's crazy ass starts dousing the whole damn tree. We could'a burned the whole mountain down—dumb ass kids, but we didn't know any better. Scabby Mike lit that bitch up, and it took off faster than shit."

"The whole tree?"

"The whole tree. We just sat back and watched it burn. When the fire took to the hornet's nest, I swear I could hear 'em screamin'. Whistlin' like fireworks. It felt good."

"Then what happened?"

"Deddy saw the smoke from the house, and he and Uncle Jimbo come haulin' ass out there. We cut a break to contain it, and managed to get the fire out before it spread."

"Was he mad?" I said, and immediately regretted asking.

"Well goddamn, Clayton, what did you think? Hell yeah, he was mad. I toted a legendary ass whuppin' that night. So did Buckley." Hal paused again, and brought his voice down, "I gotta tell you though, little brother, it was worth it. It was worth it to hear those little bastards screaming."

I forced down the rest of my beer, and tossed the can on the floorboards like my brother did. Hal stopped the truck and cut off the parking lights. He popped open the last beer and downed it in three huge gulps. His belch was hearty, loud, and long. Man, I wished I could burp like that.

"We gotta walk from here," Hal said. He grabbed his shotgun from the mount behind our heads, racked it, and quietly got out of the truck. I followed right behind him. I thought maybe I'd been out this way before with Deddy, but couldn't be sure in the dark. This part of the mountain was peppered with stills, but a lot of them were in disrepair. Ever since the family's focus shifted to the crops under the northern face, this area was tended to less and less. It wasn't abandoned, just not a priority.

We walked about a quarter mile into the woods before we could see the dim light of a campfire through the trees.

"Hey, Hal," I said, "Whatever happened to Big Merle? I haven't seen him around for a while, did his family move off the mountain?"

"He's dead," Hal said, "Buckley beat him to death with a piece of stove wood, and dropped him in a hole. Fat bastard wasn't happy with his place in the pecking order—got greedy. It happens. Now be quiet, we got a job to do."

Hal crept slowly through the trees toward the glow of the fire, and I mimicked his every move. The closer we got, the quieter Hal became until I could barely hear him myself from just a few feet away. When we were close enough, I saw I was right. It was one of Deddy's stills, one that was supposed to be decommissioned. It wasn't. We stopped at a deadfall of rotten pine and watched a blonde haired man with a patchy beard stoke a fire under a massive copper boiler. The heat coming off the barrels felt good on my face after the long hike through the cold woods. I tugged at Hal's shirt to get his attention, and he leaned in close to me.

"There's only one," I whispered," That's good right?"

"It's good, but it ain't the one we want."

"So, what do we do?" I asked.

"What do you do, when you can't reach a hornet's nest?"

It didn't take long for me to come up with the answer my brother was looking for.

"You set fire to the tree." I said.

"Very good, kiddo," Hal said, and ruffled my hair with his thick calloused hand, "I think Deddy's got you all wrong. Now stay here." Hal put a finger to his lips and vanished into the darkness. He reappeared less than a minute later directly behind Blondie, who was now copping a squat by the small campfire, thumbing through a titty-mag. His rifle propped up against a tree to his left.

What a dumbass, I thought.

Hal drew way back and hit the man in the temple with the butt end of his Mossberg. Blondie never knew what hit him. He went down hard, face first into the dirt. It was hands down the coolest thing I ever seen. My brother was awesome.

"Clayton," Hal said, snapping me back into the moment, "Get out here, and tie this pig-fucker to that hemlock tree."

I shuffled out of the woods and did as my brother asked with a quickness. I'd always been good with knots. I was sure Hal knew that. He pulled a length of Paracord from his jacket, and tossed it to me. I bound the unconscious man in no time. Hal kicked over the huge metal boiler—the heart of the ancient still, and the coals spilled out all over the small clearing. Once some of the underbrush started to ignite from the coals, Hal used the high-octane hooch in the barrels as an accelerant, dousing the entire site. Almost instantly the small patch of woods became a blazing inferno.

"Holy shit," I said, "How we gonna put this out?"

"We're not. They are." Hal pointed to the man tied to the tree. I was confused.

Hal explained; "This fire is going to be seen by the fella we were sent here to find, and I promise you he'll be along shortly. When him and his boys are tuckered out from fightin' a woods fire, we'll pick them off like fish in a barrel." He tapped the grip of a black handgun sticking out of his belt, "It'll be fun. C'mon, let's go find a place to watch."

"What about him?" I said, and pointed to the Blonde man, who was starting to come around due to the intense heat.

"Fuck him," Hal said, "Come on."

"But he'll burn alive."

"And?" Hal said, beginning to lose his patience, "Get your ass up that path before I leave you here to burn up with him."

I couldn't move. I just stood there like a dumb ass kid.

The man tied to the tree by my expert knots awoke completely when the fire started licking his feet and legs. He swiveled his head back and forth, wide-eyed and frantic, taking in the scope of what was happening to him. He struggled to free himself, drawing his knees up to his chin. He screamed at me to help him. He begged me. I just stared at him—horrified. Hal gripped me so hard under the arm, he nearly ripped it off dragging me with him back out the way we came.

From a safer distance, I watched my oldest brother get comfortable against a tree stump, and pack some chewing tobacco into his lower lip. He looked rested and content, as the burning man's screams became something else. Something unnatural. I'll never forget that sound. I wondered if Hal could even hear it at all, or if all he heard were hornets.

Life is nothing but a competition to be the criminal rather than the victim.

~Bertrand Russell

Rubes

Terry Rietta

The sun bakes the wealthy by the pool. I wish it would just finish the job, but since when do the stars listen to me? As Johnny and I stroll through the marks at the Ritz, I feel the heat of middle-aged eyes on my ass. I don't blame them. All modesty aside, this caboose is carved out of granite and looks a whisper over eighteen. It's worthy of gawkery. The greys and the baldies think their sunglasses can hide what they're up to, but an ass like this comes equipped with radar. It's not like I did anything to earn it. No gym. No diet. No infomercial devices. Just a few pairs of chromosomes that jigsaw puzzled just so. Maybe the cosmos aren't so cruel after all.

Life gives you opportunities. You exploit them or you don't, but you got no one to blame but yourself for leaving money on the table. Maybe you got brains or rich parents or a dog that can do tricks. Good for you. I got an ass. And today it's in short-shorts instead of a bikini 'cause when a girl's trolling for the big spenders, she's gotta leave a little something to the imagination.

My tail is meant to keep the uber rich pool hounds at this swanky palace distracted. If they had any sense at all, they'd be looking at the man I'm dripping off of—Johnny, the shark with the smile and the shades and the linen suit. But hips on a swivel trump polish every time.

My ears pick up the low clatter of dice tumbling into each other against velvet. I give Johnny's elbow a squeeze. He's on it, already adjusted course. To Johnny's ears, that sound may as well be a dinner bell. We saunter up as cheers, moans, and a pair of double sixes spill onto a backgammon board. A chubby man in his thirties snatches a pile of cash off the table.

Johnny whistles low between his teeth, impressed. "Quite a

roll."

Chubby ignores him and winks at me as he collects the stack of money. When he puts the cash in the briefcase next to him I can see the stacks have company. I clock a dozen or so. That's a lot of cheese.

Johnny lowers his gaze to the men around the table. "You guys look serious about your dice."

Chubby swishes the ice around his drink and scooches over on his lounge chair. "It's just a game. Little bit of fun to pass the time." He tries to be casual about angling for a better view of my ass. I shift my hips millimeters to help his cause.

"That's a lotta money for a little fun."

"Makes it interesting. Gotta have stakes or it's not a competition."

"You're a grown man, you know this isn't a competition. Not a real one anyway."

When Johnny says something not-so-nice, he nods as he says it. The marks don't even see themselves nodding back. If anyone else said something like that, it'd be fuck off and move along, but Johnny has a way of smiling through his language. Somehow he gets heads bobbing instead of fists clenching. We all have our gifts.

"I don't know about that." Chubby rubs his briefcase like a letch.

"Yeah, you do."

There are two kinds of gamblers. The kind who play because they've had a lifetime of shit luck and think they're due. And the kind who think they're smarter than everyone else. Johnny sized Chubby up as the latter and the way to play a guy like that is to insult him in front of his friends.

A confident man doesn't get rattled. A pretender takes the bait.

Chubby cracks his neck by twisting his head to the side. "Why don't you have a seat? Let's see if losing some money changes your tune."

Bingo. Mr. Plus Size takes the cheese.

One of Chubby's posse looks up from his cell phone. His fingers have been tapping and sliding on it since we walked up. My ass and I would be insulted if the phone guy weren't so clearly gay. "I wouldn't roll with him. He's been taking everyone's money the last three days. Must've won over eighty grand today."

"Give or take." Chubby chews his ice.

Johnny takes the dice off the board. He tosses one of them to Chubby, just out of reach so the big man spills his scotch reaching for it.

"Tell you what then. I'll bet you ten grand that I roll a higher number than you. Simple as that. You in?"

"You got that kinda dough?"

"Baby, get my bag, will ya?"

I slink by the pool, catching some evil mojo from the ladies propped, stuffed and shoved into their swim suits. My ass has many talents, it's also equipped with a radar for hate. I compensate for the sin in my shorts with sweetness in my eyes. Don't want the ladies pulling the marks away out of insecurity. I'm back with a briefcase in just a few wiggles. The boys' club has not settled down. Lots of drinking. Lots of jawing.

Johnny opens the case and the jawing stops. He takes a brick of cash out and

looks down on Chubby in his lounge chair. "High roll. 10 thousand. You in?"

The men around the table straighten up a bit. Johnny owns these guys and it's taken all of eight and a half minutes. I always like this part. No more eyes on me. Cash beats ass. Rock, paper, scissors.

I detect a hint of fear-phlegm in the back in Chubby's throat when he answers. "Sure."

If I heard it, the dice heard it too. The cosmos don't like fear. They feast on it.

Johnny rolls. The die dances and spins on its point like a diamond. God, even the dice want to impress him. The ivory cube finally settles. Shows a 6.

Ohhs and ahhs.

Chubby licks his lips and then holds his breath. Hard roll, banks off the side of the backgammon table. Lands on the ground. He rolls a 6 as well.

More ohhs. More ahhs.

Chubby exhales. "Tie."

"You gonna count that? It landed on the ground."

"It's a 6. Tie."

Johnny snorts. "Tie?" He grins wide for the fellas. "You believe this guy? You're the one who said you like competition. If it's a competition, someone has to win. What are you a soccer fan?"

"Fine. Run it back."

"You sure, Mr. Tie?"

"Fuck off and roll."

Chubby rolls 5. Johnny rolls a 6.

Chubby pulls out a banded brick of cash, tosses it near Johnny. Tries to make him reach, but I pluck it out of the air. I've got quick hands. Tools of the trade.

Chubby scans the crowd. He's lost his hold. You can see him calculating. He's gotta put Johnny in his place or this will haunt him at every poker table and golf game he's ever at with these guys. "You wanna go again? Another 10 grand?"

Johnny flips through the bills, counting it. "Sure. But rolling dice gets kinda limp, don't ya think? You said you wanted a competition so let's make it a contest of something meaningful."

"What do you mean, meaningful?"

"Let's have...a contest of wills."

"Wills? What are you worried your luck will run out?"

"Luck's for suckers. Any bitty with a bucket of nickels can have a good night with a slot machine. A contest of wills is a contest of men."

This is where I'm supposed to pout.

"Johnny this is stupid. Just take the money and let's get outta here. "

I was born to pout the way most men were born to breathe. Pillow lips don't always come as a matched set with a high-dollar ass, but sometimes the universe smiles. Don't hate me. It didn't give me much else.

To be honest, there's not much acting involved in the pout today. I really have kinda had it with these guys and I'm bored as hell. We've put Chubby in his place, we're 10K richer for 10 minutes, and I'd like to move on. Sometimes you just take your winnings off the table, order some room service and fuck.

"You in?" Johnny grins at Chubby as he steals a sip of his scotch.

Contest of wills sounds dramatic, but the truth is Johnny had to switch games. Johnny'd swapped one of the dice out when he tossed one to Chubby and made him spill his drink. If he kept rolling sixes all day, Mr. Always On His Cell Phone was gonna be calling the police instead of checking his stocks.

Chubby licks his lips. "*So*, how exactly do we have a contest of wills?"

Shit. Chubby's chasing more cheese.

I should probably put some sunscreen on.

§

Johnny and Chubby stare at each other. Total focus. Neither blinking.

They look intense while I look bored sipping on a frozen daiquiri, trying to ignore my bladder. Of course it's not hard to act bored while witnessing two adult men balls deep in a staring contest. Then again, it *is* a staring contest for 10 thousand dollars.

Thank god we've moved from the pool to the bar. Even a high dollar ass sweats if it's left in the elements too long. Chubby's posse is still intact. They've circled around, making the standard side bets and cell phones videos. These boys haven't had this much fun since the last fight they witnessed by the monkey bars.

The trick in *contest of wills* is simple. It has to be winnable for the mark. There's no luck to it. The mark simply has to think he's better/smarter/more in control than the guy sitting across from him. Johnny was just taking what was offered. Johnny's never lost one of these, but Chubby's holding out longer than most.

I've positioned myself right in Chubby's eyeline, that is, if he were to look up. I hold my daiquiri so the coldest part of the glass rests on my nipple. As it springs to life, I move the glass and arch my back by degrees. The ass is powerful, but sometimes it sits on the bench and lets the other kids have a turn.

Chubby blinks. "Shit."

"I win."

I'm sure Johnny would've had him, but like I said, I really had to pee.

Chubby sighs, hands me a banded stack of bills.

Johnny pats Chubby on the back. All encouragement and smiles. "I thought you had me. You want more or are you done?"

I hear Chubby growl as I make my way to the ladies' room.

A quick flush and a nose powder later, I find the boys back in the bar. More drinks. More side bets. More jawing. Johnny and Chubby sit at a table with a couple of candles in front of them. Johnny's started without me, he's getting cocky.

The two men hold their hands low over the flames.

Chubby loses. Pretty quickly, too. I don't mean to stereotype, but the chunkier the boys are the faster they go down on the flame game. Maybe the excess body fat percentage gets meltier or something. Don't ask me. I didn't go to college. I'm just telling you what I've seen. Doesn't really matter. Chubby's hands work well enough to hand me another stack of money.

I switch my daiquiri to soda water and lime. Johnny cooks up more contests with Chubby.

Who can sit pantless in ice the longest.

"I win."

Who can eat more hot peppers.

"I win."

Who can stand on one leg the longest.

"I win."

Who can drink the longest-consecutive-swallow out of a bottle of bourbon.

"I win."

Poor Chubby loses every single one and Johnny's a broken record of "I wins". Part of it is just Johnny being obnoxious, but the other part is pure calculation. You goad the mark to milk him at this point. Like a carnival dunk-tank bozo who harasses you into more and more baseballs until your wallet runs dry.

This part always bothers me. Watching the mark get drunker and angrier and drunker and angrier. Not because of the money. Fuck, this guy's got money to burn. He'll just go make more. The crippling thing is: he thought he had friends and now he knows they were an illusion. He has to watch the pack of guys he thought worshipped him abandon him. One by one, Chubby's support posse peels off like fair weather fans ducking out in the middle of a blow out loss. Abandonment is not fun to watch.

Hopefully he's too drunk to process how shitty his friends are. How far they let him fall just for sport. They're probably in their rooms right now uploading the cell phone footage on youtube. They build you up to take you down.

Johnny stumbles in the hallway, clearly pretty drunk himself. He must be feeling like he owns this guy to get this shitfaced. Like any man, Johnny tells the truth when he's drunk and the truth never mixes well with the games we play.

Johnny and Chubby sit back at the pool by the backgammon table. I'm doing my best to maintain an arched back and crossed legs without falling asleep. A long day has turned into a long night and truthfully, I don't know why we're still here. We've emptied

Chubby's case of goodies.

Johnny slurs. "Thing is, you could have won any one of these contests."

Chubby spits back. "Bullshit. If I could've I would've."

"You fucking rich guys. You don't know how to fight for anything in your life."

"Come to work with me some day. It's a fist fight from the first cup of coffee"

"Maybe, but you're fighting with a bunch of other entitled pricks. Doesn't count. Doesn't count any more than that 6 you rolled that landed on the ground."

"Fuck you."

"You want what I got, you gotta take it from me." Johnny motions to a pile of money in a suitcase sitting at my feet. "I'll put it all on the line."

"What?"

Johnny's eyes are wide. "Winner take all. You guys were jacking off all over each other at the backgammon table talking about competition. *Now* it's a competition, right? You wanna know why? Because it's personal."

That's it. We are way off script. It's never supposed to get personal. He's a mark and the cash is a take and we shoulda been outta here hours ago.

I slide over to sit on Johnny's lap and pull his face towards mine. "Baby, let's just give this man a little cash back and call it a night."

"Shut the fuck up." Johnny opens his legs and I fall on my million-dollar tush. It occurs to me that I may have exaggerated its granite-like qualities. That hurt.

Chubby helps me up. "Doesn't matter. I don't have anything left to bet."

"I don't care about your money anymore. What did you drive to get here?"

Chubby dangles his keys. Bentley keys.

"Then that's what you put up. Your pride. Your ass is walking home if you lose. If you can't win with your pride on the line, I don't know how you can show your face to your so-called friends."

Chubby tosses his keys on the table. "You wanna make it about pride? What are you putting up?"

"How about this pile of cash?"

"You just said you didn't care about money. You can just go

hustle some more up as easy as I can, right?"

"Fine. I'll throw in Angela if you win."

This is a new wrinkle. My job is distraction not collateral. "What?"

"Shut up, baby. I'm not going to lose.'

"That's the second time you've said shut up to me in the last couple minutes. And to be very clear, I am not a property. I am not a prize."

"C'mon baby, you've always been a prize."

Ouch.

"If I win. Nothing changes, right? But if I lose all this money I'm not keeping you anyway. We both know why you're here, right?"

I thought I did. Clearly Johnny didn't. I fight the mist in my eyes.

Johnny stares at Chubby. "You want her? You ever had a piece of ass like that in your life. C'mon, you've been eyeballin' her all night. It'll give you a little extra incentive for the next bet."

"Which is?"

.Johnny starts taking his shoes and socks off, nods to the pool.

"Simple. Who can hold their breath the longest?"

§

Both men tread water in the deep end of the pool.

Johnny may have overreached here. Chubby actually looks comfortable in the water. His face takes on an almost supernatural look with the pool light glowing from underneath him. "You're gonna lose this time."

Johnny struggles to stay afloat. "Nah, I saw it on your face when I walked up to you. I saw you and a pile of money and thought...I'm just gonna take it. I'm gonna take his money cause he thinks he's better than he is. And now I'm gonna dangle money and a beautiful woman in front of your face and then I'm gonna snatch it away from you and the only one you'll have to blame is yourself, cause you're too damn weak to take it."

"Look at you. You can barely swim." Chubby's eyes radiate hope.

"It's not a swimming contest. It's a hold your breath contest. One. Two. Three."

Both men submerge.

It's creepy quiet. Just the pool filter and the lap of the water against the side. I watch them underwater. Squared off and staring at each other. I can imagine the pure contempt coming out of Johnny's eyes. Johnny's always hated rich people. But he always just took their money with a smile. Tonight, this was something else. Tonight was about punishment. For the wealthy. For me. For the world.

I check my watch. It's been 40 seconds.

Chubby starts to break. Makes a move to swim up to the top when I see little bubbles coming out of Johnny's mouth. Johnny grabs Chubby's leg and hauls him back down. Won't let him lose this one. Johnny's not going to quit, but he won't let Chubby quit either.

They struggle and punch, but Johnny's on Chubby's back. His arms and legs wrapped around him in a death grip.

I look around for minute, horrified. I start to run for help, but then I stop and an invisible weight leaves my body.

Life gives you opportunities to exploit. You got no one to blame but yourself for leaving money on the table. Maybe you got brains or rich parents or a dog that can do tricks. Good for you. Tonight this ass is in short-shorts. But tomorrow, what my ass is wearing or doing or thinking won't be anybody's business but my own.

I pick up the Bentley keys and the briefcase and walk away.

Tumbling After

Rie Sheridan Rose

I always wanted to be the good girl that my sister was—go to church, feed the poor, blah-de-blah-de-blah—but bad boys were my weakness. The moment I met him, I knew he was right up my alley. Looking at him, standing there in my bedroom doorway, shirtless, suspenders around his hips...still damp with the sweat we'd worked up in the bed where I was lounging, I realized there was nothing 'boy' about him. Not anymore. The shotgun over his shoulder said he was aiming to take someone's money...and I was thinking I could use a payday.

Names can be deceiving, but I'll give you some to keep things straight...let's go with Jack and Jill, 'cause he sure made me come tumbling down. All the way from the dizzying heights of suburban aristocracy to the depths of skid row flop houses like this one. And, God, did I love every minute of the fall.

Jack and I met at a high school dance—my high school, that is. He didn't get past eighth grade. Didn't see any point to it. Wasn't important to his chosen career. I had learned these things before the end of the night.

Six months later, here we were. I jumped at the chance to leave my holier-than-thou home life and take to the road by Jack's side. It took a bit of adjusting—but not much. Stealing your breakfast from a farmer's hen house is a helluva lot of fun. If you get caught... bullets are cheap.

We're earning ourselves quite a little reputation. Nothing like Parker and Barrow, of course, but people know our names—Jack and Jill, at least. But enough blather. I think Jack is ready to put his shotgun to its intended use, and it doesn't do to keep Jack waiting...

"You scribbling in that book of yours again?"

"Yeah. Sorry, Jack. I'll be ready in a minute."

"Shake a leg, dollface. Day's not getting any younger, and I have my eye on a sweet side of bacon just waiting for liberating."

Jack always talks like someone out of a dime novel. I think that's where he's picked up most of his ideas on how to be a trigger man. Some of them work, some don't, but I don't expect this ride to last long, so I let him throw out his slang and hold the shotgun.

If it were up to me, I'd pull on some overalls and tuck my hair under a cap when we pull a heist. Easier to move, and a whole lot safer, but Jack is enamored with the idea of a gun-toting moll by his side, so I have to slink around in a dress with my face powdered and painted. Takes a while to get going in the morning.

It wasn't long before we stepped into the little Ma and Pa grocery though. Jack with his hat pulled low over his eyes and his shotgun under his coat; me with my revolver tucked into a muff. This wasn't Jack's sweet score, I could tell. We'd be lucky to get a couple of sawbucks from this one, but he was hungry. Delayed gratification was never Jack's strong suit.

"May I help you?" asked the gray-haired granny behind the counter. She saw a nice young couple on their way to somewhere else, I bet. Not a clue to the wolves in sheep's clothing standing in the middle of her spotless storefront.

Jack strolled to the window and stood looking out for a moment, as if expecting someone to join us. Then he pulled the shade in one fluid motion.

"Excuse me, I'd rather you didn't touch that," Granny protested. Her eyes bulged from their sockets as Jack swung around with his shotgun. It was almost funny to see.

"We really hate to trouble you, ma'am," I soothed, stepping up to the counter and pulling the revolver out of my muff, "but if you would be so kind as to remove all the money from the register, no one needs to get hurt here."

I was lying, of course, but she didn't need to know that.

Her hands were shaking so badly she could barely manipulate the drawer, but she finally popped it open. I slid a glance to Jack, and he was helping himself to fresh made donuts piled in a basket across the store. Boy never could keep his mind on the job.

"This is everything I've got," our hostess whispered, holding out the bills with quaking hand. "Went to the bank last night."

Plucking the bills from her hand, I sighed, shaking my head in sympathy. "I'm really sorry to hear that, ma'am. Y'see, this will really gum up the works. My man over there is a bit of a gunsel. He expected a nice bit of scratch here. I'm afraid I'm going to have to rescind my original promise."

I straightened up, aimed the revolver, and pulled the trigger. The gun bucked in my hand like a playful puppy straining against its leash. Granny's eyes widened in surprise as a blood-rose bloomed over her heart. I'm an excellent shot.

Jack crowed from the other side of the room, "Murder, dollface! If you ain't the coolest customer ever lived. How much we get?"

I counted the bills. "Thirty bucks. Might as well stock up on groceries while we are here. Hurry. Gunshot may bring company quick." I knelt beside the old woman's body.

She was wearing a thin gold wedding band and a cross with a tiny emerald set in it. I pocketed those.

Jack had found a large metal bucket, and he was filling it with bread, cheese, ham, and onions—he loves his onions. A box of matches, lantern, and a can of kerosene, and the bucket was full. I swiped a pound cake and a dozen eggs.

"Let's make tracks before the coppers show up."

The whole operation had taken no longer than ten minutes.

We hot-footed it to the car and burnt rubber out of there, laughing like maniacs. It wasn't my first kill, by any means, but it felt different. I hadn't waited for Jack to tell me what to do, I had just done it. For once, I really felt like a moll and not some dame Jack had saddled himself with.

"What's the big score you were talking about?" I asked him, when I could finally pull myself together.

"Bank in Tilsbey. It's a small town, but there is a mine nearby, and the payroll is planted there every Thursday for the miners coming in Friday with their checks. We hit that bank at just the right time, and we will be rolling in dough. Maybe high-tail it to Canada for a while till the fires die down."

"Mexico, Jack! Let's go where it's always warm, and drink tequila on the beach all day."

"Mexico it is. Anything for you, dollface."

I snuggled against him as he drove. Could life get any better than this?

§

Mexico was just a pipe-dream without a stake. We might eke out the thirty dollars enough to get there, but it wouldn't be enough to live on. The Tilsbey bank job was not optional.

So we drove. Halfway across the state. All day and most of the night. Pulling off to take a leak on the side of the road now and then, eating onion and ham sandwiches. About four AM, we even risked a small fire and scrambled up a mess of eggs. Living the life of highwaymen. Silly, children's games.

When Jack couldn't keep his eyes open, he reluctantly let me take over. I never was much of a wheelman. I manage not to crash us into a tree, so just as dawn rose on a crisp, clear Thursday morning, I pulled into a motor court in Tilsbey, Virginia.

Leaving Jack snoring in the passenger seat, I stepped through the lobby door. Just one heavy-eyed clerk on duty, not much older than we were—twenty-five tops. I could work with that. Tossing my hair and adjusting my neckline, I minced across the parquet floor and leaned over the counter, making sure to showcase my assets as prominently as possible.

"Hello, there, handsome," I gushed, oozing sincerity. The pimply mouse behind the desk ate it up.

"W-What can I do for you, ma'am?"

I leaned my chin on my hand. "I need a cottage for a couple of days. You have anything available?"

"Uh, well...I have three units at the moment. The one just there—" He pointed out the front window.

"I was hoping for something a bit more...private," I murmured, leaning forward and speaking into his ear. I swear the man turned carnelian.

"There's one in the rear, with a back drive out. It's a dollar a day."

Expensive for a place like this, but I guess you pay for privacy. "That sounds fine...there's just one thing." I bit my lip, dropping my eyes as if embarrassed. "I only have fifty cents today." Reaching out, I placed a hand on his arm. "I'm expecting my brother to bring me some scratch...can you spot me till tomorrow?"

The idiot didn't stop to wonder how my "brother" would know where to find me.

"Sure...that would be fine. I trust you." He fumbled behind him without taking his eyes off me and handed me a key. "Here you go. Unit 6 in the back."

I leaned over and planted a perfect cupid bow smack on his cheek. The stench of his body almost made me retch. Did the twit never bathe? I wondered how long the lip-print would remain intact.

I sashayed myself out of the lobby putting a little extra bump in my grind. At the door, I paused and blew a kiss at the genius behind the counter. A little sugar always goes a long way.

I pulled the car around back, and let Jack out of the trunk.

"Sorry that took so long, sweetie. The greaseball behind the counter was a total pill. But there's a back drive over here that should come in handy, and I talked him down to fifty cents for the night."

"You're the best, dollface. We'll pull the job in the morning, so we won't need any longer than that."

The anticipation of the bank job was a powerful aphrodisiac to Jack. We didn't get a lick of sleep that night, making whoopee until the sun peered into the dirty lace curtains.

Which didn't make for bright eyes and bushy tails the next day. I put on my best face and new silk stockings. Jack dandied up as much as he ever did—he put on his hat and suspenders with a flower pinned to his shirt. It felt like we were heading for a romp instead of a bank job.

The tires squealed as Jack tore out of the back drive. My hair blew in my eyes, and I laughed in nervous excitement. We'd never even contemplated anything this big. This would be our final heist, one way or the other. Mexico seemed a long way away...

Jack pulled into the lot in front of the First Bank of Tilsbey. I took a deep breath and ran my fingers through my hair. "You sure about this, Jack?"

"Don't go soft on me now, dollface," he chided, running his hand down the side of my face. "Just remember those sandy beaches and sunny skies waiting for us." He handed me my pistol, and I tucked it into my purse. "Now get in there and do me proud. I'm right behind you."

Lifting my chin high, I shut the car door behind me and walked up the steps to the entrance of the bank. One last deep breath, and I pulled open the door, sauntering across the lobby to the teller cages on the far side of the room.

I laid my purse on the counter and smiled winsomely at the

togged up dandy behind the cage. Hair pomaded, parted ruler straight, he obviously fancied himself a pip. "Yes, madam, may I help you?"

I batted my lashes at him. "Why, yes. Yes, you can. I need to make a withdrawal."

He reached for a banking slip. "Of course. How much would you like to withdraw?"

"All of it." I pulled my pistol out of my purse, sticking it through the bars of the teller cage.

His eyes widened and he stammered, "Y—yes, I see..." Hands shaking, he reached into the till.

Jack came through the door, gun peppering the ceiling with holes. "Everybody down," he ordered. "All the bread out of your pockets. Place it on the floor above your heads. Jewelry too. Quickly. I'll plug anyone who doesn't snap to."

Patrons all over the lobby dove for the floor, but I saw the teller's hand slide under the counter. "Goddamn it, Jack! He's tripped it." I shot the smarmy bastard in the face.

I jumped up on the counter and reached through the bars, straining to reach the cash in the open till. My fingers brushed the bills, but I couldn't grab them.

"Get the dough from the floor, because we're out of luck on the till."

"Hell's bells, Jill! We needed that lettuce."

I scanned the counter, trying to figure out a way to get the cash. There was a wail of sirens in the distance screaming closer. "Shit!" I screamed. "I can't get to it."

Behind me, I could hear whimpers as Jack poked at the customers with his scatter-gun. "Who's in charge here? Someone can open that cage. Who is it?"

The sirens were closing in on us.

"Jack! We gotta go!"

"Not without that stake. If I have to shoot every last one of you, I will!" To drive home the point, he painted the floor with the blood of a woman crying in the corner. "Now, who can open the goddamn cage?"

An older gentleman with mutton-chops and a shiny suit raised a shaking hand.

Jack grabbed him and jerked him off the floor. He shoved the man toward the cage. "Get it open."

The old man fumbled through a ring of keys.

"I know what you are doing!" shouted Jack. "Don't play with me. Get that money. Now!"

I began scooping up the cash from the floor, stuffing it in my purse, down my dress, wherever I could stash it.

Jack jammed his gun into the old man's back. "Open that grate, or I will shoot you right now."

There was a squeal of tires and a spray of gravel against the windows as the sirens screeched to a halt outside the bank. Heavy doors grated open and slammed. There was the sound of running feet on the stairs.

"Jack! What do we do?" Tears filled my eyes. I wanted to be home with my mother and father. I wanted to wake up from this dream and go to school. I wanted...

...but it was too late.

The front door burst open. The first bullet hit Jack before he could swing around. Then he was dancing in a hail of gunfire.

"Jack!" I pulled my pistol in line and took aim at a big man with a star on his chest. "Damn you!" I screamed, pulling the trigger. As my gun bucked in my hand, I felt hot lead tear into my body. The pain bloomed in fiery red roses.

And then, Jack fell down, and Jill came tumbling after.

Prison isn't so bad as long as they let me have paper and pen. It's been nearly forty years now. I didn't even get to bury Jack, and Parker and Barrow grabbed all the headlines, stealing even his shot at notoriety. The gun molls and gunsels are gone now.

Ashes to ashes...we all fell down.

They're Pros, Each and Every One

Ryan Sayles

Jugs was screaming threats and orders but none of the people in the bank were listening anymore, even though he was waving his gun as wild as he could.

Women were shrieking and a dude in a business suit fainted a split second after Tony shot himself.

Stupid ass.

Everything was going south. *Everything*. It was planned meticulously; they had trained and drilled. There were no variables. Jugs was orchestrating everything from his stopwatch. Nobody jumped out of the getaway car and tripped flat on his face before it all began. There was no Hollywood heist-type new jack who was a last minute replacement for a regular guy who wound up being a bloodthirsty psycho to hose up everything. There was the plan, the training, now the execution.

Monty dropped them off and circled the block twice. Jugs led the charge, ski mask and Ray Bans on his face, money bag in his left hand and .45 in the right; Cuz and Lizard in next, each taking a flank and Tony's goofy ass pulling up the rear. He was there for the added appearance. Four guns instead of three. He was *in* the plan—a favor to his brother Monty—but the rest of the plan read like this: *Tony gets a gun but no rounds. Got it? Don't* actually *arm the retard; just make him look good for the crowd. That's the plan.*

Then Tony ran in the bank door with his finger on the trigger—all the training said don't do *that* until you're ready to plug a fool—and tripped on some broad's purse loop. The round that cut through Tony's left thigh and took a chunk out of his femoral artery wasn't supposed to be in the gun. Tony must've put it there. He would have seen the guys—pros each and every one—checking their firearms and re-checking and re-re-checking again. He'd do the same. Find it empty. Go to WalMart or whatever and load up.

"I'll prove to them this isn't just a favor to Monty but a favor to them. I'm quality." Tony'd say standing at the checkout counter, box of ammo on the conveyor belt, on its way to killing him later.

Stupid ass.

So Jugs was screaming his very simple directions: *face down. Fill the bag. No tricks. No heroes. Nobody gets hurt. Face down. Fill the bag. No tricks. No heroes. Nobody gets hurt.* Then Tony trips, lights off a heater right into himself. Blood everywhere. Dude faints. People scream. Chaos, which was held in check by fear, now busts loose like an 80's break-dancer busts loose on a sheet of cardboard. Shit just got wild.

The female teller, chosen by Jugs during the dry runs because she looked young, naïve and easy enough to scare to where she wouldn't drop a GPS or a paint bomb into the money bag, turns ghastly white at the blood. Faints. Money bag goes down with her on the other side of the counter.

"Mother fucker!" Jugs shouts. His watch says he has thirty seconds before it's time to scram. Jugs runs to the teller counter. Jumps it. A man in a banker's suit gets stupid as Jugs lands. The guy reaches out—he's a freakin' behemoth so he's probably got Big Guy Balls—and grabs at Jug's .45. Jugs knows the risks. He offers the guy the muzzle as he fires off three rounds in one second. Maybe less. Have to check his watch for the official count.

Mr. Behemoth gets cured of his Big Guy Balls affliction real quick. He drops, three rounds worth of his guts come crashing out through his lower back.

Jugs grabs the money bag, takes the remaining handfuls of cash, jumps back.

"Let's go!" He shouts. Steals a glance out the window. Monty's pulling up. Right on time. No cops yet. That'll change real soon. Thanks for the gunshot, Tony.

Tony is writhing like a bitch on the polished marble floor. Screaming, crying. Even yanked his mask off. Cuddling his thigh like it's not trying to kill him. He stuffs one palm into the wound, trying to stave off the flow. No use. He looks up at Jugs. Their eye contact is all Jugs needs to know that in two seconds Tony is going to die but before he does he'll do something even stupider than trip and shoot himself with a gun that isn't supposed to be loaded. He's going to say *Jugs, help me.*

Jugs don't want his name out there with all these ears listening. Tony better die in one second, then.

Jugs put two rounds in Tony's face and turns to the door. Cuz and Lizard are standing there, holding the space. Just like in the drill. Notice those two don't deviate from the plan. They're good. Jugs runs out the door, the guys follow.

Jugs runs around the rear of the car and up the side, opens Monty's door, pulls at him. Yanks him right out of the driver's seat. "Change of plans," Jugs says, swinging Monty out onto the street. Monty knows the phrase *change of plans* should never come from Jugs' mouth. Something was indeed very wrong.

"Where's Tony?" Monty asks, that near-avalanche of *oh shit* looming above him. No Tony. Disconcerting, seeing as how Monty promised his whore mother while on her deathbed made of cancer and STDs that he'd watch out for her idiot youngest son. Maybe letting him get in a robbery crew wasn't a good definition of "watching out for," but that's a debate for another time.

Monty looks around, his heartbeat making it obvious things went wrong. Very wrong. "Where is Tony? Where's my fucking brother?"

"Half-brother." Jugs says as he grabs Monty by the shirt and heaves him out into traffic. Monty hits face first into a trash truck easily doing forty. Goes under the wheels. Flops around as the bulk of the thing crunches along overhead. The brakes lock up trying to avoid the inevitable. Too late.

The three remaining guys jump in the getaway car. Tires screech like a banshee getting a surprise ass-fisting. Burn rubber. They're gone.

On the way, Jugs says, "You guys know why Monty died, right?"

Both nod. They're pros. They know. It'll be hard finding another wheel man who could plot eight different to-and-from routes, time the lights, know the traffic patterns and controls, prime the cars, have the schedules down to a habit and then *drive* the same way. Monty could do all of that, but a good wheel man who is distraught by his dead kid brother is a loose end.

They're pros. They know.

§

Back at the place Jugs walks up to the same table where he laid out the plan, the same table where they played cards and ate out of drive-thru sacks and he dumps out the money bag.

All three sit around as Lizard brings the cash counting machine. Grand total, $56,117. Luckily, two out of the five had forfeit their shares. Divided by three it comes to $18,705.60 apiece.

Jugs stacks it evenly into three wads, ties up the bills. Sits one in front of each dude. Game over, then. Job done.

"Cuz, how's your mom doin'?" Jugs asks.

Cuz looks at Jugs and crumples his eyebrows. It's his tell; Jugs figured it out during Texas Hold'em. "Fine. She's just the way she's always been." His tone has that fake, quizzical sound to it like someone who isn't very good at hiding things is trying to hide something important.

And Cuz, he's not good at hiding things.

"The reason I ask is because you're behind on her debts to that casino over on 8th Street."

"What?"

"Yeah. Mommy likes how warm the seats are at the higher roller table. You like mommy so you shoulder her burdens."

Things go from celebratory to tense the way a stoplight suddenly goes from yellow to red when you're already speeding and too far out to brake. The room gets too hot and too cold all at once.

Cuz's balls crawl up into his abdomen. Lizard just looks back and forth, back and forth. He's hoping this is all an act. He's hoping that when Jugs gets done with Cuz he don't turn on him. He's hoping to hell that he's ready for him if he does.

Cuz finds his voice and says, "That's horseshit Jugs and you know it."

"I know it to be to the tune of almost forty-five large."

"I—" Cuz looks to Lizard for support. Lizard likes Cuz, but if he smells what Jugs is putting out there, this is bad. Lizard finally looks at Jugs and just says it point blank, "You sayin' Cuz is goin' to fuck us for the dough? Pay off his mom's debts?"

"That *is* what I am saying." Jugs says, all of a sudden the too hot and too cold room is real quiet. Tomb quiet.

"You don't know nothin'. Give me my cut. I'm outta here." Cuz says. He twitches just enough to light it off.

Guns out. Just like that. Too hot and too cold becomes too electric. Mexican standoff.

Everybody's a quick draw. Lizard and Jugs on Cuz, Cuz with his one piece erratically going back and forth between both of them.

"This the plan, Jugs?" Cuz asks. "All along?"

"I caught wind of some things. Figure we'd sort it out afterwards. No use in shortening the team on a heist, or ruining the morale beforehand."

Jugs smiles, says, "But yes. It was in the plan."

Cuz's face boils with indignation. "See what he's doin', Lizard? He's peelin' dudes off the score. Tony wadn't supposed to have no damn bullets in his gun, but I bet Jugs hooked him up! He probably knew that short bus kid would shoot his self! And then he whacked Monty. *Monty!* We'd been rollin' with him for years!"

"Monty wasn't going to take his half-brother's death very well." Jugs says, cocking the hammer on his .45. "He would have tried to blame us for not helping Tony—he would've blamed me for blasting the fat retard—then it'd be a matter of seconds before he shot or called the cops or both. Not in the plan, gentlemen. Now, Cuz, were you going to kill us as well?"

"I ain't gonna do nothin'! I just want my cut!"

"We can work it out," Jugs says. "Put down your gun. Give us a show of faith."

"You gonna kill me?" A whine. He needs to hear "no" the same way someone needs to hear it when they're asking the doctor if their spouse is going to die.

Jugs does his best reassuring laugh ever. "No."

Cuz slowly leans to the ground, sets the gun on its side. "There. Show of faith. Now we work this out."

Jugs swallows hard. "Do you—"

BOOM!

Jugs drops like an I-beam falling from a skyscraper's roof. He pumps two rounds into the ceiling before he pretzels his entire body in agony. His knee is missing; sprayed along the floor behind him. His gun falls and bounces out of reach the way they always do in those moments where the bottom drops out when you least expect it.

And Lizard stands there with a second piece out at arm's length, barrel smoking and aimed where Jugs' knee used to be. He's a pro. Carries a back-up.

Jugs roars with anguish and fury. Clamoring at his knee, writhing. Every vulgarity known to man spilling from his mouth like a hole punched through a dam. "No one was supposed to have a second piece! It was in the plan!"

"Yeah, well. The plan ended as soon as we entered the bank." Lizard says. Holds up the second heater. "Insurance, my man. Please don't tell me I'm the only one packing a back-up?" He casts a sidelong glance at Cuz. Cuz shakes his head. Cuz also notices Lizard's original gun is still pointed at his head.

Lizard says, "Cuz, you gonna fuck us?"

Cuz nods slightly. "I was gonna fuck Tony. Victimless crime as far as I can tell. That's all. I promise. Just a down payment to keep mom from getting—" he looks down at Jugs, his face purple-red and straining "—kneecapped."

"And when Monty came around?"

Cuz, with a little laugh, a silvery, warm one that reeked of cruelty, "Monty was in on it, bro. We was gonna split it. And that's the truth."

Lizard kneels to Jugs, motions the wound with his gun. "You wanna live?"

Jugs, sweating like his saint mother just caught him masturbating to the men's underwear section of her Sears catalog, nods furiously. He grits his teeth like he's giving birth.

"It'll cost ya about eighteen grand. You good for it?"

"You no-good piece of—"

"Nah, you got me all wrong," Lizard says. Stands. "*I'm* only gonna charge you five for the car ride, but the doc I know who'll fix you *and* not call the cops, he's gonna cost you the rest. You want that, or you wanna go to a real ER and speak with the police?"

Jugs looks away. Vision swirling, throat dry. Sweating bullets— no pun intended. He sees the table, all the bundles of green. Looks at his gun, a million miles away across the floor. No way he'd get within ten feet of it before eating hot lead. He knows damn good and well if he says the real ER he's getting plugged right here and now. They won't take the chance of him diming them out. Jugs wants to vomit. Looks to Lizard and Cuz, says he's good for it.

Then he vomits.

§

Jugs rides shotgun, Cuz drives and Lizard is in the back.

At Lizard's feet is the money. Next to him, the grab bag of

military-grade everything his brother-in-law bought from some Mexicans last year. Lizard swiped it the night before the heist when his brother-in-law was tripping balls on peyote. And while Lizard is a pro, he's not skilled with heavier weaponry. In the last twenty-four hours after he got his hands on this grab bag, he didn't feel he was sophisticated enough to mess with it. But better to have and not need...

Now, basking in the triumph of the day, he *does* feel sophisticated enough. He digs around inside, grabs a grenade.

"Anybody got some opiates? I don't care what. Morphine, Vicodin, Percocett, Hydrocodone, anything. Anybody?" Jugs asks, as uncomfortable as a bull right after its balls are tied. "Somethin' just to take off the edge? Fuck, man..."

"I wanted to stop for a cheeseburger, you know." Cuz says. His last cigarette gave up about fifteen miles back when they first left the city limits and hit the desert. No smokes, no appetite suppressant.

"That ain't gonna take the edge offa shit," Jugs hisses. "You're a real backstabbing turd, you know that?" Jugs' good leg bouncing up and down with all the pain traveling like lightning through his every nerve. "Here I am, shot by my friends, the plan all blown to hell, and you're wanting some sloppy burger and—"

"It was gonna take the edge offa my growlin' stomach, that's for sure." Cuz says.

At the mention of The Plan, Lizard feels downright bulletproof. He tore that plan to shreds with something Jugs never planned for. How is it a plan, Jugs, if you're not planning for things?

Stupid ass.

Lizard smirks like he was a kid again, getting away with smacking his third grade teacher on her juicy heiny. Fiddles with the little olive drab pineapple. Flicks at the dangling ring. Squeezes the spoon.

From up front, Jugs says, "Fuck your stomach."

"Fuck your knee, bro. Don't forget you was gonna shoot me right there."

"I— I wasn't gonna shoot ya. I was gonna sweat you for a minute and then we woulda been cool. Dude, now my knee—"

Lizard rolls the thing over in his hands. The weight of it reminds him of feeling up Loraine last summer. She was the bustiest chick he ever did lay hands on and—

Thumb catches on the ring. Pulls it out. Man that thing came out *easy*. The spoon flicks off. Hits Lizard in the mouth. *Inside* his mouth, clicks right through his Chiclet teeth. Wedges tight up and down in the soft tissue. He's like the Rancor after Luke Skywalker jammed the bone in its gaping hole. Lizard starts screaming around the spoon, shoves his arm through the space between Jugs and Cuz. Hand grenade front and center.

"Aggghhhhhh!" Driver and passenger recognize this for what it is, simultaneously hit notes reserved for Mariah Carey and men getting racked by a misfiring piston. Cuz stomps on the brakes hard enough to snap an ankle. Lizard—sophisticated, high on success, unrestrained passenger—he flies forward. Out the windshield.

The brakes' hideous screech echoes off into nothing, one ripple at a time. Windshield shards twinkling in the sunlight. The faint gasps of Jugs and Cuz, staring at all the red-rimmed hole haloed in the windshield. How Lizard is a car's length away, rolling around in a rooster tail of dust just enough to show he ain't dead. Not yet.

"Oh dude oh man oh God oh dude man oh my God," Cuz smacks the windshield frame and it frees all in one piece, falls off to the side. There, spinning a settling pirouette on the hood is the grenade. Both men feel a sudden bout of *get the fuck outta here* come on like emergency diarrhea.

"Aggghhhhhh!" Driver and passenger start to bolt out their respective doors. A single *BOOM* barks outward and bites them in the ass.

Cuz's head and feet make it to open safety before his door slams shut hard with the blowback. His body does not make it to open safety, however, and settles back into the driver's seat.

Jugs dives and is carried on a hot breeze filled with fragments of grenade shell. He dies eight feet away from the smoking hulk of the car. His last acrid, morose thought is of a cheeseburger and a pain pill and a perfectly legit plan.

Slag and debris peppers the old road around Lizard. He rolls onto his back, sees the empty sky overhead. His body broken. Tasting copper with that spoon still in his mouth, Lizard doesn't fight when the black comes for his vision.

§

"Hey Brian, you see this?"

"Of course I see this. Who do you think I am, my brother-in-law?"

"The dude with the two black kids?"

"The white dude with the white wife and two black kids. That dude ain't seein' somethin', but I'm seein' this."

"You know man, the way you talk about your family tells me all I need to know about you."

"Like you're any better."

The ambulance rolls to a gentle stop next to Lizard. The blasted car, close enough to taste the scorch on the air. Brian the paramedic gets out, makes a slow tour. Chris the not-paramedic leans out the door. "Anyone alive?"

Brian scratches his head, sees Lizard raise his hand just enough to feel his heart sink. *Damn it, I've got to do something now.*

Both men drop to their knees beside Lizard, readily see he's dying. Lizard, mouth rammed open by some metal object, parched lips, motions for them close. Brian leans in some, watches Lizard's car-wreck mouth trying to form a sentence around the grenade spoon.

Finally, "*Hell.*"

"What?"

"*Hell.*"

"I bet it's hell. Just hang on—" Chris the not-paramedic says. Brian stops him, points to what Lizard is writing in the dirt.

Help. No cops. Got cash.

"Oh...help..."

Brian the paramedic leans back, stares at the car. Stares at Lizard. Puts two and two together and as the light bulb pops on overhead he feels as proud as his six year-old kid spelling cub, mug, tub and hug. Brian raises an eyebrow, looks at Chris the not-paramedic. "Hey, didn't those cops say something about a bank robbery earlier?"

Chris lights up. "Escaped in a car which—"

"Looked just like that one," Brian nods towards the ruined vehicle. They had spent the day at a multi-agency training out in the desert. Something mass casualty-related. Cops gathered around their car's radio, listening to static and reports of the deadly bank robbery pouring in for a few hours, then nothing. But now, this.

"Hang on, hang on..." Brian the paramedic stands, goes to the car, careful to step over Cuz's bits and pieces. He rummages around inside, pulls out the duffle bag. Picks through it. Walks back over.

"Money."

Chris the not-paramedic sticks his nose in the thing, smiles.

"Well, some of it is burnt, but not enough to change my mind about this," Brian the paramedic says.

Lizard stares at the duffle bag. It had beaten the odds; survived his sophisticated screw-job. He should have never sold his brother-in-law that peyote. Not even at the profit he got for it. This is really all his brother-in-law's fault.

"I'm on board." Chris the not-paramedic stands, and they both look down at Lizard like he's a hurt child molester instead of a hurt bank robber. As if the Hippocratic Oath applied to some but not all, and only when fifty large wasn't at stake.

"You call this in when we landed here?"

"Nah. Didn't think about it."

"Good. For once I'm glad you're not very good at your job."

"How long you give him?"

"An hour, tops."

"Wanna shoot him with a pain killer, help him along?"

"Nah. I'm not explaining why I popped open the drug box. The sun will set real soon. The coyotes will help him along then."

"Word."

"Word."

The ambulance pulls away. Tires screech like a banshee getting a surprise ass-fisting. Burn rubber. Lizard mumbles "Fucking queefs" as best he can around the metal.

Brian glances in his mirror. Sees an arm rise. Sees a finger flipping him the bird.

Trinity

Richard Thomas

The three pale women haunted a corner of The Lucky Lady, smoking cigarettes and emptying the bottle of red wine that sat in the center of the table. They'd driven off the waitress with their sneers and verbal abuse, snapping at each other as they tried to forget.

Daphne's face was flushed, her ivory skin in sharp contrast to the blooms that filled her cheeks. With her right hand she kept placing her cigarette in the ashtray so she could pick up the glass of wine, her left hand severed at the wrist, a knot of stitched flesh that ended where her hand should have begun. There are fates worse than death, self-inflicted punishments that remind us of how we continue to fail in our redemption. Inhale, exhale, lift, swallow, and repeat. Despite her handicap, she was dressed to kill—short skirt, high heels, cat-eye mascara and a dark glare that cut through any man that dared to approach the table. She made her money in basements and nightclubs, prowling the darker side of the Chicago underground sex scene, a tattoo in script running above her collarbone, "Pay the piper," marking her flesh.

Jennifer sat in the middle, her long, blonde hair paid for at a local salon, her clothes painstakingly selected, ironed, dry-cleaned, color-coordinated, and expensive as hell. She did the same thing that Daphne did, but she didn't charge any money. She married well, and ran as far away as she could from Conway, Arkansas, never looking back, blocking out the incident, the shrill screams that still echoed when the nights ran long, the boy that she murdered out of spite, anger, and impatience. The twitch in her left eye was worse tonight—her long, thin, imported cigarettes crackling down to stubs in record time. On the wine glass her lipstick was a blood meridian, smudged and repeated, as a lover might ring a neck with kisses. She kept opening her mouth to speak, and then closing it with snap, morphing into a barracuda.

Marcy was emaciated, cold sores ringing her mouth, her hair a rat's nest, her hands always moving, two birds flitting about the table, pecking each other to death. Her knuckles were cracked and bleeding in spots. Her jeans had holes in the knees, dirty tennis shoes untied, constantly licking her lips, disappearing to the bathroom as often as the jukebox played a new song. She blinked her eyes and sighed, picking up the wine, placing it back down. She wanted something stronger. She wanted to ask Jennifer to do something different, to change the past, to change their present, but that wasn't going to happen. It would end like it always did, these reunions of guilt, these efforts to understand. It would end with Jennifer buying their silence.

A faded red pick-up truck with a twelve-pack in the front seat; an endless sea of cornfields and darkness that stretched out forever; and nothing but boredom and time stretching out for eternity—this was how they came undone. They were laughing, the three girls crammed in the cab, Daphne with her hand on Marcy's thigh, a dark little secret, Bobby driving down rock roads looking for niggers, and Jennifer holding her breath, leaning into him, muttering under her breath, *quarterback*, reassuring herself, *honor roll*, pretending it would all be okay. The bruises on her forearms, she hid them with makeup. The dull throb way up inside her special place a private beacon of pain.

When he saw the boy, Bobby accelerated and reached down beneath the seat to a shoebox he kept for exactly this kind of occasion. He pulled a baseball sized rock out of the box and gunned the gas, gravel spitting out behind the truck, the headlights fracturing the night, the kid turning around, his McDonald's uniform still on, his backpack slung over one shoulder, barely registering the noise before the truck was on him, and the rock was in the air.

The girls stayed in the car as Bobby hovered over the kid, splayed out on the road, blood seeping from his head, his backpack by his side, spilling out textbooks, cds, and a large plastic calculator. He kicked the boy, *nigger*, and laughed, swaying on his feet, *nigger*, finishing off the Budweiser, turning to the girls with a smile on his face. He urged them to come on out and get them some, to be a part of this darkness, to bond over the ritual. They did. He unzipped his pants and started to urinate on the boy—and that was when Jennifer picked up the rock.

She let out a noise unlike anything they'd ever heard—an Indian on the warpath, a pig at the slaughter, a peacock calling for its mate—high pitched, squealing, shattering the dark, the headlights flickering, her arm coming down on the back of Bobby's head. She didn't stop. Daphne and Marcy clung to each other, mouths open, the engine running as the flurry of motions broke the swath of light, up and down, Bobby on the ground, Jennifer on her knees straddling him, a sound like wet lettuce meeting a fist.

The girls leaned into the darkness and vomited, holding each other up, the kid on the gravel moaning, coming to. Jennifer stood up, splattered in blood, and heaved the rock out into the field. She walked in a trance to the back of the truck, took out the gas can and went back to her boyfriend, dousing his body and stepping away. The kid opened his eyes, took one look at her marbled face, and grabbed his backpack, sprinting down the road and out of sight. Jennifer reached into her purse and took out a lighter and cigarette, hovering over his still body, inhaling, her hand shaking, a stuttering of air in, and a stuttering of air out. Her eyes went to the girls as they swayed at the side of the road, and flicked the cigarette onto the motionless body. A dull whoomp and she walked away.

"Get your shit," she said. "We're walking."

They left the truck running, and started down the road. It would be a long night of crossing fields, cutting through woods, and hiding in the shadows, as they made their way to the nearest house, Marcy's. Back door, shower, and a change of clothes—it was easy.

Jennifer cleared her throat and reached into her purse. She took out a picture of the three girls from when they were little ragamuffins, shoes on the wrong feet, dressed up for church, standing by the apartment complex where they first became good friends. Best friends forever, they said. And they meant it.

Jennifer pulled a wad of bills out of her purse, paid for their drinks, and then stood up. She edged past Marcy, trying not to touch her, unable to look at Daphne and her mutilated arm. Two thick envelopes were placed on the table, smoke billowing around the girls, the red wine in the glasses catching light and flickering, the depth of the Merlot abysmal, no words spoken, the trinity intact.

The Last Croak

John Weagly

"Don't do this," Balthazar said, going down onto his knees on the grimy warehouse floor, his thick Cajun accent blurring his words. "I get you the money."

"You've been sayin' that," Colin said, taking the Ruger out of his coat pocket. "Mr. Walden is tired of waitin'."

"Think about this. If you let me live, I can work, I can earn, I can pay your boss back. If you shoot me, you never get the money. Surely he can see that!"

Joseph shook his head. "An example needs to be made for the other deadbeats."

"And you're it," Colin added.

"Don't do this," Balthazar repeated, defiance sneaking back into his voice. "If you do this, if you kill me, you will pay."

"Sure," Colin said. "We'll pay."

Joseph shook his head again.

"I curse you. As the seventh son of a seventh son, as a resident of the land where earth, water and magic meet, as a participant in all that is seen and all that is not seen, before I go to the dark I call the darkness within myself and curse the man that releases my spirit. I curse the man that sends me to the other side. I curse the man that..."

Colin pulled the trigger. In the empty warehouse, the gunshot sounded like a sharp, final laugh.

An hour later, Colin and Joseph were sitting at Joseph's kitchen table, each drinking a bottle of Bud Light Lime. A cassette of *Rust Never Sleeps* by Neil Young & Crazy Horse played on a boombox on the kitchen counter.

They couldn't think of anywhere better to go. Neither of them felt like sitting in a bar—when they did go out for a drink after a job was finished they both felt like everyone else in the bar was looking at them. If they went to a restaurant to get something to eat afterwards, they felt like everyone in the restaurant was looking at them. They spent a lot of time together as partners and friends, and a lot of that time was spent sitting around at Joseph's, where no one could look at them.

Neither Joseph or Colin had said anything in the last six minutes. The smell of burnt toast lingered in the air from much earlier in the day. Joseph looked at his fingernails while Colin looked at his beer bottle.

Colin hiccupped.

Joseph looked up from his hand. "What's that?"

"I didn't say anything," Colin said. "I've got the hiccoughs."

"The hiccups."

"Hiccoughs, hiccups. Whatever."

"It bugs me when people call them hiccoughs," Joseph said.

"Fine. Hiccups." Colin hiccupped again.

"Thanks."

They sat in silence for another moment, Joseph looking back at his fingers and Colin looking at the scratched and stained surface of the wooden table.

Colin hiccupped again.

"I'm tired of doin' this," Joseph said.

"We could watch some TV," Colin said. "Or I could go home..."

"Not this. I mean the threats, the strong-arming people, the killing."

"I always do the killing."

"I know, and I appreciate that!"

"When did you ever kill anybody?"

"Never," Joseph agreed. "And I appreciate that! Believe me!"

"Then what's the problem?"

"I still have to be there. I still have to act like an asshole. I still have to help with the body."

Colin hiccupped.

"Honey-covered Christ!" Joseph said. "Drink some water or somethin'!"

"Maybe you should scare me."

"Right," Joseph said. He waved his hands in the air. "Boo!"

Colin smiled. "That guy tonight," he said, the smile leaving his face, "He was pretty scared."

"That's what I mean. The begging, the crying, a curse for Christ's sake! I don't like makin' people act like that, makin' them feel like that. I'm tired of it."

"Mr. Walden isn't gonna let you stop."

"I know that." Joseph took a drink of his beer. "I know."

"You're stuck."

"I suppose we both are." The song "Sail Away" came to an end and the cassette clicked to a stop. Joseph stood to turn the tape over. "I'm just tired of it."

Colin hiccupped. A deeper, darker, twisting, wrenching hiccup. With this exceptional auditory spasm, a greenish-brown blob shot out of Colin's mouth and landed on the table in front of him with a gaudy wet plop.

Joseph stood and looked at the blob.

Colin sat and looked at the blob.

After a second, the blob tried to hop away.

"Holy shit!" Colin screamed, jumping away from the table and knocking back his chair. "That's a frog!"

"Holy shit!" Joseph agreed.

"Holy fucking shit, a fucking frog just came out of my mouth!"

The frog reached the edge of the table, but couldn't seem to figure out how to get down to the floor.

"I could feel it," Colin said. "I could feel it squirmin' in my stomach, then wrigglin' up my chest, then crawlin' up my throat. I felt it come all the way up, burning and scratching. Holy shit, a fucking frog!"

Joseph crouched and took a closer look at the animal. "It might be a toad."

"What?"

"It might be a toad, not a frog."

"What's the difference!"

"Frogs tend to have smooth skin, while toads have more dry, bumpy skin. Frogs have teeth on the top of their mouths while toads don't have any teeth. Also, frogs are aquatic animals while toads live in wooded areas. Of course, if you want to get technical, toads are in the frog family, so, technically, toads are frogs."

"I meant," Colin said, "What's the difference as in why does it fucking matter? Whether it's a fucking toad or a fucking frog it doesn't change the fact that it just came out of my fucking mouth!"

"Right. I guess it doesn't matter."

Colin hiccupped and another frog splatted onto the table.

"Holy shit!"

"Holy shit!"

"Holy fucking shit, my insides are turning into frogs!" Colin said. "Take me to the hospital!"

The two frogs looked at each other on the table.

"Hold on, now..." Joseph said.

"Hold on now? Do you get what's happenin' here?"

"I do, but let's think about this..."

"Let's take me to the hospital!"

"What's going on here isn't natural."

"No, shit!" Colin agreed. "No, it isn't natural, it's not somethin' you hear about, but maybe I ate some frog eggs and now they're hatching. Or maybe I swallowed some water with tadpoles in it. Or... I don't know! But maybe a doctor can tell us what's goin' on!"

"I don't know."

Colin hiccupped and a third frog came up. This one landed on the kitchen floor.

"Holy shit!"

"It's the curse," Joseph said.

"What?"

"It's the curse," Joseph repeated.

Colin looked at him. The kitchen was starting to smell like stagnant water and dead vegetation. "You think that guy from earlier..."

"What was he, Cajun? Don't they have a lot of Voodoo down there in Louisiana"

"I suppose, but do you really think..."

"It makes more sense than you swallowin' tadpoles!"

"Then how come it's not happenin' to you?" Colin said. "You killed him, too."

Joseph thought for a moment. "No," he said. "I was just there. You pulled the trigger. He said somethin' about cursing the man that killed him, the man that sent him to the other side."

Colin pulled his chair forward and sat at the table in a daze. "That man was me."

One of the frogs croaked.

"I'm sorry, dude." Joseph sat back down, using his arm to brush the two table frogs onto the floor.

"How long do you think it'll last?"

"I don't know," Joseph said. "But, you did take that guy's life, so..."

"A life for a life."

"That would make sense."

Colin hiccupped and a fourth frog came up, landing on the kitchen table. Joseph brushed it away with his arm.

"Jesus that hurts! I feel like I'm being ripped apart."

"You want some Pepto Bismol?"

"I doubt that'll help." Colin's hand shook as he took a drink of his beer.

Joseph tried to look hopeful. "Maybe it's not for life, maybe it's just for a little while, then it'll go away."

"No," Colin said. "You were right, a life for a life. I can feel it. Maybe because it's me that the curse is on, but I know I'll be puking up frogs until the day I die."

"Maybe. But..."

Before Joseph could finish, Colin stood from the table and shambled into the living room, his right hand clutching his stomach as he walked. After a moment, he came back with his Ruger. He placed the gun on the table in front of Joseph. "I can't live like this," he repeated.

"What?"

"You have to take care of it. You have to take care of me."

"Wait..." Joseph stood, putting space between himself and the firearm. "I can't kill you."

"You have to."

"Maybe you were right," Joseph said. "Let's take you to the hospital."

"No. They can't do anything. That Cajun bastard knew how to place a curse."

"But..."

"You don't get it. It hurts. It hurts like nothin' else has ever hurt before. You have to end this for me."

Joseph picked up the gun and looked at it. He held the gun out to Colin. "Do it yourself."

"No. I can't."

"Try."

"I can't. I don't have it in me. You have to do it."

The air in the kitchen felt humid and close. "I've never..."

Joseph said.

Colin gave three quick hiccups and a fifth, sixth and seventh frog came up, landing on the kitchen table. Colin moaned. The three animals looked up at him like he was their mother.

"Please?" Colin said, going down onto his knees on the kitchen floor, pain hitching his breath. "You don't know how it feels. My insides are being torn to pieces. I don't know how many more of these fucking reptiles I can stand."

"They're amphibians."

"Just fucking shoot me!"

Joseph picked up the gun. It felt warm in his hand and made his palm itch. He pointed it at Colin's head and curled his finger around the trigger. "I'm sorry."

Colin hiccupped. An eighth frog hit the floor. Blood trickled down Colin's chin.

"Holy fucking shit," Colin rasped. "Do it."

"What will I tell Mr. Walden?"

Colin looked up at him. "Tell him you're tired. That you quit. That you don't want to be an asshole anymore." Colin smiled. "And then get out of town."

"I'll do that," Joseph said, smiling back. Then he pulled the trigger. Blood and brains splattered the kitchen and Colin's body slumped to the floor.

"I'll tell him for both of us," Joseph said.

Afterword

Ron Earl Phillips

This is the part of the book where I ask with a wink and a smile, if you've read the contents of this anthology, or if perhaps you just skipped to the end to get some glimpse of what came before. I'd urge you to jump back and read each story beginning to end, and then put on a show to congratulate you on your conquest.

Congratulations.

However, that's not really my job because once you've made it this far this copy of **RELOADED: Both Barrels vol. 2** is yours to do what you will. As the editor, I hope you will read it from beginning to end, and give each and every story a moment of your time. You paid for it afterall. And for that I do thank you.

My job, and those of my co-editors, Jen Conley and Chris Irvin, was to read and review the multitude of submissions, up by half from our first anthology, and then select the 25 short stories that you found in this modest collection. An admirable task at any level.

I think we did a pretty good job selecting a diverse collection of crime stories, and I challenge you not to find at least one story that you will enjoy. All you need is one and you have opened a gateway to a new author, whose future lies in your hands. And that is where your job begins.

Now that you've read the collection in full, maybe a couple times over, and you've found that one author, or as many as you dare enjoy, within these pages I task you with the duty to spread the word on that author and their story. Sure, it benifits this collection for you share what you like about the anthology, but even more it benefits the author that you just read and enjoyed. Your positive feedback allows them to sell themselves to other potential readers, editors and publishers. Their words build stories, your words build futures.

So are you ready to accept the task? Not, yet?

If you haven't already, flip through the biographies and explore these authors more. You'll find yourself only a click or a keyboard away from finding more of their works, whether in other short story collections they have appeared or books they have written.

If I've done my job, I have not only given you access to 25 new stories, but an archive of past and future stories. To a careers worth of stories of unlimited potential.

Thank you for giving us and these authors a chance.

And if you haven't read all these stories yet, what are you waiting for? Go on, I'll be here when you get back.

Ron Earl Phillips, 2013
Managing Editor, Shotgun Honey

BIOGRAPHIES

PATTI ABBOTT is the author of more than 100 published crime stories and the collections, MONKEY JUSTICE and HOME INVASION (Snubnose Press). She won a Derringer Award for her story, "My Hero" in 2009. She reviews movies for CRIMESPREE MAGAZINE and pilots the five-year old series Friday's Forgotten Books at her blog http://pattinase.blogspot.com.

HECTOR ACOSTA is a recent transplant to the New York area and often finds himself willing to trade his soul for a Waffle House. When he's not being distracted with thoughts of smothered hasbrowns, he's at his desk writing. Previous stories of his have appeared in THUGLIT, WEIRD NOIR, and SHOTGUN HONEY Vol. 1 anthology. You can follow him on twitter at www.twitter.com/hexican

ERIK ARNESON lives in Pennsylvania with his wife and editor, Elizabeth. His stories have appeared in Otto Penzler's Kwik Krimes, Mary Higgins Clark Mystery Magazine, Needle, Grift, and Off the Record 2: At the Movies. Online, his work can be found at Shotgun Honey, Beat to a Pulp, Out of the Gutter Online's The Flash Fiction Offensive, and Near to the Knuckle. He blogs at ErikArneson.com and tweets @ErikArneson.

CHERI AUSE. The central idea behind "The Trouble with Sylvia" came from a news item I clipped years ago. The report said an elderly woman went missing and was found dead two weeks later in the home she shared with relatives. Beyond that, my story with its dark humor bears no resemblance to actual events. "Sylvia" is also my first mystery publication, so Ron and the Shotgun Honey editors will be forever dear to my black little heart. Previously my short fiction and poetry have appeared both in print and online. Links to those publications can be found at http://cheriause.blogspot.com

TREY R. BARKER, the man behind the Barefield novels, has published short fiction just about everywhere in the last twenty years, from crime to mystery to horror to science fiction and even westerns. The newest Barefield novel, 'Exit Blood' is available from Down and Out Books in both e-book and trade paperback. Barker is a sergeant with the Bureau County Sheriff's Office in northern Illinois, which provides him no end of material for his fiction. Check out his blog, 'Bullets and Whiskey,' at treyrbarker.com

ERIC BEETNER is the author of The Devil Doesn't Want Me, Dig Two Graves, Stripper Pole At The End Of The World & the story collection, A Bouquet Of Bullets. He is co-author (with JB Kohl) of the novels One Too Many Blows To The Head and Borrowed Trouble. He has also written two novellas in the popular Fightcard series, Split Decision and A Mouth Full Of Blood. He lives in Los Angeles where he co-hosts the Noir At The Bar reading series. For more visit ericbeetner.blogspot.com

TERRY BUTLER lives in the countryside near Hollister CA. His stories have appeared online at Darkest Before the Dawn, Plots With Guns, Shotgun Honey, Yellow Mama, Hardluck Stories and A Shot of Ink among others. He's been in print at Hardboiled Magazine and in anthologies edited by Ed Gorman, Dave Zeltserman, Gary Lovisi and Richard Starr. http://terryb1. tumblr.com.

JOE CLIFFORD is acquisitions editor for Gutter Books and managing editor of The Flash Fiction Offensive. He also produces Lip Service West, a "gritty, real, raw" reading series in Oakland, CA. Joe is the author of three books: Choice Cuts and Wake the Undertaker (Snubnose Press), and Junkie Love (Battered Suitcase Press). Joe's writing can be found at www.joeclifford.com.

GARNETT ELLIOTT lives and works in Tucson, Arizona. Recent stories have appeared in Alfred Hitchcock's Mystery Magazine, the All Due Respect anthology, Uncle B's Drive-In Fiction, and Yellow Mama. You can also check out his latest hardboiled novella, The Drifter Detective, available at Amazon. com.

ROB W. HART is the associate publisher at MysteriousPress.com, the class director at LitReactor, and co-host of LitReactor's podcast, Unprintable. He's the author of The Last Safe Place: A Zombie Novella, and his short stories have appeared in Shotgun Honey, Crime Factory, Thuglit, NEEDLE: A Magazine of Noir, and Kwik Krimes. He lives in New York City with his wife and two cats, one of whom he suspects is a Cylon. You can find more on his website, www.robwhart.com.

ANDY HENION writes press releases for a living, runs on a treadmill and has lactose issues, though he's never, to his knowledge, been targeted by a hit man. His crime fiction has appeared in Grift, Plots with Guns, Beat to a Pulp and Hardluck Stories; he's been nominated for a Pushcart and shortlisted for a Derringer. Born the day before man landed on the moon, he lives in Michigan, roots for Detroit and searches for the best sentence at andywritesstuff.blogspot.com.

JOHN KENYON is a writer who lives in Iowa City. He has published numerous short stories, and some of the best are collected in The First Cut from Snubnose Press. His novella, Get Hit, Hit Back, is part of the Fight Card Series. He also edits Grift magazine and the accompanying website (griftmag.com), where he publishes short fiction, reviews, interviews and essays. By day he is executive director of the nonprofit Iowa City UNESCO City of Literature organization.

NICK KOLAKOWSKI's work has appeared in The Washington Post, McSweeney's, Slashdot, Playboy, Carrier Pigeon, Washington City Paper, and other venues. His first book, a work of comedic nonfiction titled "How to Become an Intellectual," was published by Adams Media in 2012. He grew up on a steady diet of Raymond Chandler novels and Tom Waits albums, which continue to influence his life and writing in unseemly ways.

ED KURTZ is the author of A Wind of Knives, Control, Dead Trash, and the forthcoming crime novel The Forty-Two. His short fiction has appeared in Shotgun Honey, Needle, Thuglit, Beat to a Pulp, Glitterwolf, and numerous anthologies including John Skipp's Psychos, Ross E. Lockhart's Tales of Jack the Ripper, and Steve Berman's Shades of Blue and Gray: Ghosts of the Civil War. He lives in Austin, Texas. Visit Ed online at www.edkurtz.net.

FRANK LARNERD is an undergraduate student at West Virginia State University where he has received multiple awards for fiction and non-fiction. Recently his stories have appeared in the podcast series BLACKOUT CITY and issue two of the comic book series CHILLERS. His second anthology as editor, STRANGE CRITTERS: UNUSUAL CREATURES OF APPALACHIA will be released in the fall of 2013 from Woodland Press. For more visit: www.franklarnerd.com

CHRIS LEEK is an editor at the western fiction magazine, The Big Adios and part of the team behind the genre fiction imprint, Zelmer Pulp. He also writes a book review column for the crime fiction website, Out Of The Gutter. He still has all his own teeth and will work for beer. You can find out more at his blog: www.nevadaroadkill.blogspot.co.uk

A writer from New Jersey, **MIKE LONIEWSKI** creates stories in a variety of genres and mediums. His writing has been published through Image Comics, APE Entertainment, Alterna Comics, Viper Comics, and Shotgun Honey.com. Loose Ends marks his first published short story. You can find his creator-owned comic, Myth, on comixology.com and follow his writing on twitter at Mike@redfox_write.

BRACKEN MACLEOD is a former martial arts teacher, university philosophy instructor, and trial attorney. While he does his best to avoid using the law education, he occasionally benefits from the martial arts and philosophy training. His work has been published in Sex and Murder Magazine, Every Day Fiction, and Shotgun Honey, as well as in several anthologies including Femme Fatale: Erotic Tales of Dangerous Women and the forthcoming Anthology Year Two: Inner Demons Out. His debut novel, MOUNTAIN HOME, is available from Books of the Dead Press. You can follow him at http://luxferre.wordpress.com and on Twitter @BrackenMacLeod.

JULIA MADELEINE is a Canadian thriller writer, artist, and entrepreneur from the Toronto area. When not obsessively writing stories of mayhem and suspense, she works along side her daughter as a tattoo artist in the family business.

BRIAN PANOWICH has been showing strangers his stories for a little over a year. He's got a bunch of stuff floating around out there in the ether at places like Shotgunhoney.net, and Outofthegutteronline.com. Some of it's worth reading. Two of his stories were even nominated for a Spinetingler award. That's pretty badass. He is also the sexiest member of the entertainment behemoth ZELMER PULP. Their latest book is a Sci-fi epic so good you'll wanna slap your Mama. You should go buy it. Everything "Brian" can be found at www.panowich.com.

TERRY RIETTA is a father and a filmmaker. He hits his free throws and he washes his hands before dinner. And he has always written to woo his wife. He attended the University of Texas in Austin where he studied many things but graduated with a degree in advertising. His short stories have been published in Shotgun Honey, Jersey Devil Press and Parable Press.

RIE SHERIDAN ROSE's short stories currently appear in several anthologies with various publishers. Yard Dog Press publishes her humorous horror chapbooks Tales from the Home for Wayward Spirits and Bar-B-Que Grill and Bruce and Roxanne Save the World...Again. Mocha Memoirs has the individual short stories "Drink My Soul...Please," and "Bloody Rain" as e-downloads. More info on her work can be found on her website, riewriter. com.

RYAN SAYLES is the author of The Subtle Art of Brutality. His short story collection That Escalated Quickly will be out in the fall. He is a founding member of Zelmer Pulp, a contributor to Out of the Gutter Online and staff at The Big Adios. he has been published at nearly two dozen sources and included in numerous collections. His sideburns positively affected the lives of millions. He may be reached at Vitriol and Barbies.wordpress.com

RICHARD THOMAS is the author of three books—Transubstantiate, Herniated Roots and Staring Into the Abyss. His over 75 publications include Cemetery Dance, PANK, Gargoyle, Weird Fiction Review, Midwestern Gothic, Arcadia, Pear Noir, and Shivers VI. He is also the editor of two anthologies, both out in 2014: The Lineup (Black Lawrence Press) and Burnt Tongues (Medallion Press) with Chuck Palahniuk. In his spare time he writes for The Nervous Breakdown, LitReactor, and is Editor-in-Chief at Dark House Press. For more information visit www.whatdoesnotkillme.com or contact Paula Munier at Talcott Notch.

JOHN WEAGLY's short fiction has been nominated for a Derringer Award 4 times, winning one in 2008, and has been nominated for a Spinetingler Award. As a playwright, he has had over 50 plays produced by theaters around the world. He is an ensemble member at Raven Theatre Company in

Chicago, Illinois. His website is www.johnweagly.com

MEET THE EDITORS

JEN CONLEY's stories have appeared in Thuglit, Needle, Beat to a Pulp, Shotgun Honey, Out of the Gutter, Big Pulp, Literary Orphans, SNM Horror, Protectors, Grand Central Noir and others. One of her stories was nominated for a Best of the Web Spinetingler Award and another was recently listed as "Other Distinguished Stories of 2012" in Best American Mystery Stories. Born and raised in New Jersey, she lives in Ocean County where she teaches middle school and writes in her spare time. Visit her at jen-conley.blogspot.com or follow her on twitter, @jenconley45.

CHRISTOPHER L. IRVIN has traded all hope of a good night's rest for the chance to spend his mornings writing dark and noir fiction. His stories have appeared in Thuglit, Shotgun Honey, Flash Fiction Offensive, Noir Carnival, Weird Noir, Tropus, Action: Pulse Pounding Tales Volume 2, and The Rusty Nail Magazine, among others. He's one of the editors at Shotgun Honey and lives with his wife and son in Boston, Massachusetts. You can find him online at www.HouseLeagueFiction.com and @chrislirvin.

RON EARL PHILLIPS resides in the foothills of West Virginia with his wife, daughter and one too many cats. He spends his days writing code for a newspaper media company, his nights writing and editing fiction, and his weekends avoiding a neverending honey-do list. His work has appeared in anthologies such as Off the Record, Lost Children, Beat to a Pulp: Hardboiled, and Feeding Kate. Learn more about Ron at www.ronearl.com.